THE SURVIVORS

"…is a great tale that starts out as a lighthearted look at an unlikely alien invasion, only to rapidly descend into a grim study of humanity. Imaginative, funny, and ultimately frightening, the novel delivers. Sean Eads knows his stuff. You should know his stuff, too, so pick up *The Survivors*."
—**Lee Thomas**, Bram Stoker Award and Lambda Literary Award-winning author of *The German*

"Reading *The Survivors* is like discovering the young, edgy Thomas M. Disch last century. This novel is classic New Wave SF refracted through a sharp 21st century prism. Author Sean Eads purely amazes."
—**Edward Bryant**, multiple Nebula Award and American Mystery Award winner

"Eads (*Trigger Point*) offers up a short novel reminiscent of 1970s 'big idea' science fiction. Starting with slapstick but descending into nihilism, the narrative revolves around would-be journalist Craig Mencken's increasingly frantic attempts to come to terms with an invasion of obnoxious aliens."
—*Publishers Weekly*

THE SURVIVORS

Sean Eads

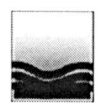

Lethe Press
Maple Shade, NJ

The Survivors
Copyright © 2012 Sean Eads. ALL RIGHTS RESERVED. No part of this work may be reproduced or utilized in any form or by any means, electronic or mechanical, including photocopying, microfilm, and recording, or by any information storage and retrieval system, without permission in writing from the publisher.

Published in 2012 by Lethe Press, Inc.
118 Heritage Avenue • Maple Shade, NJ 08052-3018
www.lethepressbooks.com • lethepress@aol.com
ISBN: 978-1-59021-299-8 / 1-59021-299-1
e-ISBN: 978-1-59021-408-4 / 1-59021-408-0

This novel is a work of fiction. Names, characters, places, and incidents are products of the author's imagination or are used fictitiously.

Set in Warnock, Incised 901, Amerika, and Amerika Sans.
Interior design: Alex Jeffers.
Cover artwork and design: Niki Smith.

LIBRARY OF CONGRESS CATALOGING-IN-PUBLICATION DATA

Eads, Sean, 1973-
 The survivors / Sean Eads.
    p. cm.
 ISBN 978-1-59021-299-8 (pbk. : alk. paper) -- ISBN 1-59021-299-1 (pbk. : alk. paper)
 1. Aliens--Fiction. 2. Vigilantes--Colorado--Fiction. 3. Gay men--Fiction. 4. Denver (Colo.)--Fiction. I. Title.
 PS3605.A3723S87 2012
 813'.6--dc23
                              2012010109

For my parents, Ivan and Edna Eads. I love you.

"We will now discuss in a little more detail the struggle for existence."

—Charles Darwin

BOOK ONE
Roommates

Chapter One: Squatters' Rights

1.

The aliens had sex again in my bed last night, making a mess on the walls and ceiling. If I was just renting maybe I'd leave it alone, but goddamnit I *own* this place. I also own the food they've been eating. A steady stream of televised scientists keeps insisting it's unlikely they can digest our food, but I've looked in my refrigerator and can tell you the aliens handle cold pizza and Coors just fine. The scientists are just trying to ignore the problem. Each day the networks show aliens leaving grocery stores with food they haven't purchased. Of course they're eating it. And no one will stop them. The police are just as bad, griping about dangerously overcrowded jails to avoid doing their jobs. Should human criminals be freed to lock up a few nuisance aliens? That's what Denver's finest asked when I called to have these two arrested for breaking and entering. I said I knew all about cramped jail space. I've been made a prisoner in my own home.

Not that the aliens restrain me. I *wish* they'd do something that dramatic. Just watching them is enough to make me think I'm dead, a ghost. But yesterday the larger one—and if their genitalia are even slightly analogous to ours, the male—sat down on my lap as I watched CNN's tedious invasion coverage. The bastard had two open couch cushions but instead he flopped down on top of me. He *kicked back* across my body like I was just some comfortable pillow. I'd like to think he did it on purpose. That at least would make me feel alive, if they showed some genuine contempt for my existence.

But instead he truly didn't seem to feel me beneath him. I'm not even sure if he watched or even comprehended the existence of the television. When I yelled out he was crushing me, he didn't turn up the volume or anything. And when I pounded my fists into his back and neck, the blows had no impact on him at all. But I felt the jarring contact and bruised my knuckles on his flesh. Still he didn't move; he didn't even make a sound. The bastard outweighed me by two hundred pounds and I knew I wouldn't last much longer. Darkness edged my vision, framing sudden bright explosions of colors as I suffocated. I was saved only when he suddenly got up to stare at the wall. I rolled onto the floor sputtering and slapping sensation back into my crushed thighs. Then seeing him turn and afraid I'd be trampled, I gave a panicked whimper and clawed my way upstairs toward that slimy bedroom.

The phone rang. Neither alien reacted. "I'll get it," I said, wheezing. Back when I still felt curious and experimental about my new roommates, I once turned off the answering machine, set the volume at maximum, and called my own landline to let it ring. It rang a blistering one hundred and seventy-six times before I broke. The sound just became too grating, but the aliens milled about oblivious to it. Were they deaf? I jotted the hypothesis down in my journal for further exploration.

"Craig?"

I don't know why I tensed so much when I heard Mr. Morrison's voice. My big crime was poverty and to remedy it I'd become a freelance journalist. To become a freelance journalist, I lied. I buttered up a sheet of résumé paper with a list of journals that either didn't exist or weren't searchable online and like that I had a new identity. This happened just before the rockets—rather old-fashioned looking rockets at that—started falling like Earth was bullseye in a galactic darts tournament.

Mr. Morrison owned drag strips and racetracks. About two years ago he'd decided to buy out a floundering local magazine called *MotorRev*. It was his burnout of a wife's idea, so she became the editor. Somehow years of coke addiction had given her incredible editing skills; she cut verbiage with the same razor precision she cut lines. And they paid so well that you didn't think of it as getting paid, you thought of it as *booty*. Their reputation spread and soon guys who specialized in Broadway reviews for the *New Yorker* were pitching pieces on the difference between the 05 STI and the 05 MR. Substance didn't matter. Mrs. Morrison bought everything.

Or almost everything, but I patiently ignored the rejections. I had dreams. When the rockets started touching down I wasn't thinking anything about the end of the world or galactic invasions. I was thinking of my first real freelance sale and an IKEA sectional. The tenth rocket landed just forty miles away. The media had swarmed the joint and besieged anyone who'd talk to them. I decided to call *MotorRev* one final time and lucked out into getting Mr. Morrison rather than his wife. It was the first time I'd spoken with him and I found him amiable until he finally asked a question I hadn't even considered.

"So why the hell would a car magazine be interested in some UFO story?"

"They must drive some pretty bitchin' rides." I felt inspired. It was the first time I'd ever said *bitchin'*.

"That's an interesting angle."

"The angle is *everything*. It's what separates a great piece of journalism from—well, why embarrass the *New York Times* any further?"

I pictured him nodding in his office. There was a long moment of what seemed to be silent agreement, the contract mentally drawn and all but signed; and then: "But how do we know they even have cars?"

"How else are they going to get around?"

I became his Johnny on the spot. That was three months ago and since then I've been Mr. Craig Mencken, professional correspondent for *MotorRev*. And every time he calls I fear he finally got around to doing a background check.

"Craig, I want you down in New Mexico. There's been another rocket."

His voice carried a laughable urgency, like this New Mexico landing was the first, second or fiftieth touchdown. I had watched just over two hundred on television and each had a banal sameness. The major networks no longer bothered to show the rockets and even the cable channels relegated the invasion to a ticker scroll at the bottom of the screen. The first signs of us going numb to our new reality were there for all to see. The most spectacular aspects of the invasion no longer even warranted a nightly summarizing montage. But that was the nature of their assault. We used to say the truth was out there; well, the truth that had been out there was now here, and the truth seemed immensely dull.

I wondered why Mr. Morrison seemed so anxious for me to go to New Mexico. Did he not know the statistics? Did he not know that one rocket touched down across the planet every five minutes since the first one landed sixteen weeks ago? Did he expect this particular rocket to be different in some way? Did he think it would carry more than the usual complement of thirty aliens? Did he expect any of these new invaders to actually say something?

"Craig?"

I remembered my paycheck. "Yes, I'm here."

"I know you're here. I want you there."

"Of course, Mr. Morrison."

"I want something big this time."

"Big, Mr. Morrison?"

"A scoop. No, more than a scoop. An interview. I want the first interview with— *Get out of that!*"

"Sir?"

In the ensuing pause I heard his phone smack the floor, followed by something like a scuffle. I pressed my ear into the receiver as he came back. "One of the aliens was rifling through my underwear drawer."

I dropped the phone down to my chest, feeling a little lightheaded, a little hurt by this sudden intimacy between an alien and Mr. Morrison. He'd never even mentioned he had one in his home. I thought only I suffered so uniquely. Sure they were in shops and banks and malls. But these two had picked my *house*. I staggered down the hall and perched on the top step. My aliens were both in the living room, the female leaning head first into a corner, almost as if in some sort of meditation or prayer. The male, returned to the couch, seemed to be grooming himself as he tossed back a beer. Neither had ever shown the slightest interest in my clothes or anything that might suggest a more personal connection.

"Craig, you still there?"

"Yes. So you've—you've made some kind of breakthrough?"

"Breakthrough?"

"It acknowledged you."

"Acknowledged, hell. It didn't say a word to me."

"But it touched your underwear. It acknowledged your personal *things*."

"Oh yeah, we're the best of friends now. Hell, one of Liz's cats sleeps in the hamper. Doesn't mean a thing. I'm going insane here. *Get out!*" Another scuffle.

"Mr. Morrison? Mr. Morrison?"

"Yeah, I'm here." He sounded ragged, battered.

"Mr. Morrison, there's something I've got to know. When you yell at them, do they acknowledge you?"

"I just said they didn't say—"

"I know, I know. But do they do anything else, like turn their head to look in your direction—like you were just a disconnected noise they vaguely hear?"

"No," Mr. Morrison said. "I'm less than a bug to them."

My heart really thumped when he said that. Mr. Morrison was the most powerful man I knew in terms of affluence. Hearing him admit such inferiority brokered the first real dread I'd experienced in weeks. Yet I was smiling into the receiver and I knew my pulse raced with a sense of my own equality. Mr. Morrison and I were identical to alien eyes; we shared the fraternity of the invisible.

"Why?"

"I don't know. Maybe it's important. Why do you think I can get an interview with these creatures?"

"I don't. I expect you to go there and be seen. Talk to people. Flash those credentials around. That way it'll be more believable when you fake the interview. And don't act all in a huff. I'll pay you a grand for every ethics code you break. What do you say?"

I said I didn't know about any ethics code, but at a grand apiece I'd take on the seven deadly sins down in New Mexico.

2.

I got no further south than Colorado Springs. I figured I'm obviously a good enough liar, why waste precious funds on some half-assed covering job? That, too, was just an excuse. The magazine would pick up my tab but going to New Mexico just seemed...futile. I had packed like I was going all the way. That was a necessity to convince myself. Until about Manitou Springs I probably believed I was. Then I stopped and doubled back to the city.

The magnitude of Mr. Morrison's demands didn't impress me until I got to my hotel. I inserted my keycard and entered a mundane, faintly musty room. But the space! The furniture was squeezed into about two hundred and fifty square feet and still the room felt empty—the most pleasing, fulfilling emptiness I'd ever known. I spent a moment surveying everything, trying to understand the special quality of the barrenness. The absence of aliens enthralled me. There were ninety of them down in the lobby, lounging like hobos waiting for a train to hop. I had to hoist my suitcase over their lazy, disinterested bodies, barely keeping myself from a vengeful heel grind on their fingers. The manager said they had just shown up yesterday, though no rockets had been reported. He apologized and said he was working to remove them; he appreciated my patience and I could call the hotel's corporate toll-free number to offer criticism and advice.

I finished detailing my criticism and advice to their customer service representative and then hung up to admire the room again. But already the space seemed narrower. My mind placed the lobby aliens inside the room; it was as if they had even managed to crowd my thoughts as well. The assignment was hopeless. Who would believe I got an alien to talk? Their numbers just in the United States were already estimated at two hundred thousand, with not a word spoken by any of them. And I was going to be the one to scoop the greatest interview in history? The irony was that even if I did, everyone would assume I made it up. Maybe that was Mr. Morrison's point. He intended it to be a publicity stunt, an entertaining hoax to spark subscriptions. Or maybe he'd figured out I was a liar and wanted to see how far I'd take it, how good I could be.

I decided I'd be really good.

I settled into the task with the comfortable ease of a professional bullshitter. Kicking back on the hard mattress, I gazed up at the ceiling and lost myself in swirls of plaster, a tumult of white wave crests frenzied by my brainstorm. I needed to invent a language and that troubled me. There's a difference between bullshitting and inventing, though both require inspiration and imagination and often quite a bit of theft. I thought of something between Klingon and Tolkien. I imagined weird sharp slashes that looked a little like English and a little like Chinese and still a little more like hieroglyphs. And clicks, I thought, becoming excited. Some of their language should just be Morse Code-like clicks that came from the back of their throat. Maybe hand gestures were also a crucial part of their language. They spoke words but their organization and grammar were in what their fingers did.

No, that was too complicated. Stick with the clicks.

Time passed and the mattress softened. I'd moved on to their alphabet and reconsidered the clicks. Would the clicks signify a different anatomy, something unique in their mouth or throat? I didn't like it. Anatomy could be verified. Okay, no clicks. That was better. I became lighter and pleasantly tired. I began to sound out their language, laughing at the quacking noises I made. I'd composed about a quarter of their outrageous alphabet when black ink spilled over everything.

I slept four hours and had a dream that felt like four days.

The dream was really a memory from just over four months ago. My boyfriend left me the day before the first rocket came down in Comoros, just in time to stop a government coup from happening there. Inconvenient location for First Contact aside, within one hour the world stood still, stores and malls closed, and good luck getting a plumber for your toilet. My situation with Scott had kept me from paying much attention to anything else, especially the news. When I discovered I needed a plumber right away and couldn't get anyone to answer their phone, I ran down to the corner gas station to use their bathroom. The station was locked and empty despite the open sign. I pounded on the door and peered through in disbelief. Was the place being robbed? Within I saw a small mess like everyone had left and closed down in a rush. Had I missed a terrorist attack?

Finding a solution to my immediate problem, I returned home to fix the toilet myself. Halfway back I stopped, listening to the silence. There was no traffic—not a single car on the busy intersection. A chill came over me. I raced the rest of the way to my house, the smallest in a neighborhood of small houses. Since I got it through inheritance I felt slightly ashamed of my pride. I hadn't worked or sacrificed for it. Still it was *mine*. That feeling was universal, right? You have something; you've staked a claim. No one could take it away from you, from me.

The Sutters next door had a little boy, Ryan, a homeschooled only child of about five who spent every day outside going nuts with his imagination. Sometimes I sat out on the porch overlooking my postage stamp-sized yard and watched him while I worked on my writing. Two months prior to the landing, when we were still tight, Scott suggested I give up on novels and write screenplays. He was a sci-fi geek and thought together we could churn out a decent robot movie. Probably our relationship started skidding when I countered there could be no such thing. But Scott persisted. He got into it much faster than I did and soon he had an elaborate plot mapped out for me, a skeleton awaiting flesh. Scott said the key was to have some funny minority characters. Watching Ryan attack invisible monsters had given me the idea to add in a funny kid who was into the martial arts. I made the kid Iranian to address the minority issue. Scott was thinking more along the lines of Tyler Perry.

Ryan Sutter for once wasn't pretending to be a ninja. That was his favorite game and I'd even taken a throwing star in the thigh as a result. Thankfully between my pants and his weak arm the star just bounced off, but I still made a big show of how he'd killed me. After that we were best friends. As I reached the porch, he came at me with his hands clasped together, index fingers extended to form the barrel of his imaginary pistol. He ran around to my right and blew my head open again and again, all the while making little whizzing sound effects.

"It's bang," I said. "Guns go bang."

"Not ray guns." He took aim at my kneecaps. *Whizz. Whizz.*
"Oh. Ray guns."
"Like what the aliens have!" *Whizz. Whizz.*

He was too hyper to waste any more time on me. He held his arms out, made a sort of blast-off sound and then ran away like he was flying. I watched him disappear around the side of the Sutters' house and then I stepped inside and happened to turn on the TV.

I spent the next seventy-two hours watching television and sleeping in brief, unsatisfying naps as the news footage switched between Comoros, the White House, the Pope, and then to endless coverage of demonstrations. Some people believed the world was ending; others believed a brighter future was beginning. Some called for the military invasion of Comoros right away, to get our troops in control and stationed for victory; others protested violently for peace, looting stores to argue the aliens were here to change our barbarous ways. Whether or not the aliens were vegetarians remained an unsettled—and unsettling—question. The Vegans positively shivered. The over/under on the aliens' hostility could make a man rich in Vegas.

I hardly ate during those seventy-two hours. I didn't shower or shave, and I took to using the bathroom in the back yard. Who wanted to go out? Who wanted to miss—what? The horrible truth was I'd never imagined First Contact to be such a mixture of excitement and tedious boredom. The rocket remained on Comoros and nothing came out. I'm quite convinced that if another week had passed without signs of life, the majority of the world would have forgotten an alien ship had arrived at all. Years would pass, turn into centuries, and as more governments rose and fell on Comoros some intrepid adventurer would find it again, buried under moss, and make the electric discovery to the world: an alien ship had crashed on Earth hundreds of years ago!

On the third day news broke that a United Nations team was preparing to cut into the rocket. A new, never-before-seen military drone would make the incision. The details were too complex for the media commentators, whose increasing desperation for *news* stoked a sour fire in their bellies. They spoke of boobytraps and biohazards. Maybe we should leave well enough alone. Maybe the crew inside was dead; maybe there was no crew and this was just a probe. Maybe whoever sent it was going to come looking for it and so we should take very good care of it in the meantime—to demonstrate benevolence. Cutting into the rocket was a natural, aggressive act, the sign of a hostile species; cutting into the rocket was a natural, inquisitive act, the sign of a scientific species. The rocket was empty; the rocket carried a great ambassador; the rocket was Christ's chariot and the End Times were now. The speculation changed depending on the channel you watched.

I too speculated in my little house, thinking great social upheaval must be coming regardless of what the rocket carried. Right now I had proof, because the television showed it, that attendance at religious services had exploded around the world. But that would fall again and eventually plummet to insignificance. People would find themselves thawing on a warm secularism that melted superstitions away from hope and faith. We had created God because we thought we were alone; and knowing now that we were not, we could abandon that old idol. We would find a bond of common sense. Yes, already I felt it happening. The pundits weren't talking about abortion or gay rights anymore. The divisive issues that diced our society into fragments would soon no longer matter. We had a new fear now, and because the fear was so encompassing and so great, it would leave us united even after we beat it back.

But at the moment we were still in the first days of dread, and so the people flocked to their churches. On television, the pundits spoke too fast and lacked their usual tone of authority. The psychological pressures they felt inadvertently revealed their darkest fantasies. One pundit feared interstellar enslavement, discussing the details of forced medical exams like a writer of fetish porn. Another proposed the aliens were here to forcibly interbreed with us in order to replenish their race. Perhaps we would be kept naked in their zoos, exposed and humiliated before galactic eyes. After so many hours of this stuff, I began to see that most of these predictions and expectations did little more than reveal the sublimated desires of the prognosticators. They all just needed a good screw and an escape into atheism. They'd find both in the new Brotherhood of Man.

But now the U.N.'s drone was ready, and the world watched the robot's slow progress up the craggy path to the silent rocket. The robot resembled a miniature tank, like a pet dwarf elephant. I imagined little kids squealing with delight as they saw it. I imagined lovers holding hands in response to such cuteness. No doubt Hasbro or Tonka were battling behind the scenes to make a toy model of it in time for Christmas.

The robot reached the rocket. Its turret, which was supposed to project a powerful laser, rested within five feet of the target.

I think this was the moment the whole world whispered. The commentators whispered even though most were thousands of miles away, safe in their studios. I imagined everyone crowded around their television sets, whispering to each other. I thought of Mr. and Mrs. Sutter whispering comfort to Ryan and Ryan for once whispering back as he shivered between them, realizing this was something even his parents did not understand. I sat up, wearing clothes I hadn't changed in three days and whispered to myself as I leaned forward holding my breath.

Everyone thought the next sharp sound was the laser activating. It was not. The rocket had opened by itself. A dark circle appeared along the dorsal and a figure emerged. This was the moment the whole world gasped. How can I describe my first look at an alien without revealing a lifetime of buried prejudices surfacing in an instant? I myself understood what it was like to be different, to feel alienated; I assumed those experiences would overthrow any initial instinctive reaction. Before seeing them, I thought I could never judge them based on their appearance.

A head appeared. I screamed. Maybe the whole world screamed with me.

The face looked vaguely like an inverted, tilted triangle, the cranium swept back with each eye positioned near the corners. The rest of the face narrowed down to large, flaring nostrils and a lipless mouth. We saw only the head and a little bit of its neck. The head began to pivot as if the hidden body were corkscrewing itself free. As its profile angled toward a better camera, I noticed the alien's ears were attached within an inch of each eye. The ears moved independently and with great flexibility; they folded over the eyes in rapid flicks, like blinking, like vision and hearing consulting each other. As the head swiveled more and the ears flexed I was reminded of some sort of living robot with a crazy antenna array that starved for radio waves.

Hair thick enough to be called fur covered the head. A ribbon of pink flesh stretched between the eyes and ran down to its nose. I focused on that. Perhaps the rest of their bodies would also be pink—or dark, I didn't care about skin color—and not so bestial, so monstrous as the shape and general hairiness of the head suggested. By now the media feed had switched to privilege us with a high-resolution close-up on the eyes, which gleamed a solid, liquid black. The head paused as the alien got its first full view of the Indian Ocean in the distance. I laughed with a warm joy and whispered, "Welcome to Earth," certain that after sailing the cold sea of space our fresh, blue-green world must have stricken it into a dumb stare.

How foolish I'd been to contemplate terrors. Bad science fiction had poisoned us all with expectations of destruction. In movies, our robot tank would have fired. The Air Force, waiting off screen, would have bombed the entire archipelago to ensure the world's safety. Even now, despite my hope, I wondered why the bombardment had not commenced. When would the nukes be used?

Five hours later the head was still there, poking through the same small hatch in the rocket's otherwise seamless surface. The U.N.'s robot had been retrieved. The mystery deepened but the tension was shattered. The commentators lost their fear. New rounds of jovial speculation commenced. They talked like frightened children realizing the terrible old lion only had a thorn in its paw. Now they were bigger than the alien. Now they had power over of it.

"It's possible he's a single traveler, perhaps an ambassador."

"I think what we're seeing here is what the Indians saw when Christopher Columbus arrived. Luckily for us we're a little more sophisticated than the Indians."

"I just hope that alien is a little more sophisticated than Columbus." It was a moderator's small, thoughtless quip that made everyone on CNN's roundtable of experts become grave.

Night fell on Comoros and on the alien head that sometimes changed the direction of its staring but otherwise gave no hint of intent or interest. The head made no sound or even indicated that it realized the passing of time. Its gaze looked sometimes at the ocean, sometimes at a tree and sometimes right into the camera lens. The face on our television screens stared back at us and through us to the living room walls behind us.

An emissary from the United Nations, Marcos García, had been appointed the planet's representative once we learned the rocket was not empty. García had become the U.N.'s most prominent negotiator over the past decade, though few of his brokered treaties ever took effect. By reputation he was an extraordinary linguistic autodidact, a man talented in empathy and understanding. The commentators had been hyping his abilities from the start and by now he seemed like some walking universal translator.

The cameras followed García's path up the craggy surface. A military attaché accompanied him to within fifty feet. Then he held up his hand and García continued alone.

At the rocket, the alien's head still poked through the opening and now it seemed like a stuck bear, a cosmic Winnie the Pooh wedged tight by girth. Was it afraid? Was it terrorized by its surroundings? I looked at the alien and thought of a frightened animal, a rabbit sensing predators everywhere. Somehow its strange behavior was *our* fault.

"Come on out, it's safe," I said to the television. "No one's going to hurt you. It's okay. You can do it. I know you can!"

The head swiveled again, and again the eyes seemed to take in everything. And nothing. The film feed was now restricted to one common pool that offered no close-ups, no revealing angles. It showed history in one broad panel that included García, the rocket and the alien. García was mic'd so we could hear every word.

As the ambassador neared, I expected the alien to kill him. I couldn't help myself. Every science fiction movie I'd seen prepared me for García's fate as the alien's head swiveled in his direction.

García stopped. He held out his hands and began to make strange gestures that must have been sign language. I thought it looked cool but it also made the microphone pretty pointless.

The alien looked away. And looked back to García. And looked away again.

"Greetings!" García called in English. "Welcome to—to—"

The head turned and considered something off in the distance.

García tried several more languages to no avail. Finally, according to the commentators, he resorted to an undignified scream in Esperanto: "Paroli al mi!"

I'm no lip reader and the camera angle was horrible, but I'm sure García mouthed "Fuck this" in immaculate English as he turned in frustration. The alien's head went back to swiveling left and right while sometimes stopping to stare at the brilliant blue sky.

That was the moment of our First Contact with an alien. We just didn't know if it actually counted as the alien's First Contact with us. It didn't seem to notice we existed.

3.

As it turned out, the University of Colorado at Colorado Springs was holding a symposium on the aliens. I went hoping for linguistic pointers but it mainly seemed like a *Star Trek* convention. The conference had been designed as cross disciplinary. Literature professors explained how the aliens were Lacanian Others trapped in their own shattered mirrors. One noted that the impossibility of "reading" the alien was a comment on the failures of Saussurian structuralism in the post-modern (and post-human) world. I ambled out of these and other smaller forums—the aliens and Constitutional issues; the aliens and Christianity; the aliens and Women's Studies—and went to the main lecture hall. Here another debate took place between theorists from the Art Bell wing of natural science and physics.

"We must seriously consider the possibility that the aliens and ourselves are not sharing the same dimension."

This announcement stirred a ripple of excitement in the packed lecture hall. I hadn't considered the possibility before and wanted to ask questions. I'm pretty shy about such things. If I have a good question I find that someone will inevitably ask it for me. If no one speaks and I determine to put it forward myself, I find the question comes out either too tangential or stupid or otherwise worthless. I write well; I talk poorly.

Another professor on the panel spoke up. "It is important to be rational here. Look at what we know. Do the aliens respond to our voices? It seems not. They show no obvious awareness of any sound. This could merely mean that they are deaf—or deaf in the way we ordinarily consider it. Would a dog think we were deaf because we don't respond to all the sounds that only it could hear?"

I found myself nodding to this line of thought.

"Then what about sight? Touch? How many here have actually shoved an alien?" He raised his own hand high, prodding the reluctant audience. Finally I raised my hand too and joined the other five or six people out of about two hundred courageous enough to admit it.

"And what happened when you shoved the alien? Did it respond?"

"I really don't see where this argument is—"

"It's simple. Appealing to biological arguments seems foolhardy in this case. There must be more."

"Foolhardy? Who knows the actual nature of their sensory perception? Perhaps they see and hear in ways so different that they cannot comprehend our presence."

"And touch? What happens when you strike them?"

"*Shove* them," the panelist defended. "They don't respond."

"Precisely. And how can that be? What creature, regardless of its level of consciousness, doesn't respond to physical force? Let us say the alien in question cannot hear us, see us, or feel us. We therefore become an invisible force. What happens when this invisible force suddenly knocks it forward—or backward? Or simply restrains it? Wouldn't a conscious organism respond to that in some way? Surely at the least it would look around in puzzlement. My explanation suggests a reason."

"Frankly, I think the only person here not sharing our dimension is you."

An argument ensued. The moderator gaveled away.

I wondered, thinking back to just three days ago when the male alien almost smothered me as I pummeled his back and neck. There'd been no reaction from him and yet I *felt* like I'd hurt him, like he knew I'd assaulted him. The idea agitated me so much that I shouted, "Maybe they don't feel pain."

Unwanted attention landed on me and wouldn't leave. The panelist arguing from biology nodded with approval. He said I'd given a perfect example of how we were imposing our norms on misunderstood neuropathy. I felt proud to have done that. The other panelist shook his head. "Maybe they don't. Must they? If you physically move them or knock them off stride, that does not necessarily equate to pain. My explanation is that part of the aliens does not share our dimension."

"But they're here!" I said. "*They're living in my home!*"

A lady one row ahead turned to me. "You have an alien in your home too? So do I. I can't get rid of it. I tell it that it's trespassing and it walks right by. My husband and I came home last night and it was—it was lying in our bed. My husband got mad. He told it to leave. He shoved it off the mattress and all it did was stay in the floor when it fell. I thought it was dead."

"And the goddamn police won't do a thing about them!"

A quick glance found several heads nodding in frustrated solidarity. The symposium seemed ready to become either a very large support group or a raging lynch mob.

"Please," the moderator said from the front. "There will be future sessions dedicated to the psychological and sociological implications of the alien presence here!"

"Go fuck yourself, sympathizer!"

I snuck out when significant portions of the audience began shouting down the panelists and then each other. I left the Science Building and walked over to the University Center hoping to see some decent college flesh, a sunbathing frat boy. But the campus was disappointingly devoid of humans. I did find the quad awash in aliens lounging on the grass like a bunch of bored co-eds. Funny, I thought, that the symposium on the aliens was being held inside one of the few places on campus that lacked them. That gave me a chuckle.

I took out my notebook and pen and jotted some notes. Nothing these aliens did was any different from how the two in my house behaved, but I had never bothered to observe them in groups. In many ways they acted exactly like any gathering of humans, except for one crucial difference. I noticed that the aliens did not even seem to acknowledge each other. I watched a group of six standing just thirty yards to my right. They did not simply ignore each other. One or another alien crossing the quad would actually bump into the group, bare feet stepping across bare feet and bodies in a blind jostle. Then they all stopped moving and stood still and silent. After a minute they reminded me of total strangers waiting for an overdue bus, staring straight ahead and adrift in their own lonely thoughts.

I went on, at last coming across a human student, a young woman smoking a joint like it might be her first. I took out my cell phone to take a picture, as a young college girl's first toke had all the innocence of a Norman Rockwell painting.

"You know this isn't Boulder. The campus police might frown on that," I said with a smile.

She gave me the same disinterested look I was accustomed to receiving from the aliens. Fuck this bitch and her too-cool-for-Craig attitude. I moved past her with my open notebook and walked up to a nearby cluster of loitering aliens.

"Excuse me. Got a minute for an interview?"

None of them even shifted in anticipation. Their gaze darted about, sometimes passing over me but clearly not accepting my presence. I waved my hand in front of their faces.

"How are you enjoying Earth so far?"

I scribbled an answer judiciously into my notepad. They liked Earth fine. I smiled and nodded, telling them I needed to move on. No matter that I couldn't use such a simple question in the interview I was to fabricate. I was a method liar. I needed to practice questioning them, going through the physical motions of a real reporter. It would help me later with visualizing my dissembling.

I asked about what they ate and where they came from. That was the money question, I suppose. But how could I even dare to write an answer that wouldn't immediately run afoul of the experts? No, it was better to stay clear of any question that smacked of science. Anyway, I felt a lot more grounded making up their cultural practices. I'd taken anthropology classes in college and could steal from the Maori or some African tribes.

"What are you doing?"

I jumped, startled to be noticed after being awash in alien indifference. Stoner girl was practically in my back pocket and I reacted with a yelp. She was really pretty if you were into that sort of thing.

"What does it look like I'm doing? I'm conducting an interview." I raised my pen and pad toward one of the aliens. "You were saying?"

"Is it really talking to you?"

"No."

She leaned against me like we'd been sleeping together for months and peeked across my body. "You liar!"

"What?"

"You've got stuff written down there. So they said something to you."

I flipped the notebook shut and shoved it into my pocket. "I better go."

"Wait a minute. Why are you here?"

"That's classified."

"No, it isn't," she said. "Are you here for the symposium?"

"Now that's a pretty big word for you, isn't it?" I smiled.

Her head bowed a little and her eyes went sideways as she considered my response, perhaps wondering if she had heard it right. "Fuck you."

"As I said, my purpose here is classified."

"You're not a student?"

We started walking across the quad. Behind me some of the aliens stared at the sky and others at the grass, and another sat down on the steps in a crooked pool of its companions' shadows.

The girl who'd ignored me before now wouldn't leave me alone, so I decided to fuck with her. I returned to my notebook again. "Tell me how the aliens have affected life on campus."

"They're in the classrooms. Security has started locking the doors to buildings to keep them out. Sometimes they get in anyway and just roam the same hallway back and forth. And sometimes if you don't get into your dorm room fast enough, one barges in and won't leave."

"What about the showers?"

She didn't answer. Instead she smiled, seeing an alien, and said, "Watch this!" She took her joint, which she never once offered me, and wasted a perfectly good shotgun in the alien's face.

"Watch what?"

"That's just it. Nothing." She giggled. "They don't get high. They don't even get a buzz. Isn't that amazing?"

"What's so amazing about biology? If it doesn't affect them, it doesn't affect them."

"But it *does* affect them, silly. It's just that they're so—they're so—*in control*. Like at the molecular level their minds are stronger than the drug."

I dropped my notebook and pen to my sides and studied her seriously for the first time. "How do you know that? Have you been doing experiments?"

She giggled again. I couldn't tell if she was very high or just goofy by default. "Experiments!"

She babbled on in a mishmash of tales and confessions ("So yeah I've showered with an alien so far, but that's it") while I considered a basic profundity utterly lost on the blowhards at the symposium. For the first time I wanted to find some frat boys and do more than ogle them. Frats had been getting dogs drunk and high for decades; it was impossible to think that by now they hadn't herded up an alien or two and tried the same tricks. If the aliens were acting somehow, playing some game, and if they shared any similar somatic response to our recreational drugs, then surely—*maybe*—just once their façade had been broken.

The notion blossomed like a flower of light and then the petals curled up into extinguished ash. I frowned.

She misunderstood my expression. "Hey, the showers are communal so it's not like you can judge me."

"Sure I can. Slut."

I went back to the hotel.

4.

The door opened on an elevator packed with aliens. Soft music played and none of them exited. I stood there glaring.

"Better just take the stairs," the counterman called.

"What the hell is this?"

"Sometimes they all take a notion to ride up and down in the elevator. It's like a migration or something."

"Migration? To the elevator?"

"Like lemmings," said another man, walking past breathless. He had taken the stairs down.

"To hell with this. I'm a paying customer."

I tried to muscle my way in but there wasn't an inch of room. The door closed on my face. I looked at the counterman. The counterman gazed at some paper on his desk. It must have been nice just to stare your problems away.

I huffed up the five flights to my room. It was like a whole rocket had spilled a fresh horde of aliens since I left for the symposium. I found them in the stairwell. They loitered in the hallway and near every door, ready to invade the rooms if some poor bastard gave them an opening. I found one camping out close to my room and went up to it.

"I know you can hear me. I know what game you're trying to play, so don't even think you're getting in my room."

"Because you're *not*," I added.

The alien's gaze seemed to pass through me to the wall. It was looking right at me yet gave no indication of noticing me. Maybe the expert had been right. Maybe there was some dimensional flux going on here. We were all sharing space yet somehow, in the end, not sharing it.

I swiped the keycard, bolted into my room and locked the door in a single motion that deserved its own highlight reel. There was just the slightest thud on the other side of the door. I saw the back of the alien's head in the peephole. Clever bastard, I thought. If the alien stayed there with its significant weight slumped against the door, it was bound to fall into the room as soon as I turned the knob. God, I was trapped. I began to laugh and tapped my forehead on the wood. The only way to avoid sharing my space was to die of starvation within it. The alien's occupation was…inevitable.

I spent the next hour fidgeting. Anyone looking at the situation would think I felt like a prisoner under guard. In reality I felt more like a guard imprisoned by his own sense of duty. I was the caretaker of this private room. I couldn't let it be defiled. Protecting it was my hateful job, and if I failed the failure would be more profound than I could realize. I turned on the air conditioner as I began to sweat. I called down to the front desk to tell them my situation. They told me they would send someone right up. Minutes later the manager came and said, "Step aside at once," followed by, "I'm afraid you'll have to leave now." Then the manager left. I looked out the peephole and the alien was still there. A minute later the telephone rang and the manager apologized.

"What do you mean, just open the door?"

"Just open the door, sir, if you want to leave."

"No shit. I'm not a child. But that will let the alien inside."

"There's nothing we can do about that, sir."

I gripped the receiver and tried to stay calm. "There's no way that bastard's getting inside this room." I slammed the phone down and paced, sometimes returning to the peephole whenever a sudden movement suggested the alien might have left. I shrieked in surprise the last time I checked. The alien had turned and now faced forward, looking directly into my eyesight. The idea that it might stand there staring ahead for hours on end made me shiver.

About thirty minutes later, weakness struck and I yearned to walk outside. I was starting to think about Scott and the sound of his voice. My mind filled this empty room with memories of him. I saw him stretched across the bed watching television or kicking back in the chair reading a magazine. Even though we were finished, he'd always feel like security to me, like a baby blanket that's long since disintegrated to a few cherished scraps. I hadn't gone silent on him out of awkwardness or even spite. I just knew I mustn't talk to him. Probably he felt the same. In the end all that stuff he screamed at me before walking out the door were just words. I was always told that some words, unlike thrown rocks, could not be taken back. But no ill-tossed word ever broke a window. My windows were all intact and, deep down, I knew I kept a special one reserved for Scott, made of stained glass.

I checked the peephole one more time to make sure the alien hadn't gone anywhere and then I dialed his number.

For a while, after mutual hellos, we had nothing between us but the unique sounds of prolonged telephone silence, the hint of breath, the soft grind of a receiver being angled and readjusted against the ear. I thought our silence had no awkwardness to it. The silence of people who communicate without speaking never does.

"What do you want?"

"There's an alien outside my door," I said.

"Look, Craig, I've got aliens of my own to deal with."

"They're in your place? Where is your place now?"

"No, my car."

I stood up. "You bought a car?"

"I didn't have you for a chauffeur anymore."

"What kind of car?"

"Used."

"Wait, you've got a place, right? You're not sleeping in your car, right?"

"Don't be stupid, Craig."

"Okay. So how long have they been in your car?"

"Three days. I tried to force it out but it wouldn't budge. I left the back passenger door unlocked, I guess."

"You've got a four door? Is it a sedan?"

"Yeah."

"Is it a Chevrolet?"

"No."

"Is it blue? Blue is still your favorite color, right?"

"I couldn't afford my favorite color."

"How many miles does it have on it?"

"I don't know."

"Where do you drive it? Any of our old spots?"

"I don't drive it, Craig! There's a second alien now and it's in the driver's seat. It won't budge. I'm looking at it outside my window now. How can they survive? It's hot today. Not unbearably hot like summer, but in the car with the windows up.... What goes through their minds? What do they think? Why don't they talk to me?"

"I am talking to you, Scott. I am talking to you."

"Why won't they acknowledge my presence? Why don't they move?"

"I never ignored you. I never meant to, anyway."

"I don't like this, Craig. They treat us like dirt. Like we're hated minorities."

"In a way, you and I always will be."

I heard something from his end that I could not identify. Like something snapping.

"Is the alien still outside your bedroom?"

"It isn't my bedroom, I'm calling from a hotel." I stopped, hearing myself, and then simply said, "Yes."

"Did you look?"

"I don't have to."

"I'm going to walk to the grocery store now."

"I'd like to see you when I get back."

"Good bye, Craig."

"Good bye."

I looked at the phone a while, trying to think of someone else to call. There was Mr. Morrison, but he'd want to know why I was only in Colorado Springs. Why was my existence parceled out between so many lonely, silent hours? That's what this room meant. I looked to the door. Hadn't there been a few moments when I felt glad to have the aliens around, after all? A few small moments when I had to admit my house seemed less empty just because of their constant movement?

I opened up the door wide and dodged the alien falling across the threshold like some old tribal booby trap. I looked down at its sprawl and realized I couldn't shut the door until it moved.

I went and lay down on the bed. After several minutes the alien stood up and ambled in. "Shut the door, would you?"

The alien went to the window. It ran into the glass, turned and walked into the dresser. It seemed a toy robot with wild, broken gears.

"Please talk to me."

The alien looked at me for about a second, scanning me as its gaze took in the entirety of the room. Whether it saw me or not, who could know? It headed toward a wall.

"At least you'll be a good listener." I asked it to close the door again, and then with the door wide open I told the alien all about Scott and how there had been mistakes on both sides.

The door stayed open the whole night and when I woke up I was wedged between three aliens on the bed with nine more sprawled across the floor like co-eds at Spring Break in Daytona. I hoped it had been a good party.

Chapter Two: A Few Answers

1.

Marlow notwithstanding, there isn't the slightest taint of death in a lie. In fact most people have saved their necks with a few well-placed lies, and probably seventy-five percent of all babies are born as the direct or indirect result of multiple parties lying their ass off. Flavor of mortality in a lie? More like the flavor of a birthday cake. So go ahead and make your wish before you blow out the candles. Wishes are lies too.

I had plenty of lies to juggle as I hammered out the details of the interview with Mr. Morrison and we worked on getting our stories straight. Everything was going fine, straightforward man-to-man plotting, until finally Mrs. Morrison entered the scene, fresh from powdering her nose in the bathroom.

"This is good stuff, Liz," Mr. Morrison said. I squared my shoulders and smiled at the praise.

"Oh, are you the editor now? I must have missed the memo."

I couldn't figure out their relationship at all. Some guys stick with shrews because they owe them their success. As far as I could tell Mr. Morrison had earned his fortune on his own. I guess there were some other sex things involved, though I couldn't get a handle on that aspect either. You see some rich dweebs with beautiful wives and you figure out the nature of their relationship pretty quickly. But Mr. Morrison wasn't a bad looking man. Take off twenty years and I'd have gone for him. Take twenty off Mrs. Morrison and you still had a Shar Pei with a line of coke dribbling out the bottom of a broken hourglass nose.

She started reading. I leaned forward and my hands wrestled each other in the space between my knees. I had no idea if she was in on the scheme or not. Mr. Morrison seemed to be holding his breath.

"What the hell is this?"

"It's your interview from the latest landing in New Mexico."

"We can't use this. Have you no common sense?"

Mr. Morrison looked crestfallen. "Why not, Liz?"

"You don't stretch your neck out if you're going to the guillotine."

"What are you talking about?"

"I'm talking about raising our readership, not destroying our credibility forever. We're not a tabloid. We're journalists."

"It's a car magazine, Liz," I said.

"Call my wife Mrs. Morrison," Mr. Morrison said.

I blushed and gnawed at the inside of my cheek. I tasted and swallowed blood. I used it to wash down my pride. "Mrs. Morrison, it's a car magazine. Car magazine writers aren't journalists, they're hobbyists. Or *enthusiasts*. We're talking about people who actually write 'vroom' in their articles along with sundry other onomatopoeias."

Mrs. Morrison sat back with a smirk. "I'm glad to see you're thinking about our audience. It's too bad your piece doesn't."

This bit of criticism actually stung, as absurd as it was to admit. "You mean I should write some car questions," I said.

"Oh, *absolutely*." Her pounce suggested she was exasperated by my dull mind. "Imagine what it must be like, to travel hundreds of miles across space and not being able to take your hotrod. I would imagine it's like going across country in a RV without a car hitch. Sure you get to your destination but once you're there, you're stuck. You can't go anywhere interesting."

"You're brilliant, Liz," Mr. Morrison said.

"Here," she said, taking out a pen. In a few moments she scribbled out several questions along the margins and slid the interview back at me. "I've given you human questions. Look those over and think of good, interesting, *alien* answers. Read a few articles from past issues, get to know the terminology a real enthusiast uses, and then give it all a good sci-fi treatment. Make everything *bigger*."

"Jesus, Liz. That's just awesome thinking."

Mrs. Morrison got up. Mr. Morrison followed.

"Okay, I like what we've got started here. A little rough, but that's okay. I like rough." She grabbed Mr. Morrison's ass and I thought he might try to gnaw her ear off as he pressed his mouth into her hair.

I left as the two of them started making out. Just before I finally shut the door I was able to admire how they mixed work and pleasure. They were panting out the details of a photo spread even as he groped both hands into her pants.

I went to a movie. The dollar theater had another sci-fi invasion fest showing. These had become extremely popular after the initial landing, when the aliens' bizarre obliviousness seemed so hilarious. Movies from the fifties were in particular vogue, like *Invasion of the Saucermen* and *Earth vs. the Flying Saucers*. They were all so dire, so violent compared to our reality. And yet it seemed that these nostalgic aliens were not really more sinister than those that walked among us now. Those old movies had a black-and-white innocence to them and an underlying faith in right and wrong, good guy and bad guy. Our aliens, precisely because they seemed to have no plan, remained murky. They did not pull out disintegration rays; they did not bare fangs and try to eat us. But there was the sense that our culture was disintegrating and our society was being consumed. We flocked to laugh at the worrywart imaginations of the past, our worst-case scenarios of karmic judgment plunging into us from across the galaxy, and saw the old perfect order restored again. On film the 1950s survived, indomitable, and therefore we survived too.

I settled in for the original *The War of the Worlds*, a movie I'd seen once as a kid and never much liked, though the Spielberg revisioning was no better. Even when I was eleven, the original movie's forced Christian message felt like the heroes were grasping at fantasies. So God put germs on the Earth to save us from an alien invasion? In my head I'd already written a sequel where the shortsighted aliens come back fully inoculated, establish their hegemony, and herd the humans into labor camps. Not that I welcomed such an ending. I just hated calling a silly bit of biology the hand of God. If you thanked God for something, then logically you could blame God for something. At the age of eleven I didn't have much empathy or any understanding of tragedy. I was just pissed off the Martian military's science advisory council had been so inept.

Halfway through the movie, I noticed that a quarter of the audience consisted of aliens who kept wandering in and out, crossing the screen and ignoring the shouts of "Go away!" and the hurled containers of popcorn and soda. One alien sat in the chair next to mine but one row down. I leaned forward to see if its eyes actually watched the screen. For a moment I thought that they did. And then, sensing me, the alien adopted that unfocused, disinterested gaze we all recognized. It was the same stare drivers have when stopped at intersections right next to a homeless man with a cardboard sign. *Focused obliviousness.* The alien watched the ceiling and then the wall for the next few minutes.

Taken completely out of the movie now, I realized other events happening around me. There were two kids who seemed too young to be making out, making out. Another man had his eyes closed and seemed to have fallen asleep. An alien went up the aisle, tripped, and didn't bother getting up.

I heard a woman sobbing. I tried to ignore it, to thrust it into the background with the movie. The crying became more sincere and insisted on my attention. I scanned through the darkness and found her two rows ahead and about seven seats down. She sat hunched over, dabbing her eyes. The shaking outline of her body suggested she verged on an emotional breakdown. I sank back in my seat and tried to watch the movie. Her sobbing had become palpable to everyone by now. We went on ignoring her for our own reasons. For me, I just couldn't bring myself over the hump. Not for a woman. Had it been a guy I'd be sitting there beside him with my arm draped over his shoulder.

Only curiosity conquered me because I couldn't believe the movie itself could move anyone to tears. There must be some terrible secret boiling out of her and I had to get close enough to catch the spillover. I eased over one seat and then another until I was right behind her. Looming ahead of us on the screen was a map that showed how many cities the Martians had destroyed. I looked behind me and found all the rows empty. I stood up and climbed into the next row so that I was now directly behind her.

"If only," she whispered, "if only."

If only what? I leaned forward to catch more tearful whispers, but the damn movie drowned them out.

I gave up and looked around again. Few humans remained in the theater. I'd been oblivious as the audience bled out either from frustration with the constant alien interruptions or from boredom. Even the two horny kids had left. The aliens still lingering in the chairs and aisles showed no signs of leaving early—or at all. I imagined that, as with so many places these days, the management would simply close for the night and lock the aliens inside. There just weren't enough police to forcibly expel them anymore.

By the time the movie ended and the lights came up, the sobbing woman and I really were the only people left. I watched her gather herself; she seemed surprised the film was over. She still had more crying to do and now she must find another spot where no one would care. She started down the row with her head hanging, only to run into one alien standing at the end, impassable, ignoring her.

"Please move."

The alien stared at the silver screen for a moment, and then looked at the ceiling a bit and then at the wall.

"Goddamn you," she said, her voice barely there. "Move. *Please move.*"

I sidled up beside her in my row. "You should go out the other way. It's clear."

"I don't want to go out the other way. I want to go out this way."

"Then let me help you over the chair. My row has a clear exit."

She swung her purse at me with a vengeance I couldn't duck. I don't know what the hell she kept in there, but it felt like a bowling ball had struck my shoulder. I fell into a chair. With me out of the way, she turned her attention to the alien. "If you don't move right now, I'm going to—to—"

She struck the alien with her purse. The alien swayed slightly. She swung at it again and once more it swayed on its feet. Except for the force of the blows rocking its balance, the alien gave no indication it felt pain or otherwise even noticed the assault. Its attention was as languid and obscure as ever.

On the fifth swing I jumped over and stopped her. She struggled briefly in my arms before collapsing into fresh sobs. "You don't understand, you just don't. It won't move! Why won't it move?"

My arms came around her in a light grip. "Why is it such a big deal? Just go out the other way. It's a lot easier."

She trembled, soft and hot and malleable. Holding her was like cradling a creature composed of wax and rage. "*Why?* Why won't they be like *them?*" She flung her gaze toward the blank screen.

"Like the Martians? Shit, do you want to end up crying in the ruins of a church while they destroy our world?"

"We could *fight them*."

"Why would you want to? They're not hostile."

"Not hostile?" She looked at me, laughing with her eyes wide and brimming. "No, they're not hostile, they're just *rude*! I'm tired of being ignored all the time! I'm tired of having to—to walk around them. Tired of not being shown any courtesy."

At first, in the dark, she'd seemed young to me, in her early twenties or possibly even her late teens. But now as the bitterness surged out I felt her age into the frumpy crone she would become. In reality she was probably in her early forties and with an obvious dye job. I shook my head at her. At her and everyone else who felt they understood the awfulness of the alien presence just because it sometimes meant making compromises in leaving a theater. She had no idea how true inconvenience felt. She had no true concept of their passive-aggressive ruthlessness. She'd never been to my house.

"I'm sorry. Everyone's got problems. Why don't you just turn around, go out the other way and leave it alone?"

"Are you a man? I mean really."

"What the hell is that supposed to mean?"

"I know about your kind. Pushovers. Our grandparents had a name for people like you. They called them appeasers. And now we're all Jews."

"That's fucked up," I said.

"You think so? At least I know I'll go down swinging."

She unclipped one side of her purse so that the bag now hung long and dangerous off the single strap. She swung it with potency, picking up force as I fled. At my back I heard a sharp impact and the woman's triumphant shout. I exited the theater with no heart to watch a battle that would no doubt last all night.

2.

I parked my car in the driveway, got out, and stared at my house. The lights were out. I thought of the aliens sitting in the living room, the darkness just as interesting to them as the light.

For the first time in my life, I found myself hesitating to enter my own home. My feet just wouldn't move. The night sky showed clear patches between moon-silvered shreds of clouds through which I spotted the vaguely reddish dot of Mars. The aliens were not from there—that had been proven despite many wild rumors to the contrary. But as late as last week some nutcase had spouted the Mars theory on Fox News. The rockets had never been seen because they were buried deep underground; we did not detect the rockets in transit because an alloy rendered them invisible to radar. It surprised me that any reputable news source could air such discredited nonsense—another powerful reminder that one superstitious echo can drown out a thousand scientific voices.

I opened my front door and stood there with my shadow cast ahead of me. I listened. Could the house possibly be empty? And if so, how could I keep it that way? I stepped forward and waited. They had gone. I imagined they had trashed the place in totality before leaving. I felt along the wall for the light switch. Would I be able to cope if I suddenly saw complete devastation in front of me? My furniture gutted, my dishes smashed, my clothes ripped and strewn like a hundred surrendered flags over the carnage? I took one deep, choked breath—

The light flickered. One of the two bulbs popped and died, leaving the room a somber yellow instead of bright white. But the living room looked fine. The carpet seemed more threadbare than I recalled, the couch lumpier. But nothing broken, nothing smashed or ruined. I bent down to retrieve a long strand of alien hair and held it up to my eyes. Their hair was coarse. I let it drop. Gone, I thought. Finally gone! I'm free of them—

The creaking on the steps came too sudden and too loud to even startle me. The male alien came down the steps, its engorged penis slowly deflating. I looked up toward my bedroom and my eyes narrowed. Meanwhile the alien entered the kitchen and opened the refrigerator door, grazing on the food with its stare.

"You fucking bastard," I said.

I ran over and shoved the alien just as he grabbed the mayonnaise. As always the act felt like shouldering a brick wall, but the mayo went spilling over the alien's fur and splattered across the floor. The alien himself barely budged. I glared into the refrigerator. I had shopped just yesterday but now saw only unappetizing scraps. The beer was gone. Had they been eating and drinking all day?

I slammed the door shut. The alien stood very still, its gaze drifting toward the ceiling.

"You could at least look at me," I said. "You owe me that much."

The alien did not look at me. I heard a slight dripping sound and looked down in time to follow a stray drop of its stringy, purple semen pooling between its feet. I screamed out and in a blind fit struck at the puddle with my foot, as if my shoe could absorb the mess. "You—you—you," I repeated, a stabbing syllable I tap-danced to as the alien headed into the living room.

"Not on my couch!" I didn't follow him. I'd recovered enough wits to dampen a wad of paper towels and plaster them over the mess on the floor. As I finished mopping up another creaking descent told me the female had also entered the living room. The television came on, causing me to stand rigid.

"That's astounding," I said in a whisper. I'd never known the aliens to manipulate the remote control. The implications were too many and too large for me to handle.

I ran into the living room to find them both on the couch, side by side like lovers. No, I thought, more like an old married couple who'd fallen out of love. They did not touch each other; they showed no affection at all. And neither looked at the television screen. As the channel was CW, I could hardly blame them.

I flashed a wolfish grin and said, "I've caught you." The statement felt foolish, as if I could credit years of laborious spy work for the payoff.

The female shifted her weight to the right. Suddenly the television's volume exploded.

"Goddamnit! No one needs it that loud!"

I saw the volume bar filling like a thermometer taking a volcano's temperature. How was that? Neither of them held the remote. Where was it? I glanced around as the television reached its ear-splitting maximum. Finally I spied it poking out from beneath the female's powerful thigh. All my hopes sank at once. I hadn't caught them in anything. They hadn't acknowledged the television. The fucking cow had just sat down on the remote, oblivious to its existence, and her weight had activated the power button. Shifting her weight had pressed the volume control.

I went around and tried to dislodge the remote but it was too securely lodged under her bulk. I slapped at her thigh. She ignored me.

A quick burst of rage and contempt like I've never known flooded me and I struck the female in the face. Her head snapped back on its sinewy neck and my fist came away bloody. I stood there shaking. Her blood was cold, not warm at all but chilled and thick like fresh paint against my skin. I saw blood coming from both black nostrils at the end of her tapering face. Her head turned right, her gaze swept me up and then went past me. The blood ran unstanched down her hairy torso and seeped into the couch. I was the only one who seemed to notice, the only one to make a sound.

I shrieked from an impossible mix of emotions. I shrieked to release the building terror inside me and the shame I felt for what I'd done; I shrieked to cover up what otherwise would have been a laugh of madness at divine absurdity.

I had a walking blackout. The next thing I knew, I was standing over the kitchen sink with the faucet running full blast and a cloud of steam rising toward my face. My flesh was on fire and I jerked my hands back against my chest, seeing them red and white in patches, lobster raw. I got the water off and as the steam cleared I saw traces of vomit in the drain and on my shirt.

I didn't remember puking or running the water full blast on its hottest setting. My hands remembered, though, and screamed a complaint up my arm. I ran cold water and gave them a mercy drowning. My skin wasn't blistered, but any notion that the cold water could magically reverse the burn was quickly revealed as pseudoscience. I shed my soiled shirt and then tore wads of paper towels into strips that I soaked and layered across the tops of my hands like gauze. Soon I looked like a mummy that had been caught in Hurricane Katrina.

I needed ice and opened the freezer, discovering a very old box of frozen fish sticks behind an unopened fifth of Jägermeister. I had forgotten about it and my hands hurt less as I considered this symbol of a more profound ache. I took the green bottle and swiped at a layer of frost, admiring the revealed label as if it were a cherished, rediscovered photograph. Jägermeister was Scott's favorite drink. Finding it made me realize just how fast he'd left, like an evacuee fleeing a toxic spill. But maybe leaving the bottle here was code, a sign that he meant to return. He'd left other things, like a few stray articles of clothes I'd discovered in the hamper. I could see him not caring much about dirty socks, but his Jägermeister was different. I found myself rubbing the frosted glass with my exposed fingertips as I wished for the return of my genie.

I should have shoved the bottle back into the freezer, but the more I thought of it, the more sacramental it became. I could see Scott there at the kitchen table getting drunk as we played poker with some friends, the noise of laughter blending with the steady hum of a box fan in the window blowing a pleasant summer night's air onto us. The memory proved too powerful. My hands worked the cap off and tipped the bottle to my mouth. I drank and gulped down a mouthful of that awful cough syrup. I supposed it was fitting, that this one reminder of Scott should have such a wrenching taste. And as always, I came back for more, the second swallow never as bad as the first. But never as vital, either.

I took a third, smaller hit on the bottle and looked back in on the box of fish sticks. I had already vomited once tonight; what were a few more times? I groaned. My stomach was too upset for food. I went and got my interview draft, a notepad and a pen, and brought them all to the table. I placed the Jäger bottle and a shot glass at the seat to the left where Scott always sat. Then I started thinking. I had all these ideas. Sometimes I quit thinking long enough to pour a shot, which I drank on Scott's behalf. Going through this motion made me laugh, knowing that I looked like some lonely fat kid throwing a tea party for invisible friends. But I did not feel pathetic; indeed I felt great, like I had fifty best friends in my home instead of two creatures that ignored my existence.

Maybe it was the sudden shifts of emotion, from anger to regret, regret to sadness, but my muse felt like it was on amphetamines. I studied each of Mrs. Morrison's new questions and thought of brilliant answers. I did not bother to write them down; there was no doubt I would remember them, and my hands hurt too much to hold the pen. I dared not stop the free flow of my imagination with crippled handwriting. There on the paper in front of me, the written questions had become a field of stars with rockets leaving a dying planet. I was in one of the ships, hearing my alien couple speak in an unguarded language. I understood it and I understood them. I loved them. My pulse quickened and I drank some more for Scott. I loved Scott.

The pain in my hands subsided and became a pleasant buzz. I brushed aside the shot glass and took up the bottle, giving its neck a quick kiss before taking a long drag. My eyes dampened. Hope must be a thing like the universe, a force always in expansion, sometimes thinning to invisibility but never breaking. Hope was no dark matter. The stars themselves were born out of it, and from those stars came lives unknown and undiscovered, but just as valuable as mine. Eternal distance and time made everything possible. I was at the same kitchen table where I'd sat as a boy flustered by basic algebra homework. Now I was a man grasping for assurances in my mind's dim, drunken calculus.

The paper towel gauze had dried into matted indentions of my hands. I peeled them off and took another swig for Scott. The Jäger was room temperature now and burned my throat. Scott always joked that you couldn't taste the deer blood when Jägermeister was cold. I laughed, hearing him say it in my head. "Scott, that's gross," I said, teetering. "There's not really any deer blood in this." My head lolled to the right with an amused, relaxed giggle.

From the living room, the television's volume increased again and I thought that no one would know if I killed those two aliens. Would they even fight back? Knowing I could slaughter them in uncomplicated leisure gave me a queasy feeling, as if I were planning to drown a kitten. They're in my house, they're invading, and they deserve lethal force. Anger burst across my vision, hot and thick like the liquor. My stomach burned. It was an empty, wood-burning furnace I'd flooded with gasoline to fuel the engine of my vengeance. Dimly I remembered my disgust, my remorse at striking the female alien. Was I like the woman in the movie theater after all? Wasn't it better to scream at them and strike?

Maybe I'd be doing myself a favor by letting go instead of pursuing a perverse self-control. And what could it hurt if I did scream or beat them, since the aliens ignored acts of rage as readily as acts of love? Still I found I could hardly yell at them any more than I could go yell at a cow standing in the field; or, I thought darkly, at a tumor suddenly growing on the top of my head. The bovine nature of the aliens made me forget how vastly superior they must be to humans. They had mastered space. I could not even master myself.

I had another walking blackout. Next thing I knew, I stood in the living room with a meat cleaver in my right hand and the half-drained Jägermeister bottle in my left. The aliens had a glaze over their eyes, like any tired American couple at the end of another sixty-hour workweek. They paid me no notice.

"I refuse to be Patrick Swayze in *Ghost*." I swung the meat cleaver. I was hoping for some badass whistling effect but the cleaver made no noise at all. I almost fell over but managed to right myself.

"Hello, I'm Craig Mencken. I'm a reporter. I need to ask you some questions that you will answer or—" I stumbled again but caught my balance—"or face the consequences!"

The aliens stared. A tremor ran through my lower lip. I looked down and saw half my face distorted in the dull reflective edge of the cleaver: mouth open in an exaggerated snarl, teeth huge pikes entwined with a serpent tongue. This wasn't my face. This was the gay basher I'd seen in my nightmares since I was sixteen, chasing me down in a world composed only of alleyways. I threw the cleaver down and backed up against the wall.

What happened next seemed like Scott's idea, like I'd drunk so much he was in my head directing me. Somewhere in the back of my mind I thought I'd only grabbed the bottle in the first place because I wanted to experiment with getting them drunk. I'd never meant to drink it myself. I hated alcohol, hated how it stripped me of control. *Throw it.* Scott's voice, Scott's command. I obeyed. The bottle shattered against the wall just above the couch and burst over the aliens' heads in a shower of green shards. Liquor stained both the wall and their fur. The aliens didn't flinch.

I ran into the kitchen, tripped, and slammed my face on the floor. For a moment I knew I mustn't get up, I deserved to be left lying facedown and discarded. But then I was standing, sort of, and back at the table with my interview questions all jumbled up, the letters sifted and raked into nonsense and new sense. I pushed at the words with the cap of my pen, getting them all arranged right and herded between the lines. Aliens? Planets? *What was the galaxy's position on NASCAR?* "Why, the *pole* position, naturally," I said, coughing up a mouthful of stinging liquor that dribbled from my lips as the darkness made everything numb.

3.

I woke to an eyeful of kitchen floor and groaned, rolling over to discover that I had vomited again at some point in the night and it had dried into a crusty, brownish purple island on the linoleum sea. I tried to sit but managed only a few inches. The lower part of my spine felt screwed into the ground.

The phone rang. I was content to ignore it but it kept going, driving into my head like a nail through the ear. By the thirteenth ring I was half up and stumbling. On the fifteenth I held the phone in the vicinity of the right side of my face.

"The aliens are still in my car."

"Scott?"

I slumped against the wall, exhausted and aching. Hangovers were a lot more fun when you could sleep it off with someone. I verged on asking him over when he repeated the bit about his car.

"You mean all this time you haven't been able to drive?"

"Yes."

"That's insane."

"I mounted a camera to watch them. They're good. They don't give away their game at all. They don't leave the car."

"How do they eat and drink? Does another alien bring it to them?"

"I guess they can go a long time," he said.

I hardly took notice of his words, too absorbed by the tone and texture of his voice—my soft pillow, my warm blanket. He seemed as weary as I felt. Wasn't it logical to face the aliens together? Wasn't it right to become a couple again, at least until the crisis passed? I swallowed these sentiments just in time to keep from expressing them. I risked too much becoming a beggar for his company.

"I think the one behind the wheel may be dead."

"I could—come by and pick you up, if you need to go someplace. I'm cool with that." I waited for his answer with too much heart in my head, pounding there between my temples, flooding and drowning my calculating self with romantic delusions and gravelly pain.

"I'd like you to come over sometime, maybe."

"When?"

"Sometime, maybe."

I nodded, resigned. "Look, Scott, I have to go. I have a hangover. I was up too late last night."

"Doing what?"

"Working on an assignment. Actually, I could use your help—I've got an idea for some photos."

"What of?"

My gaze darted over to the interview on the other side of the table. I blinked and gave my head a puzzled shake. The page looked different. Darker, heavier. *Complete.* I leaned forward and snagged it with my fingertips, which were still tender from last night's boiling.

"Well?"

"Just something for the car magazine." I stared down at the page, tension starting to build with the mystery—with the fright.

"You still there?"

"I've got to go, Scott. There are still aliens in my house I've got to deal with. I'll see you around sometime, maybe." I hung up on him and rested the phone against my chest as I read, squinting, trying to conjure some sense.

The draft had changed. I thought I might be hallucinating or misremembering, but now I had no doubt. I knew my own annotations and I saw the recent additions made by Mrs. Morrison. But there was new writing here. Writing done in a third hand that addressed the questions written in the first and second.

I stared at the words, experiencing a thrill tempered only by sheer astonishment. All the questions had been answered in a small, tight print that went across the page so orderly you could mistake it for word processing. I blinked and blinked. The real answer is right there on the floor, I told myself, eyeing the dried vomit. I drank myself into schizophrenia; I blacked out, and woke up in the middle of the night as someone else, complete with his own unique handwriting. The Jäger bottle had held a genie after all, a genie that had gone and made my mind its new temporary headquarters. It had granted my single wish—to complete the interview—and now it was departed forever.

Yes, I thought, beginning to nod. *No,* I realized, afraid. My hands now shook so bad I couldn't hold the paper. Part of me was so scared that I wanted to throw the pages away and pretend I'd never seen them.

One of the aliens wrote these answers.

I took a deep breath and released a long exhale. I did this again and again until I felt I had some self-control. I studied the paper once more, reading the complex answers, awed by their authenticity. Could I publish this? Who would credit me with this much imagination? Mrs. Morrison would arch her eyebrows at me, swipe at her nose, and scold me for being too fanciful. My absolute certainty about her response made me feel better. Of course she'd think I made it up. Everyone would. I'd be straightforward that the whole thing was bullshit. There was just one thing I had to do.

I went to confront the aliens.

They were gone. I sensed it before exploring every room in the house. When I found my bedroom empty, I froze for a moment. Then I smiled. Weeks ago I'd gone to bed one night having forgotten to close a window, only to wake up with the male alien standing in the bathtub while the female blithely drank my milk in the kitchen. Since then one or the other came and went, but never both at the same time. One always remained to keep up their squatters' presence.

Their absence was the one thing that could make me forget the interview. I had my house back! I had been patient, I had not lost my cool too much, and I had outlasted them. I checked every window lock and put the deadbolt in the door. In the bedroom, feeling certain they were gone for good, even the aliens' dried sexual secretions no longer seemed impossible to clean. I'd ditch the mattress, change the carpet, put on a new coat of paint and make the room a modern paradise. I'd planned on doing these things after Scott left anyway. I felt so good that all the weariness and pain of the hangover and a night spent on the kitchen floor just evaporated. This called for a big breakfast. I'd shower and go out to stuff myself at a Golden Corral. Then I'd come back and evaluate the mysterious interview answers and ponder the magnitude of all these new developments.

Chapter Three: New Developments

1.

It was the largest rocket I'd ever seen.

    It landed in a Chicago suburb, demolishing half a city block as it planted itself vertically out of the sky like an elephant's foot against an ant colony. It rose from the rubble about four hundred feet with a base the width of a football field, the remains of five entire houses splintered and pebbled around it. If any humans died, no one seemed to care; the sheer size and scope of the new invader trumped all other concerns. As I watched, edging closer to the screen over the following hour until my nose nearly touched, I felt for the first time since Marcos García's failed diplomacy an eschatological dread. My attention strayed away from the rocket to the hint of green grass and trees at the fringe of the lens. The rocket's vastness pushed all other images aside, like a big rock that lands in a little bit of water and splashes it all away, denying space to everything that was not itself. The green, vital periphery of our lives had been pushed away by the aliens. This rocket was the elephant in the living room, and we acknowledged it at the expense of ignoring the drapes and chairs—and those sitting in them.

I'd had the house to myself for nine days and was still luxuriating in my reclaimed estate when the titan's arrival sparked panicked interruptions on every station. I stood in my living room with my arms crossed and thought I should probably upgrade my homeowner's insurance in case something like that ever happened here. I started to think about the people inside the flattened houses and how I could not recall the prior rockets landing on occupied space. The broadcasters were arguing that very point, with one side suggesting it was proof of some kind of intelligent guidance system—of *awareness*. The opposition noted that as many as one hundred rockets had touched down in the oceans and sunk immediately, presumably killing everyone on board. No, they argued, the landings were entirely random, the alien passengers guided by an absurd fate that proved they were just as disinterested in their own lives as ours.

I switched channels for a cascade of opinions. People seemed to be screaming at each other on one station. Suddenly a scroll of figures rolled across the bottom of the screen. Christ, I thought, was that number accurate? It said scientists estimated the alien population on Earth to be nearing two million. The previous rockets always carried exactly thirty aliens. With one ship landing every five minutes across the globe for the past six months, their numbers really were starting to add up. I put my hand over my mouth and shook my head. Somehow the total only startled me because of the new rocket. The new rocket changed everything. It looked like it could carry a thousand aliens.

As it turned out, the massive rocket carried only equipment. A reporter gasped, cutting the pundits short. The rocket was opening up, splitting itself right down the middle and collapsing in a controlled, mechanized tumble. It rearranged itself into something that looked like an oilrig or a landing platform. There was an expansive flat surface about one hundred and fifty yards across, with the rest of the rocket forming an encircling ramp that battered down still more houses. Screams came from everywhere even though I saw no people. They too were on the fringe, pushed just outside the edge of the camera's vision, left as disembodied voices that cried out for help.

We were all used to rockets opening by now, but they'd always followed a routine of perfect banality. After a period of thirty minutes a portal opened and an alien's head poked out and swiveled much like a periscope. After another thirty minutes that alien climbed out, followed by twenty-nine more. They exited single file during the next seventy-five minutes, each ambling on in a directionless direction. When the last alien left, the rocket sealed itself and no tool of man could pry it open again.

The change in procedure with this new rocket was therefore just as unnerving as the rocket's ominous size. On the platform sat a single machine, its obvious but mysterious monstrousness rendered more powerful by how minuscule it looked on its massive pad. Even granting the machine's own impressive size, it seemed like placing it within such a massive transport was ostentatious overkill, like sending a single boxed present across country inside an otherwise empty semi. I heard my own feelings of hopeless inferiority in the commentators' words as they grappled with the machine's meaning. "Fifty meters long, at least. How high?" "We're guessing fifteen meters."

Someone whistled off camera.

I wiped my hands on my pants as the camera jerked and wavered, zeroing in for a close-up of the machine. It had a dull yellow sheen that did not seem to be paint. The color innate to the metal, shaped with magnificent skill, no seams, no rivets, no intersections or evidence of construction. As different cameras now gave sharper views, a renewed admiration for their technology gained ground against my terror. The shape on first glance seemed a mixture of bulldozer and crane. The front—or at least, the side facing the camera—sloped down from a general box shape and narrowed into scooping blade that stretched from side to side. From the top of the machine, near its center, a sort of crane arm rose another twenty meters. Hanging down from this arm—or rather, suspended, as it seemed to float free and unrestrained—was a spinning globe not much larger than a wrecking ball. Someone coined the name *dozer* in a passing remark. The name stuck. I looked at the floating globe and had no doubt as to its purpose. It *was* a wrecking ball.

The telephone started ringing.

"Scott," I said. Noise blasted into my ears. I thought it was static and muted the television.

"*Scott?*"

"Craig! Good news!"

"Mr. Morrison," I said, straightening my posture as he suddenly put me on hold. On hold meant him laying the phone down while he yelled at someone. Behind his voice I detected a terrible racket, like massive construction. Perhaps he was renovating a racetrack.

"Craig, your interview just went to press! Are you ready?"

"Ready for what?"

"The publicity. You're going to be the most notorious man in the world, you know that?"

"No."

"It's true." The racket behind him intensified and ran in erratic bursts. "You're not to speak with anyone, is that clear? Change your answering machine to direct all calls to my number. From now on Liz is your PR rep. You've really impressed her, Craig. She swore out loud when she read your additions. I thought you'd fucked up good but she was really into it. She had to admit what I already knew, kid—you're *good*."

I shifted my tenting pants and tried to be calm. Praise had always excited me and enthusiastic, masculine praise had always given me an erection. I *was* good. Mr. Morrison had said it and that made it absolute.

The noise in the background sure was strange.

"Mr. Morrison, are you at a shooting range?"

"What makes you say that?"

"The sound of machine guns going off."

"Oh that." He laughed. "I'm watching a movie."

On the television screen, the alien dozer began to move down the ramp on its heavy treads.

"Mr. Morrison, put the news on. You've got to put the news on!"

He laughed again.

The dozer finished its descent, turned right and stopped at the nearest upright house. The crane rotated forward, bringing its suspended ball with it. The ball slashed forward, exploding into the side of the house, which crumpled inward as if made of straw and stick.

The dozer moved forward into the rubble. It looked like a Kodiak bear foraging in a trashcan it had just bullied open. The muted sound added to my horror. I imagined the screams, the noise of chaos. The camera footage shook and then the picture went black.

"Mr. Morrison," I said, my voice distant. "You don't believe what's happened. In Chicago..."

But Mr. Morrison was yelling indistinctly in the background again, and there were more angry bursts of gunfire. If he was watching a movie, it was because he was directing it in his own backyard.

2.

That night the president addressed the nation from a bunker. His approval rating had fallen to three percent because of his benign approach to the aliens. It had been at ninety percent for the same reason at the start of the invasion.

I expected a declaration of martial law. Instead he assured everyone the government was working with local authorities and consulting with the world's best experts to solve *the problem*. What *the problem* was he did not say. There were now so many problems that it seemed safer to use the singular to refer to the plural. Clearly, though, our thoughts now focused on the new alien machine rather than the aliens themselves. Even then it proved hard to pinpoint a precise threat. After destroying the one house, the Chicago dozer just stopped. It just went dead and dark and remained that way. This did not stop a full military encampment from guarding the silent machine. Stripped of context, pictures of the army encircling the dozer perched in rubble made the scene look like one of total human victory.

After the president's address, our governor made a speech of his own, detailing how the National Guard would soon be on our streets. Our governor had always seemed to be envious of disasters in other states, as if regretting lost opportunities to show his decisive leadership. Once during his speech he misspoke about the alien dozer being in Denver and not Chicago. He corrected himself, telling us that no doubt a dozer would arrive in Denver's near future, and he was preparing us for a fierce response.

I responded with a yawn and a call in to Scott. It was time to see him.

The next day I drove downtown seeking evidence of a police state around the Capitol building and the Central Library. The Guard hadn't quite mobilized yet, however, so all I got was traffic and the dirty transients camped out in the parks. It might have been any day from the past thirty years, except now the homeless shared their oblivion with alien neighbors. Businessmen went on ignoring the homeless and aliens went on ignoring the homeless and businessmen alike.

I was taking a very indirect path to Scott's house. None of my calls to Scott last night had been answered, so he didn't know I was coming. He also didn't know I'd discovered his address—a trifling matter for an ace journalist like me.

As I got closer, I checked the digital camera Mr. Morrison had given me a while back, when I'd described Scot's car situation and thought it'd make a great photo layout for my interview. It still gave me a plausible reason to see Scott even though Liz had nixed the idea. The interview answers had gone far past hot rods, far past being some sort of novelty hoax. I knew it and the Morrisons knew it too. What I'd given them had the ring of profound insight for the simple reason that it contained profound insight. They couldn't acknowledge what they felt from reading the piece because the writing bore my name—and who the hell was I? I had no idea what would happen to me when the interview went public. Hoaxes masquerading as truth had bright but short lives. What of truth masquerading as a hoax?

I pulled up to Scott's house, thankful that I had resisted previous urges to locate him. I would have spent too many hours driving by at night, looking to see if the lights were on, adding up the lights and dividing by the number of lit windows in my heated psychological algebra, where X equaled Scott's social life without me. Now that I saw the house I did a double take, certain that Scott not only had a roommate but a rich boyfriend—perhaps a sugar daddy. I at most had been a Splenda or aspartame partner, a decent substitute in a short-term crash. Before living with me, Scott had been an apartment dweller born and raised. Now obviously his pride could not let him go back to that. He had stepped up to the idea of home ownership through me; now he had somehow attained a small mansion. Darkness spread over my vision, blackening the immaculate grass of his yard as I approached.

"You could have parked in the driveway."

I looked up to find him on the porch, standing beside one of its four ostentatious Doric columns. I smiled despite myself. He had light brown hair with hints of red and a fair complexion that easily blushed and burned. He was the rare Nordic better suited for Grecian settings.

"I didn't want to block your roommate's car there."

"Nice try, but don't bother with all the circular bullshit. I live here all by myself, to come to your point directly. Now I'll come to mine. Why the hell are you here?"

I backed up a step and held the camera up and out, like an offering. "Didn't I mention the photo shoot I wanted to take a while back? I was hoping maybe today—"

"You mentioned it right before you hung up on me. Weeks ago."

"Oh." It occurred to me that I was staring too long at my feet and forced eye contact with him. "I wanted to take photographs of your car with the aliens crammed up inside of it. It's part of an article I'm doing."

"You could just drag every alien you see and stuff them into your own car. Use that for your picture. It's not like they're going to mind."

"But then I'd be in your situation."

He smiled at that and I brightened inside. The smile was natural, proving I'd caught him off guard. I was caught off guard myself when I glanced at the one car in the driveway.

"Wait. If you're living here by yourself then that's your car. But it's empty."

Scott nodded. His lips bent into a little smirk. "I had it cleaned out."

"What do you mean? Who did it?"

"Just this company."

I raised my eyebrows. "What company? How did they do it?"

"I didn't really ask questions. Besides, the company is sort of private."

"They don't advertise?"

"If you've got a big enough problem, you can find them. Or they'll find you." He stared at me a moment, then dropped his gaze to the ground. I stirred on my feet to see it, remembering all his enduring expressions and postures. This was the mannerism I liked the best because it made him seem shy. Scott was not shy, but every so often, usually during a long conversation, he would find himself with nothing to say. Then he'd lower his head like that, as if embarrassed.

"Scott?"

"You want to see my place?"

I pocketed my camera and we went inside.

3.

He started warming up to me over coffee that I forced myself to drink. He'd become a teetotaler since our breakup, a fact that made our past somehow even more distant and fantastical. "What's wrong?" he asked.

"Nothing," I said. "It's just that—"

"You don't like coffee," he said, as if he'd had to remember this fact from a forgotten past.

"I've swallowed worse."

I took a sip and we let our gazes relax on each other's bodies. He sat differently too, more rigid underneath his clothes. So he'd given up drinking? I shook my head, not caring if it confused him. People always went overboard on their radical life-changing resolutions, valuing even the most insignificant abstention, such as foregoing potato chips, as a major step up on the rungs of perfection. But giving up drinking was usually the act of alcoholics who realize their problem only after some tragedy, like vehicular homicide. Did he consider our relationship to be such a huge misstep?

"So you had them in your house? In the bed?"

"And you thought you had it bad," I said, laughing.

"I should have told you about the company."

I saw an excuse to push the coffee away. I did so and leaned back. "Tell me about it now."

"They're not really a company. More like a group of people in the Denver area loosely doing business together."

"For how long?"

"Since the aliens threatened to become unmanageable."

"Unmanageable?"

"What's with the sarcasm? Or can you give me an example of anyone who's coping with the situation? I don't see any coping going on in Chicago. I don't see you coping with the aliens in your house—"

"They're gone now," I said.

"Because they decided to leave. *They* decided. So the aliens are managing just fine. But us? Where's the police? Where's the government?"

"You want the army on our streets?"

"Better a human soldier in the street than an alien bastard in my living room."

I took up the coffee again and noticed my hands shook. Scott's fierceness had unnerved me more than I realized. "So this company of yours does alien management, is that it?"

Scott sipped and sat back, grinning. "They make the aliens go away. Let's leave it at that."

"I'm a journalist, I can't just leave it at that."

"You're not a journalist, Craig."

"I've been taking it up. So tell me about how they make the aliens go away. Or should I guess?"

"Guess all you want. I don't know. I didn't ask."

"I'd like to talk to someone about it. Give me a phone number."

Scott smiled. "I don't think so."

"Why not? Was it something in the contract you signed?" I laughed. "Would they make *you* go away if you told?"

"I might need them again, that's all. And if I set you up with an appointment and they found out you don't really have the need—well, they might not offer me that help."

"You're still damn stubborn."

Scott sipped coffee and looked out the window. Was there nothing left between us? I was about to drift off into self-pity and loneliness when he put the cup down and said, "Take my picture."

I took two pictures. He had a triumphant smirk in both.

We went to the porch. "How are your finances? Getting rid of the aliens probably set you back a bit."

Scott shrugged.

"Here." I pushed a grand in twenties into his palm. It was part of my advance from Mr. Morrison. I don't know why I gave it to him. He looked like he was doing better than I was. But I couldn't give him a hug or a kiss, so the money was all I had left. Scott stared at it in the same way the aliens stared at something—unfocused, not comprehending any meaning, perhaps not truly seeing it at all.

"What's this?"

"It's good bye, I guess."

4.

The same type of carrier rocket that fell in Chicago landed outside Denver three days after my visit with Scott. Like the first stray drop of rain signaling a coming downpour, the rocket's touchdown in Aurora seemed to start an assault across the planet. One hundred more fell the following week, in cities, forests, jungles and swamps. In every instance the rockets followed the Chicago pattern, opening to reveal a terrifying dozer that launched down toward the closest target (a house, an office building, half an acre of trees), destroyed it, and then powered off. I and a few thousand other gawkers watched our city's designated wrecking machine exit the Denver rocket and start rolling toward I-25. It took up all three lanes and mowed over trapped cars with oblivious abandon. It destroyed one bridge overpass with the ease of man's leg shearing through a spider web, and then it stopped right in the middle of the freeway.

"It's war," a man standing next to me said. "Pure and simple, it's a war."

"No one's declared war," someone else said.

"They have. Just because they don't say it doesn't mean they didn't declare it. They just did it amongst themselves and didn't tell us."

Three more rockets, regular sized, streaked overhead and pivoted into a landing cycle about one hundred miles to the east.

"This is bullshit. I-25 North is completely blocked. It feels like the state's been cut in half!"

I had to agree, and there was no way to move the dozer or destroy it. The governor tried to capitalize with a photo-op that showed him striking a defiant blow against the dozer's right tread with a sledgehammer. A week later the governor was assassinated by a paramilitary nut who accused the government of treason against the planet. He said politicians had cut deals with the aliens in exchange for their own welfare and the governor wasn't going to get away with it. The president was next. That sentence quickly became headlines in a lot of newspapers. *The President Is Next.* I saw people nodding to themselves as they read it in their cars, passing time in the new traffic jams caused by a few hundred thousand people looking for alternate routes to work.

Traffic now went up and down my street like it was some freshly discovered Northwest Passage. The police had yet to put up signs and establish emergency routes. Sometimes drivers caught me on the porch and summoned me to them to ask directions. I could not help them. They were on a street they'd never heard of trying to find a street that I'd never heard of. They looked at me like I was crazy when I shook my head. The street they needed was the most important place in the world, how could I not know it? What could I say? We all have our own worlds around us made up of certain roads, certain bars, and populated by a select few. These are our orbits. What did I care about twenty new neighborhood restaurants as long as I had the old ones? What did I care for the names of all the other nearby suburbs and roads unless I needed them to find my own house?

The traffic chased me inside for good. I leaned against the closed door and saw how darkness crept into the living room earlier with the fall season. I couldn't stand it. My hand strayed to the doorknob. The knob turned and I was outside again, running as fast as I could down the sidewalk like some con freed from prison. I crossed one street and then another, coming to the same gas station that I thought was being robbed the day the first rocket landed. A car pulled away from the curbside payphone leaving the receiver dangling on its silver leash.

I walked over intending to reset it. Then it was at my ear as my fingers worked Scott's number on the keypad. Maybe he would pick up if the number on his Caller ID didn't belong to my cell or landline. I missed entering the last digit as a weight came crashing into me, bowling me aside.

"Watch where you're going!" I said, turning. An alien went ambling past like a homeless drunk, acknowledging nothing, and twenty yards down smacked itself into the side of a bus stop shelter. It kept walking in place, forehead against the Plexiglas like some kind of mime.

I looked back at the keypad. What was I doing? Scott didn't want to talk to me. I reentered his number anyway The phone rang five times and then I got his voicemail. I did not even get the pleasure of his voice, just an impersonal recording telling me to enter a callback number.

I replaced the receiver and stepped back to stare at the alien. It still walked in place against the deserted shelter. I'm not sure if watching it walk in place like that imposed a feeling of loneliness upon me or just made me realize how lonely I naturally was. What the aliens did in public was not so different than what many of us did in private, walking aimlessly from room to room with no one to talk to except ourselves. We walked to escape the sound of the television altogether or to escape just far enough to pretend the television was really the noise of an engaged dinner company amusing themselves until our return. Every channel showed the world filling up with extraterrestrial mutes; every step we took outside confirmed how they filled all space with abandoned gazes and a silence that became more silent with each alien arrival. *Between stars on stars where no human race is*—that line ran through my head and I tried to remember how it went. Just more noise to contend with in a world where poetry had always been a sort of foolish luxury. What poet ever conceived a desert place made more deserted by the addition of teeming life?

But then what poet could capture my schizoid emotions of need and dread as I thought of calling Scott *again*. If only I could be certain that he was sitting at home doing nothing. Somehow the idea of both of us doing nothing separately was like when we used to do nothing together; if we were both in our houses watching television alone, somehow we were therefore watching television together. My imagination was powerful enough to concoct the notion but not quite strong enough to carry it forward without proof of his participation.

I picked up the phone again. By now the streetlamps were on and the gas station behind me was an island of light, green and yellow, red and white, like someone's industrial Christmas. *Pick up, Scott. Just pick up so I can hang up on you and move on with my life.* Once I confirmed him as a shut-in for the evening I could go on with my own rituals. I'd go to the grocery store across the street, get something great from the deli, and go home to catch up on the invasion. There was no way I could really feel hungry if I was just pretending he was home alone too. I needed concrete certainty.

On the sixth ring my palms started to sweat. I'd gotten further than last time; something had to be different. He was home. He had to be home. This call was just a silly verification I needed, kind of a game we both enjoyed. On the eighth ring I actually felt sick. Why wasn't he answering? Why wasn't I getting his voicemail? My bottom lip trembled. I damn near spoke when he picked up on the tenth ring. That would have ruined everything.

"*Hello?*"

I choked back an answer.

"*Hello?*"

I hung up with a stunned delicateness, applying the sweetest, gentlest pressure to the switch hook. Cutting off his voice was like letting something precious yet heavy fall into a dark lake and sink forever out of sight.

I stepped away from the phone and put my hands in my pockets. I looked up. The night sky was crowded with natural and unnatural bright pinpoints, stars and planets, our own satellites and streaking alien rockets. This fierce pageantry that once filled us all with wonder and dread now seemed as rudimentary as shooting stars.

Still I counted the rockets anyway, getting to fifteen when another alien jarred me on its way into the street. A wild rush of horns sounded on top of squealing tires and cars slamming into each other. I jumped back, startled. The alien had just walked right out into traffic. It survived only because human instinct made a driver brake. Unfortunately those behind the car were not so fast. As the alien finished crossing the street to enter the supermarket, I watched people get out of their cars, everyone shaken but uninjured. The accident snared five cars but only one of the drivers sounded angry. "You should've just run the son of a bitch over and saved the rest of us a headache. Probably stop for ducks in the road too, right?"

The first driver said that as a matter of fact, he did stop for ducks in the road. I moved fast, taking advantage of the paralyzed lanes to also cross to the grocery store. Once inside, my thoughts refocused on Scott at home and remembering how he used to cook dinner whenever we stayed in. This was a special night. Tonight I'd get the food and enjoy a meal for both of us.

Chapter Four: A Meal for One

1.

I approached three National Guard troops near the pharmacy who were taking a break by chatting up a pretty cashier. "Some people crashed their cars outside, you might want to see if you can help," I said. They ignored this suggestion and I headed past them and toward the deli. The path proved indirect because the aliens had effectively seized the store through sheer unresponsive numbers. I'd start down one aisle needing to make a right only to find that way blocked by five aliens standing shoulder to shoulder, each looking in a different direction and all eerily silent. They might have been movie props. I turned back and found four more aliens now capping my escape. I was trapped by blockades that might as well have been concrete.

I cried out for help.

A stock boy eventually answered. All of seventeen, he wasn't tall enough to be seen over the aliens so we spoke as close as we could, a supermarket Pyramus and Thisbe with a wall of extraterrestrial flesh between us.

"I don't know what to do. No one's ever gotten trapped before."

"Get the manager."

"He's really busy locking down the meat, mister."

"Goddamnit, do something now or I'm going to die in Aisle Five! My life is in your hands!"

The stock boy suggested I try to scale the aisle itself. The shelves might support my weight so I kicked the few remaining cans onto the floor with the rest and tried to hoist myself. The shelf's metal support arms snapped right away and sent me skipping back.

"Next idea?"

He came back after a few minutes with a stepladder that he heaved over the heads of our barrier.

"Just climb up the two rungs and then use their shoulders to heave yourself the rest of the way. I'll catch you."

I did as he instructed and landed sprawled over him on the ground, both of us looking at the stark, wraithlike alien backs.

"Thanks," I said, dusting myself off. "What were you saying about locking down meat? I'm after hamburger."

The stock boy's face went pale. He hurried away.

I continued on more carefully and pushing a buggy now, fully intent on using it as a battering ram if I ever got stuck again.

The aliens had destroyed the store with their mindless foraging. As I got closer to the deli the debris became more evident, reminiscent of broken barricades from some desperate last stand. Broken shelves and their contents were all over the floor. One aisle ran red with thick tomato sauce that flowed like a lava bed atop a river of spilled cooking oils. Surviving these gauntlets, I reached the meat section and understood why the stock boy's face had paled.

I felt I'd stepped into the scene of a grisly slaughter. The aliens had groped their way through the hamburger, pork and chicken, tearing open packages to fling the fleshy carnage everywhere. The floor here was riddled with grimy footprints like on days of snow and mud, except they were dressed in pinkish red from treading through drained animal blood. I saw the manager, his white dress shirt smeared with the raw juice of beef and poultry. I peered into the refrigerated bins to find only handwritten signs saying all meats had been moved to a secured area. The aliens' obtuse, disregarding nature had always made a havoc of our stores, but I'd never seen this level of disrespect and violation. Was the invasion reaching the point where we couldn't even shop for food anymore?

When I saw the situation at the deli, I swallowed hard and walked past, thankful I still had any appetite left. Tonight Scott and I would enjoy frozen pizzas and a pint of ice cream. As I finished at the register and stepped outside, a voice shouted: "Stop him, he didn't pay!"

I turned in shock. I'd never been accused of shoplifting, though I'd done it a few times in my teens. The three National Guardsmen rushed forward. My hands rose in protest but the troops shot past and sacked another man just ahead of me. He struggled as a small crowd gathered. The store manager joined the guardsmen and took three bags from the suspect's hands. I had a good view of him and saw every pocket was crammed full of candy bars as well. The thief had been brazen, maybe thinking that with all the carnage inside, no one would bother to stop him.

The manager shook his fist. "Who the hell do you think you are?"

The thief burst into another struggle. "I've got a family to feed!"

Just then three aliens cut between the manager and the shoplifter. Two were wandering into the grocery while the third came wandering out with goods spilling from its arms.

The manager sidestepped to let them pass and then returned to the matter at hand. "You can't just take things that don't belong to you."

The thief gestured emphatically at the departing alien. "They do it! Why aren't you stopping them?"

Several mutterings of agreement from the crowd made the manager scowl at us. Even the guardsmen relinquished their hold and backed off a step, as if the man had become white hot.

The manager gave a nervous cough. "It's complicated."

"No, it isn't," a woman said. "They get special treatment. I've been watching at all the stores, even the malls. They take a loaf of bread or a watch or something off the shelf and walk out like they've never even heard of paying for it, and every time they get a pass. But let one of us try and *we* get arrested!"

"No one's arresting anyone," a guardsman said.

An alien came out with a box of donuts. It went past the jeering crowd and didn't seem to hear any of it. Someone behind tossed a full bottle at it. It struck the alien's head with a sickening crack. The alien dropped—a reaction that silenced everyone in a snap—and stayed down for about twenty seconds. Then it pulled itself back up. It never dropped the donuts. It never turned to see what had struck it, nor did it even probe the bleeding wound. It ambled on past the parking lot, ran into a light pole, crossed against the slower traffic (sparking more snarling horns, more squealing brakes), and turned out of sight.

The thief grabbed the bags out of the manager's paralyzed hands. "I hope you burn in hell. You and the president and all the other appeasers. You let the aliens get away with everything and sell us out. You'll see what happens when the people take power again. When the *fucking humans* take back this country!"

"This *planet*," another man roared. Everyone applauded.

As we clapped, I studied the thief. I didn't believe he had a family at all. He looked to be still in college. He wore a baseball hat turned backwards and a tuft of brown hair sprang out from underneath it. He was cute and in his anger he seemed somehow familiar. I couldn't keep myself from stepping forward.

"Maybe I can help," I said, digging into my pockets. "I'll pay for all his stuff. It's cool."

"No, it's *not* cool," the manager said.

I rolled my eyes at him. "Oh, c'mon. You're making an ass of yourself out here. Just drop it."

"Mind your own business. I can't stop the aliens but I can stop the people. Just because the aliens do it isn't an excuse for the rest of us." He stopped, wanting to continue but obviously short of excuses. "We should be role models for them."

I handed him money anyway and offered a smile at the thief, who repaid my generosity with undisguised contempt. The manager looked at the money, knowing he couldn't give it back. What I'd given him could not possibly cover what had been stolen, but the crowd was going to make sure that didn't become an issue. Already several people had clapped me on the back like I'd just offered a little dying boy my kidney. The manager's last resort was an appeal to the guardsmen, a pleading glance that the troops chose not to notice. Everything was fine, no crime here. The crowd dispersed and suddenly it was just the thief and me. The National Guard troopers went back inside to secure the pretty cashier.

We looked at each other. "I was just trying to help," I said.

"Fuck you." He pulled the bags against his chest. "I'm out of here. I don't want your fucking food. I guess my kids will have to starve."

"That's too bad."

"Too bad," he mimicked. "Fuck you, Bill Gates. You've got money, so stealing isn't an issue to you."

"Do you mean it's an issue to you?"

He did a frustrated sort of single movement tap dance in response, as if he could not believe I was questioning him. I began to wonder if maybe he had a family after all.

"Well, if you've got to steal, at least get smart about it."

"Smart?"

"Sure," I said. "Make the new system work for you. Stand here and wait for the aliens to come out. If one has something you like, just take it out of its hands. It's not like the alien is going to stop you, right?"

His mouth opened.

"That way it's the aliens that stole it in the first place, and since no one inside cares what the aliens grab it isn't stealing on your part when you take it away. And like I said, the aliens won't stop you. They don't notice anything."

His contempt for me had vanished before I finished. He grinned at me in a way that got me all warm. "Goddamn, that's brilliant. That is fucking brilliant." He gave me a bag of M&Ms out of his pocket. I tore off a corner and tipped the bag toward my mouth like a full wineskin.

"Let's see if it works. Hold these."

I took his three bags as an alien came out the door with two loaves of bread. The thief shuffled back and forth on his feet and squared his shoulders like a prizefighter waiting for the bell. Then just as the alien passed he reached down and grabbed the first loaf of bread. The bag tore a little but the alien went on. The thief looked at the fresh loaf in his hands as if it had simply materialized there.

"What's your name?" he asked quietly.

"I'm Craig." I offered my hand but he simply took the bags back.

"You're a good man, Craig."

Another alien came out with stained, dripping brown bags. I smiled at the thief's new enthusiasm. He let out a cheerful roar.

"I'll just take that off your hands, bitch." He fell into pace with the alien long enough to wrestle the bag away. As before, the alien continued walking as if nothing had happened.

"Go get me a shopping cart, Craig."

"What's your name?" I asked, but he just motioned me to hurry with the cart.

When I got back he set his growing pile inside and then looked at me with pride. Now he remembered some manners and extended his hand. "I'm Ron."

His grip was warm and strong. His eyes sparkled. I noticed the start of a goatee on his chin that I'd just mistaken for shadow. Then he squinted at me and I realized I'd been staring and scrutinizing him a little too obviously. He created a distance between us without moving a step, a verbal barrier without saying a word. I sensed he wished I'd just go, that I was poisonous and unwanted. His attitude made me determined to stay even though I felt ridiculous. He talked a bit more, nothing but generalities and never actually addressing me. He might have been speaking to the grocery store itself. The real insult came as he began to boast about his exploits to customers passing by. The first woman he scared out of her wits and she hurried inside. Then a man came up, in his forties but dressed in similar sports drag, a clear indication in Ron's mind of his potential *bro*-ness. The man waited and watched, rubbing his jaw as Ron explained how the scheme worked. It wasn't long before another alien came out. Ron had struck the mother lode with this one. The alien's right hand carried a case of beer, the left hand cradled the store's largest bag of potato chips. Ron captured both into his cart in about thirty seconds.

"I'll be damned," the newcomer said, and in even less time he had his own shopping cart parked beside Ron's.

"I just need a family-sized Stouffer's lasagna and I'll wait all night if it means getting it for free."

"I hear that," Ron nodded, and introduced himself.

Besides dress, the newcomer also shared Ron's need to brag about the scheme, and in doing so only attracted more competition. Within fifteen minutes there were six people with shopping carts jockeying for strategic position around the entrance, determined to intercept aliens the moment they left the store. Alliances formed, with people pledging to secure one product in exchange for another. Now Ron was complaining bitterly and seeing how no one else wanted to listen, he turned back to me.

"Fuck these jackals, right? This was our idea, man."

I nodded. In point of fact, however, it wasn't my idea at all. The drunks had been doing it for weeks outside Applejack Wine and Spirits, which after many futile attempts at inventory control now kept their door locked with an employee beside it to literally usher every individual customer in or out before locking it back. But as everyone else had come to discover, there was always a crevice, an open door briefly unattended, a cracked window that let an alien slip in and occupy space.

"I better run with this at another store. It won't take long for the concept to spread now that all these bastards have the same idea."

"I could help you, if you want."

"I work alone, dude."

"All for your kids, right?" I said with a knowing smirk.

He gave me a *go-fuck-yourself* scowl but then snapped his attention back to the store as there was a commotion. "These two are loaded!" someone shouted.

That someone was right. The aliens, male and female, came out like a pair of young lovers going home to prepare a candlelight meal. The male had a loaf of French bread and a whole rotisserie chicken; the other carried boxed candy, a bouquet of flowers, grapes, cheese, and a skillet and barbeque tongs. I starting laughing at the absurdity of the aliens' identical above-the-fray expressions, but the laughter died as the mob started stripping away their loot.

"Hey, help me with this. I can't get the chicken out of its grasp."

The alien's grip overmatched three people, who all seemed to be sort of dancing with it as the couple walked on like nothing at all was the matter. Finally Ron turned his cap forward on his head and cleared them off. "You want the chicken? Here's what you got to do."

He pulled back and slammed his fist into the alien's forehead. I heard something crack but I wasn't sure when the crack happened— when the fist struck, or when the alien's head hit the pavement. I just felt—I don't know. Sick, certainly, like somehow I too had been punched, only right in the guts. Ron and the others were hooting as they took the chicken out of the alien's limp hands.

Then Ron kicked the fallen alien in the ribs. Ron was a big guy, a great buck of a young man who probably excelled at every sport he tried. In that one moment he killed all the easy physical lust I still harbored for him. His virility became a horrible thing, a gross mindlessness. But he possessed that physically imposing power that demands emulation. All six, men and women alike, followed his lead, gathering in a circle and just stomping with their feet wherever they could. I barely grasped the sound of a body becoming soft from pulverization. It was a dull noise. The slaughter was so soft that if it had happened in my bedroom in the dark, it would not have woken me from a deep sleep. I forced myself to stare down and see. The alien wasn't unconscious—at least its eyes were open and rolling in their sockets from point to point as its ears flapped with usual casualness. I wondered if it even knew it was being killed for sport as the stomping increased to a fever pitch, and I actually smelled—*somehow*—the odor of a collective psychological pressure point exploding. I felt the entire world's patience had just ended, closing a door that had always been only half open anyway.

I turned, looking instinctively for someone to intervene, and found only the companion alien, still clutching the candy and flowers, the grapes, the cheese, the skillet and the tongs. It had stopped with its back to us, a creature locked inside a fog that seemed to be lifting. Its ears rotated about. I thought it might turn. I know I wanted it to turn. I wanted it to be flooded with the vengeance that was appropriate, the same vengeance that had lit a fuse within me. The skillet and the tongs were enough; with its size and power the alien could not ask for more effective weapons, for more *appropriate* weapons in the bludgeoning justice I imagined. I stared hard at the back of its head, willing it to fight. But it didn't. The oblivion inside its mind continued and it continued on alone and crossed the street. I did not care whether it felt loneliness or not; I felt lonely *for it* even as I fought against a madness in my head that told me I recognized them from someplace. They were a couple and she was leaving him to die even though they'd spent hours fucking each other. Maybe it was too close to home. Scott and I had spent hours fucking each other. Would he leave me to die like this? Would I leave him? No, never. But she was going to, despite the history they had together. But how could I know that? How could I explain what I felt—what I *recognized—*

I knew them.

I sprinted to catch up with her. I looked the alien right in the eyes, backpedaling in front of her as she marched resolutely forward. The idea was too crazy, but the familiarity I sensed exceeded more than just some stupid empathy, some genetically-inspired hatred for mindless bullying in the mind of a gay man scared that it could just as easily be him back there getting stomped. I couldn't help but recognize them despite my mind's tendency to lump all of the aliens together. This alien and the one dying back in the parking lot had lived in my house, fucked on my bed, eaten my food, and finally one of them had turned my phony interview into the real thing.

I held out my hand against her bulk. "Please. Please don't go. Please come back with me. You know my house. I want to shelter you."

But it was like talking to an automaton. The alien walked my hands into my chest and then brushed me aside with her weight. Maybe part of them was robotic and programmed to do only certain things. Maybe the explanation given at that symposium back in Colorado Springs was right and the aliens did only share ninety-nine percent of our dimension, and in that one percent they saw a different world, an empty world; maybe they were so advanced that their senses filtered us out the way humans filtered out everything that did not directly concern us. Maybe we could never be a concern to them and they would never see us, even as we kicked them down or cracked their skulls. But wasn't there at least some concern for each other? I stopped trying to halt her and watched her go. Didn't she sense something was missing, that her partner was gone? Could she really not care?

Behind me the sudden report of a gun made me flinch. I refused to turn back and look. Someone just fired into the air, I thought. Just to disperse all those people. Then I allowed myself to believe someone—one of the National Guardsmen, perhaps—had come out to end the battered alien's suffering. That wasn't such a bad spin on the truth. But had the alien suffered? It was more awful to think that from start to finish the alien never felt anything at all, that its life and death were insensate and as meaningless as one long, random walk taken in any direction.

    I staggered home with the ice cream melted all over my clothes. I fixed my special dinner, which I forced myself to finish even though I retched after every swallow. I called Scott again and he didn't answer, and I realized it had never meant anything when he picked up. It wasn't proof that he'd spent the night at home because of course he had only a cell phone.

Chapter Five: Secret Agent Man

1.

On the nine-month anniversary of First Contact, the news channels were all running with the same staggering estimate for the alien population. It was even the cover of the latest issue of *Time*. Just a black background and a seven-digit number printed in stark white contrast. I looked outside my window expecting to see the entire neighborhood overrun. There were only four or five aliens milling in sight, over in the Sutters' yard. I'd become so accustomed to a few stragglers here and there that I never noticed them. But I saw them now, through the window and through the ghost of my reflection, and I let out a long whistle of disbelief. Who would look at those few and think they represented so many? Several million aliens on Earth and to my knowledge no one had yet heard them speak a single word or in any way acknowledge our existence.

No one, that is, but me.

I picked the latest issue of *MotorRev* up off the kitchen table and reread portions of my interview. My hands still shook when I reached the parts that were not written by me. I wondered if casual readers could sense what felt like a dramatic shift between my bullshitting and the stunning truth? The magazine had been delayed when the Morrisons got cold feet, and only hit the stands two weeks ago with a cover that had nothing to do with cars. It was a collage of captures from half a dozen sci-fi flicks for background, and in the foreground, holding an enormous ray gun, was a hot semi-naked woman. At first glance you could not tell it was an issue of *MotorRev* at all. It seemed Mrs. Morrison's coke habit had finally spilled over—perhaps literally—and she'd lost all sense of reality.

The phone rang. Mr. Morrison's hearty laughter blasted through the receiver. "Craig, you bastard, how about that cover?"

"What cover, Mr. Morrison?"

"You haven't seen it yet?" I expected him to be stern but instead he broke into more laughter, exuberant, spilling over with its own cleverness. "Wait until you see the girl we got. She's amazing. You'll still be pulling it to her a year from now, I promise you. She's worth ten thousand sales all by herself. And when people read your interview—"

There was a knock on the door. I went to the peephole while Mr. Morrison promised me that I'd be so famous I'd probably be fucking the girl on the cover if I so wanted. I did *not* so want. The guy outside my door, however, had serious potential if he wasn't a Jehovah's Witness. He was clean cut with a nice suit and tie, and something just a little strict about him in the face. I angled my gaze down to see if he had any literature in his hands, which were at his sides.

I opened the door with the phone still to my ear. I wanted to present the right image of efficiency. Here was a man who could walk and chew gum at the same time. Here was a man with an active social life and a lot of friends, an easygoing, confident man who thought nothing of waving a stranger into his house as he took yet another phone call. Just as I started to motion him, however, he raised his own hand and flashed a gold badge. FBI. CIA. In my shock, I forgot the initials right away. He said my name as a statement of fact and then smiled. He reached inside his blazer and pulled out a rolled copy of *MotorRev*.

I hung up on Mr. Morrison and just looked at the agent. He no longer seemed handsome and boyish. Everything about him screamed threat, harassment, and torture. My pulse went too fast for me to speak without my voice shaking, so I said nothing.

"May I come in?"

I nodded.

He walked past me, looking about, taking mental notes. The inside of my house was like the inside of my world, the place where I was out and open to the point of flamboyance. The wall art—a prized black and white Gerhart print called *Together* that I bought three months ago while thinking of Scott, which therefore made it ironic, since we weren't—left no doubt that I was gay. The agent gave a passing nod, as if he'd already pegged me. He smiled again with what I thought was a touch of condescension and disgust. Outside I would accept it and let it pass, but inside, invaded, a fierce courage and pride rose to challenge anything he might throw at me. I was ready to fight and throw him out when instead he said, "Good taste."

"Thanks," I said. He smiled as if to acknowledge he understood how the remark had deflated my intentions.

"I'm gay," I said.

"That's fine."

"You don't care?"

He shrugged. "Lots of boats, lots of seas. Yes, seas. That's the right word. I'm here to talk about this." He waved the magazine at me.

We entered the living room.

"I presume this is a publicity stunt, right? You made it all up for the publisher, who paid you five thousand dollars—"

"How do you know that?"

"That question can't be serious." He chuckled again, and again my sense of outrage shrank when it should have ballooned.

"You received five thousand dollars to come up with this piece of fiction here. Is that right?"

"That's right," I said, hoping he'd just go away.

He dropped his copy on the coffee table and stared at me so intensely that I felt uncomfortable meeting his gaze, despite being desperately eager to study his youthful face.

"Wrong. We have a problem here." He began to pace. "People in the know—people much smarter than you and I—have looked at your interview. They've looked at the information there. It set off, oh, a few hundred warning bells, I guess. Seems like what they read in your piece squares with some of the information they've been able to determine on their own. But a lot of what they read came as a big surprise. A big, pleasant surprise, you know that? Seems like you put down some puzzle pieces they were missing."

"Coincidence," I said. My tone sounded insincere, even to me.

The agent rubbed his jaw. "I'd like to believe that. I really would. Because the government of the United States has made its own best efforts to 'interview' the aliens. Yes," he turned, as if talking to some moral angel on his shoulder, "I like that, let's call it an interview. I was present at one such interview a month ago. The alien died while it was being conducted. Do you know why it died?"

"Coincidence?" I said. My voice was small.

The agent smiled.

"Relax. I'm not here to 'interview' you. I just need to ask some questions."

"I made it all up!"

"Not without help. Tell me about Ralph Morrison."

I retreated. My calves struck the sofa edge and I fell back, sitting with my fingers combing through my hair. Was he after Mr. Morrison? Did he think Mr. Morrison could actually write anything other than his name on a check?

"He's the publisher!"

"What other relationship do you have with him?"

"Nothing."

The agent reached into his sports coat and pulled out a photograph. I figured it was going to show Mr. Morrison and I was right.

He wasn't alone. I barely kept my eyes from widening when I saw Scott standing beside Ralph in the photo. There were other men there too.

"Have you ever seen Mr. Morrison with this man?"

"No." I found the agent looking at me with obvious distrust. But I wasn't being false. I'd never seen the two of them together. As long as he stuck with that question I could pass any lie detector. In the panic that was boiling just under my flesh, I thought I should try to redirect his questioning somehow. "What's this all about?"

"Do you love your country, Craig? Do you—" and here he turned his head again to consult his angel—"yes, do you love your *world*, Craig? Are you a patriot of your *world*?"

"Yeah, I'm pretty sure I love my world."

"So do these men. I firmly believe that. I think they're patriots of the Earth. They see their world under attack and they act on it. But the government thinks differently. The government thinks these men and others like them are endangering the world. And when the government thinks like that they send men like me out to stop them. That leaves me in a delicate—yes, delicate—situation, don't you think?"

"I'm not sure what to think. What are Mr. Morrison and the guy in the photograph doing that's so dangerous?"

"Fighting back," he answered with automatic urgency, like he'd been dying to unleash the words the entire time. "You see, some Americans believe the government has sold them out. Every government. They do nothing to stop the aliens."

"But what can they do? I've seen them try to open up the rockets. We don't make a dent in their ships. If we can't destroy—"

"We don't have to destroy the rockets, Craig. We have to destroy the *cargo*. That's what these patriotic men have decided to do. Come here." He opened the door and led me to the porch. Ryan Sutter was in his yard, running in circles, his arms outstretched like wings. The traffic along the road continued unabated, saturating the air with noise and fumes. The agent took a deep whiff of it.

"What do you see, Craig?"

I told him.

"What do you *not* see?"

I looked around. Then his point occurred to me all at once. I shivered. "I don't see any aliens."

The agent nodded. "To look around, you would think that the events of the past months never happened, that everything you hear on the news is a practical joke, an elaborate radio play translated across all media, on television and the Internet. You know why? Because people like Ralph Morrison are doing something the government refuses to do. They've seen the problem and they've developed a simple, patriotic plan. One that plays to our strengths and their only weakness."

"The aliens don't fight back," I said.

"Exactly."

I nodded. But could I imagine Scott or Mr. Morrison directing mafia-style hits against alien enclaves? Or leading brutal gangs of machete-armed thugs to hack away at any alien they saw, as if our streets could become home to some Rwanda-style ethnic butchery? I scanned around again, saw Ryan spinning in ever-tighter circles, saw the traffic, saw not a single alien, and fretted.

"So you're going to help them?" I asked.

"Oh, no." The agent sounded almost shocked. "I intend to stop them cold—with your help."

"*My* help?"

"You already have Morrison's trust. And let's be frank, Craig. You have intimate—no, carnal, that's better—*carnal knowledge* of the other man in the photograph. Let's not bullshit each other further on the matter. I couldn't ask for a better spy."

"But why should I help bring down patriots?"

"Because they're not patriots. They're against the government."

"But you just slammed the government—"

"I suppose I'm not very patriotic," he said, "but I still have a job to do. And now you do too. I'll be watching you."

He headed to his car.

"But what do you want me to do?"

"Just be observant for now. I'll contact you again when the time is right."

As he got to his car, Ryan Sutter ran up to him as if to attack. The agent reached into his jacket and whipped out his pass case. He flipped it open revealing the badge and I.D. The boy froze, hypnotized, swaying in front of it like a charmed snake. I had never seen Ryan impressed by anything until now, but then all I'd ever been able to show him was a rock collection I'd started—and stopped—when I was twelve.

Convinced he owned the boy's mind, the agent grinned and smartly snapped the pass case shut, tucking it back into his blazer. He gave Ryan's hair one condescending tousle, palming the lad's head like a basketball, and then got into his car. He backed into the traffic, just missing two oncoming cars, and crisply gunned into the flow. As I came down to where Ryan stood staring after him, still mesmerized, the confusion I'd felt the past twenty minutes gave way to basic American male admiration for the agent's effortless car mastery. I could barely parallel park.

"Hey, Ryan."

Ryan practically yelped in excitement. "Did you see that?"

"I sure did. He was here to visit me."

The boy turned to look up and there was a glimmer of hope the agent's coolness had transferred to me.

"Why?"

"Because I'm important. What were you doing a while ago?"

He informed me he'd watched his bathwater circling the drain last night and how little pieces of paper he tore up got sucked in and pulled down into the "abbess" and how he was playing a game called *submarine sucked into the center of the world*. I smiled and asked if he'd gotten tired of playing alien and astronaut.

"The aliens are boring," he said.

I nodded. "They don't do an awful lot, do they?"

"They don't have any cool stuff."

"The rockets aren't cool?"

"They just sit there like the aliens. Do the aliens have a name?"

"Not that I know of. What about their big wrecking machines? Aren't they cool?"

The boy made a face at me like I was crazy. Then it occurred to me that of course his parents might be shielding him from the knowledge of those monstrosities. This suspicion came too late because Ryan assaulted me with a barrage of questions. What big wrecking machines? Where were they? What color were they. *How* big were they? It was obvious he'd sensed all along his parents were hiding details from him, and now he had proof. I reluctantly answered him, telling myself it was wrong to thwart his parents' will. But his worshipful eagerness goaded me. "I think they sound so cool!" Ryan said when I finished, and went inside.

About ten minutes later I caught hell from Mr. Sutter, who expected me to be psychic and know in advance that he and his wife really *were* shielding Ryan from the scarier aspects of the invasion. They'd kept him from watching any live television for months. Now, because of me, the boy had a lot of uncomfortable questions they couldn't answer with a comfortable lie. Mr. Sutter said I'd be happy to know little Ryan was hiding under the bed and crying in terror at this very minute.

"I'll just tell him I made it all up."

"This is terrible," Mr. Sutter said, not hearing me. "Thank God we're home schooling him. It'd be impossible to keep him safe with a classroom full of kids talking about it."

"That's definitely right."

"Not that the teachers themselves are any better."

"You can't trust any of them," I said.

"I don't know if you can trust *anyone*. Not now. I've been trying to wrap my mind around all this," he said, gesturing at the traffic. "You don't think they could pull off what they've done without inside help, do you? Hell, how'd they even find us in the first place? It makes you wonder about SETI and all those 'broadcasts' we've been making the last sixty years. That's one thing. But this country—I just can't believe how complacent we are. We're not reacting at all."

"The police are pretty busy, I guess."

"Not the police." He scowled, as if I were incredibly dense. "I mean the government. The military. Why are they sitting on their ass like this? What is the president thinking? I voted for that asshole and I expect results. Hell, even Canada's doing *something* to address the crisis."

Canada had established what it called *refugee camps* for the aliens, herding them to designated tracts of fenced land the moment they disembarked. I'd seen footage of it on television and it always reminded me of a cattle drive. A similar idea had been proposed in the Congress, of course, but there were too many comparisons with Japanese-American internment, concentration camps, and other shadows from World War II to make it a viable option—yet.

"It can't go on much longer. People are getting angry. You see it on the news. And who knows what the hell is going on in China and all the places where the media is controlled by the state. Maybe they already have an alliance with the aliens. I just don't like it. Somebody should do something about it."

"I doubt they have any alliance with China," I said.

"Don't be too sure. There's a lot of Chinese just like there's a lot of them. They have something in common. *Lebensraum* wasn't just a Nazi idea, you know."

This was the longest conversation I'd ever had with Mr. Sutter, so I couldn't tell if he was a paranoid right-wing nut or perhaps just sensible in a way I could never be. People like me hear his last statement and immediately we want to say, "Yeah, just ask the Native Americans. They know *all about* Lebensraum." We don't mean to annoy, we're just designed with this innate set of scales that weigh all actions equally, regardless of historical setting, patriotism, or religion. I managed to keep the sentiment unvoiced. People like him thought people like me hated our country and held up impossibly high standards for it. Speaking for myself, I just thought all people were pretty much the same regardless of circumstance; we were all individuals whose impulses trended toward the venal regardless of nationality or race, gender or creed.

"Suppose it is something like that," I said. "What do we do about it?"

"Oh, there are people out there making some good plans. You won't find them in the government, but they're out there. Citizen brigades who know how to handle things like this on the local level."

"You mean mob justice."

"I mean sweeping up trash."

I nibbled my bottom lip and thought of what Scott had told me about how he got the aliens out of his car. Weighed against what the agent had just told me, it seemed like an underground group was on the verge of making it big on the surface. Mr. Sutter seemed like the type to be up on militias. I decided to test him.

"I guess it's all about the *company* you keep."

Mr. Sutter stared at me with a sudden fascination. He gripped my arm. "What do you know about them?"

"About who?"

"The Company."

"I didn't say anything about a company."

He looked me up and down with clear contempt. "Don't be such a faggot."

I swallowed, trying to open my throat. I don't know why I was so shocked. I'd seen the slur coming, his thought process evident in his body language, the way his eyes closed and his body stiffened with bigotry. His cheeks flushed as the capillaries there burst with small feelings of superiority.

I just smirked at him. "Good bye, Mr. Sutter."

He grabbed my arm. "*Please.* I think you know."

"I'm not sure."

"Tell them about me. Tell them and I'll do anything. I won't be ignored any more. I want to stand up for Sarah and for Ryan. Like an American."

"I think you can do that by just being who you are," I said. I know he watched me go back into my house. When I was inside looking out, I saw him still there, staring right at me. I closed the blinds and didn't look out that window the rest of the day.

2.

After the grocery store incident, I found myself irritable from an insomnia that threatened to rewire my whole life. I slept maybe three hours at the most, and then I either lay in bed or got up and paced. I started leaving the windows open again, hoping the female alien would return and take up her old residence so I could protect her from the Rons and Mr. Sutters of the world. But the windows weren't much of an enticement, I guess, so I began leaving the front door wide open through the night. I'd retire to the bedroom, pull the covers up to my chin and wait to hear the noise of reoccupation. One time I got a false positive and rushed into the living room half-naked to find a drunken homeless man passed out on the floor. I was like the owner of a stray dog, hoping it'd come back in the night, only to find a raccoon instead. I splashed the bum with ice water to get him half sensible and then rolled him out the door. He stumbled over into the Sutters' yard and collapsed there.

One morning I got up at four and went down to sit on the bottom step. The door had been open all night and I thought I must be crazy to leave myself so unprotected. Before the aliens came I would have shuddered to leave my door unlocked even in the middle of the day. And if I did leave it wide open, in those days before the aliens, my neighbors would have noticed and come over to investigate. Those days were gone. Neighbors no longer existed and living beside each other meant nothing. We all felt like tumbleweeds that a wind had blown close together, and now another wind, an unimaginable gale, was coming to tear our fibers apart. We needed a new community to anchor us, a new set of values to steel our hearts.

Not a neighborhood but a Company.

The agent had left me the picture of Scott and Mr. Morrison and I studied it for hours looking for signs of forgery. It was strange to see the two most important men in my life congregating without my knowledge. How had they met? What secrets did they share? Did they even know they shared a connection through me?

I went driving, stopping whenever I found large gathering of aliens to scope out. If this so-called Company really was keeping their population down, then they seemed to do a good job. Until I got out of the suburbs and into downtown, I ran across little more than strays, no more than three to a group. This difference made downtown's situation even more shocking. The aliens were everywhere, seemingly thousands of them milling about here and there without purpose, like blown leaves; bumping into each other, into buildings, loitering in the middle of streets, sleeping on sidewalks and on top of cars. The Company, if it existed, clearly had work to do here. As I drove on, slowed to a crawl on roads clogged with aliens, I saw most of the local shops were closed. How could human customers even get to them now? In dark windows I saw the outlines of even more aliens that had somehow gotten inside and made the spaces uninhabitable. Was my alien among them? Had the Company already executed her in whatever sort of operation they conducted in humanity's shadow?

I still left the door open at night, just in case.

Chapter Six: Fun with Martians

1.

The premiere of MY FAVORITE MARTIAN VIDEO became the highest-rated debut in television history, seizing as it did on every nasty, reactionary, angry impulse inside us. I could not stop watching.

In the first clip, sent in from Beta Theta Pi at West Virginia University, an alien was secured to a bungee cord and sent plunging two hundred feet off the New River Gorge Bridge. This was done over and over again to the tune of "Yackety Sax." The host's voice-over said, "Now that must be what re-entry feels like!" and "Not used to our gravity, huh, big guy?" The alien was in the clutches of four hot frat boys, and on the ninth time all five jumped. The kids dangled and high-fived each other as the hung upside down. Finally the kids were reeled back and the alien was left to swing over the river with an expression that never shifted out of neutral.

The host jovially called the second video "Galactic Rodeo." A smaller alien had been forced to all fours with some sort of saddle lashed across its back. Little kids were lined up to take their turn riding it. When the alien didn't move, the kid on its back started kicking his heels into its side. "Maybe they come from the planet *Mule*, kid," the voice-over said. The video cut to show the same alien standing in someone's field. A man dressed like a cowboy and swinging a lasso circled it on dirt bike. After a few passes he roped the alien and leaned sideways to send the bike tearing out from under himself. Springing to his feet, he bowled the alien down, straddled it and quickly hogtied it. Twisted up and tied tight under flesh-cutting rope, the alien kept the blank expression of someone waiting for Godot.

The show started in the half-hour format, enough for seven clips, but quickly became an hour as video started to pour in showing creative things to do with our stoic invaders. The filmed situations became more and more absurd. I watched religiously, laughing when the video was cute, silent whenever one crossed into bad taste. But even those weren't terrible. Nothing in the videos approached what had happened outside the grocery store. I felt certain that, given enough time, the show was the best thing for both parties, a perfect compromise that allowed us to vent collective frustrations while at the same time establishing what was proper behavior toward the aliens.

It was not long before other enterprising people saw the full potential in the aliens' pliancy. I've no doubt that if crime statistics for the year existed, they would show rape assaults to be at an all-time low. Such urges were now directed toward the aliens, who could be grabbed off the street and used for any deviancy imaginable. An alien porn underground, similar to bestiality fetishes, festered on the Internet. I downloaded the videos again and again despite myself, though I was never aroused. What was the point of seeing an alien strapped to a cross and whipped when it gave no hint of awareness? One could only pity these subhuman productions and the people who craved them. Such men had already lost any sense of themselves a long time ago.

Mr. Morrison called while I was immersed in a five-hour marathon of *My Favorite Martian Video*'s greatest hits, as selected by us, the audience, through text-message voting. I remembered the first clip and was surprised it made the cut. I certainly wouldn't have chosen this footage of an alien lashed to a flatbed cart and shoved down various slopes—stairs, winding roads, wooded areas—just to crash in a hundred different ways. The editing did not disguise the bloody lacerations on the alien's face. I wished I didn't understand the audience's glee for such violence. If this were *Jackass* I'd probably laugh harder than anyone. But I could no more enjoy—*really* enjoy—seeing an alien used in such a manner than I could if it was an infant or a dog.

Mr. Morrison had been calling me a lot lately and I'd been cutting the conversations short. That way if the agent ever got back to me I could be truthful and say that Mr. Morrison never mentioned anything about the Company. But my curtness seemed only to encourage him. I wondered if he was on the outs with his wife. He used to call only to talk about writing assignments, all business. Now he acted very different. Sometimes he seemed to think of me as an old fraternity buddy; other times he treated me like I was a psychiatrist. His tone changed depending on his needs, but I finally realized that the gist of the conversation was always confessional. The shorter I got with him, the sooner his confessions came. Perhaps he had killed Mrs. Morrison and covered up the murder, and now felt guilty. If that was the case, I hoped he wouldn't be shy in letting me know. I'd absolve him.

"Could you kill someone, Craig?"

"I...don't think so."

"I have a gun," he said, for no reason whatsoever. My pulse quickened. Also for no reason whatsoever, I got the idea that he was calling me because he'd shot his wife. If I couldn't kill someone, I could at least fantasize about others killing someone.

"Have you used it recently?"

"What? No. *No.*"

I frowned. "I see. I don't own a gun. I think I might be too willing to use it. Especially if I was married!"

"But you won't get married, will you? I mean, you don't...*want* to be married, do you?"

"No," I said with spots of heat on my face.

"Because you're—"

"*Yeah.*"

"Well," Mr. Morrison said. About a minute passed in silence. I heard only his presence on the other side, a hint of contemplative respiration. I imagined him in his living room, quietly satisfied, ruminating.

"Mr. Morrison."

"Ralph. Call me Ralph."

"Ralph," I said, "did you use your gun?"

"I didn't use the gun."

My gaze returned to the muted television. An alien was being shot from a cannon under a circus big top. An alien was posed on a stool between two lions similarly perched. A tamer cracked his whip and the lions gestured fiercely with their paws while the alien stayed catatonic. The camera cut away and a new alien splashed into the water of a dunking booth and stayed at the bottom like a stone and no one tried to rescue it.

"Wait a minute, Ralph."

He said nothing.

"You didn't say that right. You didn't say you didn't kill. You said you didn't use your gun."

Was he still there?

"*Ralph?*"

I discerned him by the sound of subtle movement. He'd switched the receiver from one ear to the other. There was some static. He was smiling now, I was certain. Had I ever seen him smile? Did his lips part? Did he show his teeth, and were they crooked or perfect? Were they false?

"No," I answered for him. "Of course you didn't kill your wife. Why are we even having this conversation?"

"I didn't kill *her*," he said.

The emphasis jarred me. The timbre of his voice advertised the existence of some new, carnal awareness that scared him a little, but thrilled him far more. It was the sensation that maybe long-dead poets once gave to homosexuality or incest, coupling horror with exultation. I remembered my college years and the professorial pleasure of subversive symbolism. That was the period I began to change, to come to terms with myself. As I did, I abandoned both the reading and the writing of poetry. It felt stale to claim victories on paper—small, shielded victories at that. I was through with symbols and codes. Coming out in the flesh liberated me more than coming out on paper ever could. *Sodomy über sonnets.*

"Did you kill an alien, Ralph?"

"I can't answer that yet."

"Why can't you, Ralph?"

"Because I'm a Company man. Somehow, I think you know just what that means, Craig."

A trickle of sweat ran off my forehead as the quiet grew between us. There was much to say that could only be said through silence. I stared at the television, trying to think as I watched aliens running with the bulls in Pamplona. Only they were not running. They stood there getting trampled and gored.

Quick cutaway to some lady in the studio audience rolling in laughter, dabbing at her eyes.

"Ralph," I said.

"You're a good guy, Craig. The Company may have an opening for you soon. Just prepare yourself, okay? The job interview is murder."

2.

I called Scott the next day without a decent lie prepared, but as it turned out I didn't need one. He told me to come over and when I stood on his porch an hour later he came out and immediately embraced me, one arm around my back and his right hand gently massaging the nape of my neck. "You're letting your hair grow too long."

"I've been too busy to get a haircut."

"Busy with what? Watching the world end on television?"

"What's it to you? You don't like my haircut?"

"No."

"Too bad. Ex-boyfriends don't get to vote."

I'm not sure if I meant to sting him. I sounded more playful than aggressive, almost coy. His expression stayed neutral as he said, "All the same, watch out for ex-boyfriends with scissors."

For the next few minutes I was intensely aware that he never broke contact with me as he led me inside, stopping just past the door for a bit of tongue action I had no trouble reciprocating. Scott had always been a good kisser but I couldn't help feeling this was some ruse. To my regret I started feeling he had overplayed his part, like he was desperate to sell me on his intimacy. I wedged my right hand up between our chests and gently pushed him back. This was a technique he'd often used with me when I was too horny. This time I saw that I *had* stung him, and this time I was more certain that I'd meant to sting.

"I guess I've missed you a little more than I realized."

"One good thing about the invasion. It makes it tough to feel lonely."

"I've often felt at my loneliest in crowds," he said.

"You've managed to isolate yourself well enough. No aliens within a mile of this place. How is that? Downtown's practically overrun."

"The city needs better garbage collectors." Scott smiled for just a moment and then sighed. "It won't make any difference. At some point even the waste dumps will be overflowing. There won't be a trashcan left empty. And *they'll* keep coming."

"I heard on the news there was a let up. Not as many rockets are falling this month."

"You heard wrong."

"People are getting used to them now. It'll be cool."

"We're not getting used to them. We're getting rid of them."

"Who's 'we'? The Company?"

Scott fingered the nape of my neck again. "Definitely too long."

"I want to know about it, Scott. What's it compare to? The mafia? The army?"

"Why do you want to know?"

"I'm a well-respected journalist, remember?"

Scott shook his head. "How in the hell did you ever come out of the closet? You're so comfortable living from lie to lie. You must hate yourself."

I leaned in and kissed him on the mouth, as violent as a bite. He tensed under it. I felt every part of him pulling back even though our lips never parted until I broke the kiss.

"I'm sorry," he said in a murmur. "What I said went too far."

"You can atone with a little information. How widespread are they? What is their goal? What's your role in it?"

"Company men don't talk to outsiders."

"Then how do I become an insider?"

"You wouldn't want to. You'd hate yourself."

"I already hate myself, remember?"

Scott walked to the bay window. I sat on the couch. "It's tempting. You may not believe this, but I really have wanted you with me for some time now."

"Is that why you had Ralph Morrison call me last night?"

He turned around, but I thought he was only feigning surprise.

"You are a fool, Craig. A goddamn fool." Suddenly he clammed up, his expression unreadable. He turned on the television and flipped channels until he came to the first news station. For once the anchor was not referring to the aliens. Scott noted it.

"See, Craig? More fools. The talking heads gets us to refocus on all of the silly shit that went down when we were still alone in the universe. The invasion's reduced to the bottom of the screen, in the ticker line. Estimation of alien population size sandwiched between the goddamn stock exchange numbers! Do you still get online, Craig?"

"Sure."

"Well, if you can tear yourself away from downloading porn long enough, you should go to the Resistance websites. You'll find some interesting calculations there. One even keeps an *accurate* running total of the alien population. It looks like the government's national debt clock. There's a tipping point coming, Craig, unless humanity decides to get its collective head in the game."

"Now wait a minute. There's still no proof the aliens actually mean to harm us. They haven't acted out in violence."

"They've destroyed buildings and roads with their machines."

"Machines that stop within a few minutes and never start up again. Why is that?"

"It's done to fuck with us. Those machines are in place. They can be turned on again at any time."

"You don't know that. We can't assume anything about the aliens because—because they're *aliens*."

"What I know is that the machines are being placed strategically, a few in every city around the globe. Some rockets may land in the sea and sink out of sight forever, but never one that carries a dozer. How many would they need to destroy a city? You saw how quickly it destroyed that skyscraper in Los Angeles. Mere minutes."

Scott stared at me with icy assurance. I felt the pressure of his gaze. It made me squirm. As it lingered, I couldn't take it anymore. "*What?* I want to do something about it. I really do."

"It could be something you don't want to do."

Now I stared at him. "Murder. You mean killing."

"This is as real as it gets, Craig. The aliens have changed everything. It's no longer true that those also serve who only stand and wait. You're done waiting, aren't you, Craig?"

My heart was beating too fast for me to speak. I just nodded. Scott's gaze, like a zealot's, overwhelmed and converted me.

He came over and sat next to me, his left arm hooked around my shoulder. I looked at him, waiting. Scott just smiled.

"I think I'll make a Company man out of you after all."

Chapter Seven: Company Men

1.

The blindfold came off and I jerked around to see who had manhandled me down the steep stairway. Scott had me by the elbow, steering me like a prisoner. He did not acknowledge me at all. I was in a basement but not in a house. When Scott told me of the initiation, I had assumed it'd be in someone's basement. This place was too large for that. I saw no furniture and the overhead lights had the same flicker and whitewashed color of a parking garage. Everything, floor, walls and ceiling, was barren concrete. It was a warehouse of some kind. I looked toward the distant corners just as footsteps caught my attention. Scott's grip tightened and he spun me around.

About twenty men stood there watching us. They looked like rough characters, a collection of Sam Elliott moustaches and Stone Cold Steve Austin goatees, regularly doused by grease and beer, swiped clean with a brisk rake of a shirtsleeve or hairy arm. Was this the whole of the Company, I wondered, or just its board of directors? How in the hell did Craig, cleanshaven and lean in his khakis and Polo shirt, fit in with this gang?

Then there was Mr. Morrison. I spotted him toward the back. He stood an inch taller than me and had always seemed so imposing, but he looked puny next to these giants. He didn't make eye contact with me, and his meek behavior and position told me he wasn't the alpha male in this pack. That surprised me. The agent never outright claimed Mr. Morrison led the Company, but I'd assumed it due to Ralph's wealth. It dawned on me then exactly how Craig fit into the mix. I could tell by the way all the heavies looked at him. If these were the Company's board of director's, Scott was the goddamned CEO.

He seemed to sense I was about to look at him and squeezed my arm to keep me looking straight ahead.

Scott hadn't told me what to expect regarding the *initiation*. I'd assumed everyone would be wearing masks and costumes, like Illuminati or Masons. Before me stood men unafraid to show their faces, men who scorned all costumes and delayed business. Most of them looked like they'd just gotten off work but could easily do another eight hours of hard labor without complaint. Here were men to stand toe-to-toe in a fistfight with an alien and win. My face flushed with patriotism and desire.

Scott led me across the warehouse floor. There were partitions I hadn't recognized at first. It was not just one basic room. We turned a corner into a separate space and there I saw the first splatters of color on the wall and larger spills on the floor, as if someone's carefully started fresco had ended in a Pollockian rage.

"Get on your knees," Scott said.

I couldn't help but smile. I thought he was joking. "What, with all these people watching?"

"Your knees!"

"I'm not getting on my knees, Scott."

"Yes, you are," a voice behind me said. A sudden forceful shove on my shoulders sent me down. The same hands that put me on my knees now clamped down on my shoulders to hold me in place. Shaken, I looked up at Scott and found him indifferent. He stared off to his right where the rest of the group approached, dragging a huge burlap sack that seemed to have five hundred pounds of potatoes in it.

For the next minute my head was too heavy to lift, dense with hatred for Scott. Was he this cruel or was it all an act to appease this rough trade? Did they know he was gay? It seemed impossible that such thuggish, rough-hewn men would follow him if they did. Then I thought of how the agent had shrugged at my art and my pronouncements. I was behind the times. Homophobia belonged to a simpler past. The aliens were too important a target to ignore over petty bigotries of race and gender and orientation. Scott knew how to get things done, he knew how to organize and get his way. He had natural leadership abilities but never the drive and ambition to use them. The invasion had motivated him.

A ring of scuffed boot toes appeared at the edges of my vision as the men came to encircle me. I straightened my shoulders and looked up at the nearest man, a skinhead with scary tats on his neck. He sneered at me but I addressed him anyway, as I couldn't stand to look at Scott. "What the hell is this all about?"

The skinhead answered by stepping aside. The burlap bag had been opened and emptied, spilling out an alien that was also on its knees. They shoved it into the ring with me and it fell forward on its face. I jerked back but the hands held me fast.

The alien moved. Its legs began the slow piston motion of walking. The act started like a nervous jump, the last neurotic kick from a dying brain. But the alien was alive, and perhaps not even stunned. It looked a little like a wind-up robot that had fallen over. Everyone must have had the same image in their head, because the Company men chuckled as they watched. Then one thug observed, almost like a lab researcher, "Isn't that the funniest fucking thing? We captured it walking and the bitch just starts doing what it was doing before, even face down on a concrete floor."

"Flip it, Matt."

A bruiser stepped forward and delivered a devastating kick in the alien's side. The force of it took the alien an inch off the ground and slammed it onto its back. The legs somehow continued uninterrupted. *But the face!* Wasn't there a brief flicker of pain and awareness there before it reinforced its rigorous mask? I saw it between eye blinks, or within the quick, imaginative darkness of that blink. I swore I saw it. The alien's face was slack and speckled with fresh blood from a gash in its nostrils. Its eyes darted in random directions that might have seemed like panic if the movements were faster. Slow, they gave the same old impression of luxurious disinterest. Meanwhile its ears rotated like radar dishes sweeping the sky for signs of life. I got the feeling this alien was older than most, perhaps even elderly. Its hair was thinner, sparser and somewhat knotted like an elderly man's. I sniffed an odor from it that I associated with old age, a smell like loneliness and dread, mental decay, interior death.

Its legs curled up to plant its naked, massive feet on the floor. The head elevated, rising with its neck as the alien sat upright. The Company men stepped back as they would before any dangerous animal. Was I wrong to admire the alien just then? It had been overpowered by ridiculous odds and brought to this hole to be tortured, yet it still inspired fear.

The alien rose. The circle expanded another few steps in immediate accommodation. The alien stood as tall as the tallest of the men and as unconcerned as a babe.

"Back down on the ground, fucker," Matt said, the words a harsh whisper as he drove the steel toe of his boot into the alien's knobby shin. The flesh split open at once, spraying blood. The alien flailed back but remained as quiet as a mime until the thud it made on the floor. I winced. If the alien truly felt no pain for itself, then I found myself feeling it for him. And as I heard the new sound of a baseball bat tapping against a man's open palm, I prepared myself to feel even more.

I spent the next five minutes whimpering, trying not to vomit as I was forced to watch the Company's batting practice. Every man took a turn, even Ralph. Even Scott. The alien lay pulverized, sprawled on the concrete floor, its parts only semi-connected after the battering. Its head lolled back and forth like a toy's broken spring, its dark eyes a rolling liquid in a glass with spreading cracks.

It never cried out through the beating. Not once.

Now Scott came forward. "Gentlemen, this is Craig, a friend of mine. Craig has potential. He's a writer."

They studied me. I sensed I was the only thing most of them had read in years.

Scott held up a magazine. I gasped. It was *MotorRev*. My interview.

"Come forward, Ralph."

Mr. Morrison obeyed. The circle parted to receive him.

"You all know Ralph. Ralph is a Company Man through and through. Ralph has bankrolled most of the Company's training plans and strategies at considerable cost to himself. But he is a traitor. This—" he rolled the magazine into a baton and waved it—"is Ralph's publication. This particular issue is more than just a magazine. It is a historical document—far surpassing the Bible, the Constitution, or anything else you can think of. This is the only interview ever conducted with an alien. Ralph set it up. Craig made it happen. And it's *real*."

A volcano of rage had coned up the moment Scott said *traitor*. The rest of his speech seemed lost on the men. Scott led them, Scott had denounced Ralph, and now Ralph must be destroyed. Mr. Morrison turned. He looked like a caught spy trying to flee. The combination of panic and anger in the room was so overwhelming that for a moment I forgot I was the real mole, at least technically. I wasn't sure if I supported the Company or not. I hated the invasion. But I had only to look at the dying alien and hear its labored breathing to remember humanity's ugly, mean potential.

Mr. Morrison meanwhile begged for his life. He sank to his knees. One of the Company men stood over him and seized a handful of his salt-and-pepper hair. His head hung there sort of bouncing, as if decapitated. He looked right at me and confessed and begged. "It was all a lie. Tell them, Craig. We just wanted to sell more magazines!"

I tried to speak. I couldn't.

"It was a stupid publicity stunt," Mr. Morrison said, moaning.

Scott shook the rolled magazine at us both. "Tell us about what they told you. Tell us about what you told *them*."

I found my voice. He led a gang that would kill at his whim, but I was used to arguing with him as a boyfriend and I responded to him in that fashion, with exasperated sarcasm. "Gee, Scott, let me try to remember all those top national security secrets I've ever had access to—"

Hands started to throttle me. My shoulders bunched up and someone laughed and said I looked like a turtle with its head stuck between two prongs.

"Let him go," Scott said.

My freedom was instantaneous. I fell forward onto my hands and knees. Looking up at Scott, I tried to comprehend him. I rubbed the nape of my neck to demonstrate the pain and to flash vindictiveness at him. They really did not know that he was gay; they did not know that we had been lovers. I could spill all of that now and use their bigotry to take him down. Didn't he see that? He and I were also aliens to these men. But the very reason I refused to accept such a status also kept me from betraying him. I would not embrace their bigotry and crown myself with their bias out of spite.

"Craig and Ralph made a mistake by trying to profit off of the invasion. But Ralph has already atoned, haven't you?"

Mr. Morrison, dazed, snapped to attention at the sound of his name but remained utterly lost. "I—"

"Ralph joined the Company in good faith. But good faith isn't enough. So Ralph, like the rest of us, showed his will by shedding the blood of the enemy. His profiteering was a sin that happened months before you saw the light, is that true?"

"I'm sorry, yes—*Jesus, yes*— My wife's idea—"

"Then the blood you spilled has already absolved you. Step aside, Ralph."

Mr. Morrison was released but not before someone thumped him on the head as he groveled away.

Scott bent toward me. "Are you ready to make a blood sacrifice, Craig?"

I stared at him. The CEO was gone. The Evangelist had taken his place. Was this a Company or a Church?

He began to read from the interview. Talk of rockets, talk of galaxies, talk of reproductive cycles and strange religious creeds. I glanced again at the alien. It did not move. Its eyes directed a penetrating intensity at the ceiling. It's listening to us, I thought. It's listening to Scott read my interview. It knows there's truth there and wonders how we got it.

"I made it all up," I said.

Scott dropped the magazine to his side and gave me a patronizing shake of his head. "This is going to take a lot of blood to fix, Craig. A *lot* of blood."

He means my blood, I thought. How strange to think the man I loved was going to kill me.

Scott turned and stared at each of his soldiers. He met each of them eye to eye. "You all know me. A few of you were here before me. I value your trust the most because you placed it in a newcomer, a nobody who came to you with his hand out. Now that hand is closed. That hand is a fist. It is your fist and it does your bidding."

"We're soldiers!" The skinhead shouted.

"Yes, we're soldiers. Every single one of us." Scott's gaze returned to me. "Including you, Craig. You just need to free your heart. It's dragged down by your pretensions." He flung the magazine outside the circle, toward Mr. Morrison at the unimportant, murky fringe. Then he extended his hand to me. "Are you ready to show us?"

I took his hand.

The circle shifted into a smaller, tighter circumference that left the alien and me in the center. It was Mr. Morrison who handed me the bat, grotesquely discolored and splintered from use.

That bat lay across both my palms. I couldn't make my fingers move. Scott came and put his right hand over mine and closed my grip around the handle. His lips parted slightly, anticipatory, and he nodded approval. His eyes narrowed almost to a squint. I noticed his left eye closed a little more than the right—had it always done that? He resembled a diamond appraiser looking at me through a loupe. Was I flawed?

I thrust the bat at him.

"What is this?"

"A test."

"What kind of test?"

"I think you know."

I did. What would happen if I failed? This wasn't some novel where passing the test unexpectedly meant refusing to kill or torture. The Company had no such subtlety. I was to take this bat to the alien's head until its brains spewed. The bat shook in my grip.

"Hurry up and club that fucking seal!"

I don't know who said it, but a chant started. *Club. The. Seal. Club. The. Seal.* I turned around, looking at every man's face. They showed such eagerness, such passion. Grotesque as either might be, they wanted me to fulfill my promise. They wanted me to join them. I could do this. The sight of sniveling, pathetic Mr. Morrison put steel in my knees. He'd done this too. He'd managed. Was I less than him? A month ago the answer was an automatic yes. But down here, where only rage and ruthlessness counted, I had a chance to flip our status.

"Right," I said, adjusting my grip. The alien's legs moved for the first time in at least a half hour. It had taken all those beatings and still had a little left.

Holding the bat head level with my eyes, I stared at the splintered end. Was there any more primitive way to kill something, short of strangulation? To swing this club, to feel the reverberation of its impact, the reverberation of inflicted brutality, ring even in your bones and realize you could stomach it. Could I?

I'd delayed too long. They knew I was chickening. Scott put his hand on my arm. "You've wasted our time, Craig." He reached for the bat.

I jerked away and swung, shrieking. The bat head burst open and disintegrated against the floor by the alien's head. I pulled back, wheezing and inexplicably winded by the single swing. I coiled and swung again. I swung with my whole body and drove the jagged end down like a stake. The alien's face rose up to me as I went down. I was swinging on the bat handle, corkscrewing around it like a boy sliding down a pole planted in flesh. I'd stabbed the alien between the shoulder and neck, penetrating right through the meat so fiercely the shard tore through muscle and tendon. Blood geysered up in two enthused spurts that then settled into a low, steady bubbling. The bat quivered, dancing now to the internal rhythms of the alien's body, its breathing, its pulse. I let go and fell to the side, flat on my back.

The Company men loomed over me, dark, thick wraiths whose contemplation exploded into screams and hoots. I was raised and held high, passed around atop their hands and then placed on my feet. When my legs buckled they hoisted me again, one burly arm around my chest, another securing my hip. I exulted in this sudden brotherhood, aroused as the friendly touching, prodding and patting continued. I caught Mr. Morrison trying in vain to reach me through the much larger men. I found my voice and shouted louder than any of them. I stood straighter even as blind congratulations threatened to trample me. I struggled out of their grasp and they forgot me, turning on each other with a joy that was hard to distinguish from rage.

Scott stood apart from everyone else, alone in front of the alien, just staring. The bat, quivering like some wooden Excalibur, went up and down on the waves of the alien's shallow respiration.

"My God. Look at that."

"You did it," he said.

"But the alien. It's—"

"Yes. I know."

"Do *they* know? Does anyone?"

We looked at the Company men in their revels, then returned our attention to the alien. It writhed at our feet, its right hand tugging at the shard. Its strength waned by the second.

Watching it was like coming across a stricken animal and finding an awareness of death in its eyes you never supposed possible. Maybe hunters, coming upon a deer they'd mortally wounded, had experienced what I felt now. In this final moment, the alien that sprawled at my feet, the alien that was supposed to be dumb and insensate and oblivious, returned a cold stare of defiance.

"It *knows*, Scott."

"Yes, it knows."

Its eyes watered.

"Scott, it's crying. An alien—showing emotion, showing it *knows*."

The alien fixed its lancing gaze on me in a final joust. I grabbed Scott's arm. "Christ, it's in pain."

"Yes," Scott said, still quiet and thoughtful, as if he'd just heard an intriguing poem.

The alien kept its hand feebly on the bat handle. Its stare saw into me in silence. Its cries came out in its blood, which screamed.

"Scott, it *sees* me."

"I know." His voice remained low and calm. "Don't be melodramatic. Look right back at it. Let it know you see it too. Let it be sure you know exactly what you did to it. Show the bastard how it failed in the end and how that one failure has let us see through their lies. All the time they spend acting like we don't exist. It's a game, Craig. Now the game is over. Now we know they see us, every one of them, every second. They see us. They hear us. And soon enough they're *all* going to feel us. They're just like weeds in a garden. They're here to choke us out. Too bad for them the Company exists. Today it's one human stronger, and they're about to become one alien less."

Scott raised his left hand up and I jumped, seeing the gun. "Scott—" I said, but he already had it aimed at the alien's forehead just a few feet away. The alien made no attempt to ignore it, training its gaze right at the barrel and, for just a second, flashing its teeth at us.

The men rushed back at the shot. I turned to puke and was glad for my empty stomach. The dry heaves saved a little face. But the men weren't looking at me anyway because Scott was giving orders.

"Some of you men get the bags and we'll dump this trash in the usual place. Then we'll go clear a few streets. I'm feeling inspired. We'll stuff the dumpsters good tonight."

The Company men roared their approval and moved with purpose. Scott came to me. I was still doubled-over.

"I don't think I can kill again."

"It isn't killing, Craig. It's cleaning."

"I can't—not tonight."

Scott took me still farther aside as the men cleared the mess. Everyone worked at it except Mr. Morrison. Ralph stood quietly by himself with the blank look of a peddler who's lost his goods.

"What's wrong with him?"

Scott smiled. "He's just shaken from what I did to him. He didn't expect to be called out. Men like him should experience humiliation once in awhile."

"He doesn't seem to fit in very well around here."

"Well, look at him. Twenty-five years ago Ralph was the jock. He did whatever he wanted. Then he got to be about forty and woke up realizing his life had changed. He doesn't know how it happened. The wife? The job? You ever read *The Metamorphosis*? Well, that shit's real and universal. One day everyone wakes up to discover they've turned into a bug. Gay guys like us, we just wake up to it a little earlier than most. But it makes us stronger. We learn to cope. Guys like Ralph, they don't know what to do. He'll go to any lengths to fit in. He doesn't really want to be part of the Company. What he wants is a gang of guys he can lead to the strip club and impress with his wallet. But look at us. Look at all of them—misfits in their own way. And you know what they say."

I shook my head. "What do they say?"

"Misfits are the best fits."

Scott walked past me and clapped his hands while I stared after him. "Looking great, guys. No, fuck hosing away the blood right now. We've got more to shed. Let's go hunting!"

That was all it took for Scott to rope them in and lead them marching around the corner and up the stairs. They left the alien's corpse on the floor, half-stuffed into the burlap bag.

Only Mr. Morrison and I did not move. We stared at each other.

"Hey there, Craig."

I almost laughed in madness.

In a sheepish voice, he said, "Look what you've gotten yourself into."

"Whatever it is, you're in as deep as me."

He shrugged. "Guess so. But there's no law against killing aliens."

"There's a moral law," I said.

Mr. Morrison ran his tongue across his lower lip. "That's based on the Bible. The Bible is based on God, right? I figure the aliens are proof God doesn't exist. Otherwise they would have been mentioned in Genesis."

"The aliens made an atheist out of you?"

"You bet."

"What would you do if every alien left its rocket with the Koran tucked under its arm?"

"Convert," he said.

"What if it was a trick?"

"I don't know."

"Well, I still believe there's a moral law, even if I've broken it. And I don't think it has anything to do with the Bible. I don't need the Ten Commandments to know right from wrong. What I just did was wrong."

"But you did it anyway."

I trembled. "I didn't kill that alien. Scott shot it."

Just then Scott called down from above and he sounded like God. His voice echoed.

We climbed the stairs and I got my first look at the Company's headquarters above ground. It was a very large and abandoned warehouse that must have been in lower downtown Denver's industrial district, an area that never got revitalized in the push for a major league baseball team and more sports bars. The few intact windows were brown with dust and grime. Outside I heard shouts and car doors slamming and engines revving.

Mr. Morrison touched my arm. "I've always loved that sound, ever since I was a kid. I built a publishing empire to its tune."

"I don't think I'd call one small magazine an empire."

"Great writers have published in it."

"Only because it pays absurdly well."

"You've never seemed to mind."

I looked him right in the eyes, thinking of what Scott had said about him. I could see the bug he was and I hated him. I hated ever kowtowing to him. I said, "That's because I'm a poser, Ralph. I lie for money. But you know what? It's better to be the guy getting paid for a lie than the guy who's paying for it. You're just a big cunt that a lot of people have dipped in for an even bigger paycheck. Even a little faggot like me has used you to get his kicks."

The world turned over as I went down. Scott and a couple of his goons only just got Mr. Morrison off me before he clawed out my eyes. I rolled over making a choking wheeze, wild and blind with pain. When I could see again, I found Mr. Morrison struggling against many restraining arms as he screamed his case.

"Fuck this! I'm bankrolling the Company! You'd all be dead without me—"

"You're jacked up, Ralph," Scott said. "Get him out of here. Get him an alien. Let's get that rage directed at the right object."

They left. Scott looked down at me. "That was stupid of you. Can you stand?" Whether I could or not, he proceeded to drag me up and hold me.

"I've never been in a fight before."

"You still haven't. He clocked the shit out of you. It wasn't a fight."

"What does my face look like?"

"Purple and red."

I touched my nose and eyes. Scott laughed and said, "What the fuck? Are you trying to tell the colors by feel? Quit acting like you're in *The Miracle Worker* and put your hands down. All that matters is your face looks a hell of a lot better than that alien you killed."

"I didn't kill it."

"Sure you did. We both did. And we'll kill some more. I was hoping tonight, but—"

"I can't." I stumbled as we moved. He bucked me up, kind of steering me on his right hip toward the exit. I saw in splotches of light.

"I want to take you to my place. I'll put you in bed."

"You'll look after me?"

"I'll be back in the morning."

"Where are you going?"

"Back here. There are a lot more aliens who are going to get a tour of the basement tonight. We don't kill them all. Some we rough up and then dump among their kind. Just to spread the word that we mean business."

I said nothing. I had no response to the grim sadism Scott described.

Scott took me back to his house, undressed me and tucked me under covers after forcing me to swallow some pills. When I woke up later, I heard the shower going and found a mound of bloody clothes piled up on the floor beside the bed.

Chapter Eight: Conversations

1.

When I got home I felt like I'd been gone weeks. I stepped into the living room and realized that in some way I no longer lived here. I was not the same Craig Mencken who had last gone out the door. For a few minutes, I walked around inspecting furniture and trinkets and pictures as I would in the house of a stranger. Had I really lost so much in just over a day? Or was it that I had gained so much—the knowledge of carnal violence—that I no longer fit in this old psychological space?

I had to remind myself that this homecoming was not an epic return, like something out of the *Odyssey*. I had never been more than fifteen miles away. I had not even been away for forty-eight hours. So why did I feel the way I did, trespassing in the house of a dead man?

I thought of my widowed father. The accident that took his life happened almost a decade ago, too long for me to still feel much grief or regret. I had been shocked to inherit the house. He had, after all, vowed to write me out of his will because of my nature. When I stepped into my childhood home as its new owner, I was sure that my father's final gesture was not an act of love or acceptance. It was revenge from beyond the grave, his way of making me feel like I'd never make it on my own. Not that I needed much help in feeling that way. Having no place of my own and unlikely to ever have a place, it would have been insane to reject the property. I could have sold it, but the money would have just gotten me into a different house I'd have to make unaffordable payments on. No, Dad had trapped me. I changed almost everything about the place except the kitchen, which was too expensive to remodel.

Over time I trained myself to see the place as a fortress rather than a prison. Here I made all the rules and decreed every opinion. Here I was pure. Was that what bothered me now? How could I pretend to purity after what I'd done? How could I even act surprised that I'd let myself impale the alien, as if I'd never before entertained similar notions to redress personal injustices? At least I could acknowledge the worst in myself. I remembered reading once about the death of Julius Caesar. As the senators moved to stab him, he cried out, "Why, this is violence!" I'd laughed out loud when I read that. He seemed so shocked at the idea, like he'd never imagined such brutality. How many people had he himself butchered? That was Caesar's hubris: his arrogance and conceit, to commit violence without imagining it could be done to him in turn.

But I was a modern man, a liberal who believed in karma. I had never killed anything larger than an insect before, and believed I'd been punished for every spider I squashed. What retribution awaited me, then, for the alien's death? At some point in the future, men were going to come at me with their knives, just as they did to Caesar. When they did, I was not going to cry out in mock surprise. I deserved my blows and I'd take them like an alien. Maybe it would happen in this house. Here I stood already haunting it, waiting to become a ghost.

The front door opened. Expecting Scott, I instead found an alien standing there, its arms overflowing with goods. It had just been to the grocery store. I gasped. It was *her. My* alien had come back.

She seemed just as unprepared to see me. For just a second, she appeared startled. But her recovery was flawless, and in the next moment she brushed past me on a beeline to the kitchen, knocking me out of the way like I did not exist. I was again just the house spook.

I followed her, determined to win through my own silent, persistent staring. I stood there as she heaped stolen groceries onto the countertop, stopping to examine a box of Rice-A-Roni as if it were an artifact from some Atlantean culture. This gave me pause. We had all seen them stare at random things, sometimes for hours on end. But this was different. The alien wasn't just staring, she was *seeing*. I edged closer as she started taking other actions I'd never seen an alien do before. She purposefully opened a cabinet, took out a frying pan, and set it on the right front burner. I stifled a gasp with both hands. To my knowledge, no alien had ever acknowledged any appliance besides the television, and even that was questionable, considering the way they just stared at it. I'd never seen one cook food. They had swallowed eggs whole or cracked them above their gaping mouths to swallow the raw slime in one grotesquely prolonged slurp. They had scooped handfuls of raw chicken directly off the Styrofoam and pursued the residual pools of blood with their lengthy tongues. They ate potatoes raw as we would eat apples; they tugged at raw steak and swallowed, barely chewing. Their actions and their faces hinted at the bovine, which made these ravenous and sudden carnivorous displays even more unsettling. In the end their eating seemed so primal and instinctive. We often felt that some intergalactic race of shepherds had loaded their cattle aboard ships and sent them across the stars to pasture here.

Watching her now was the equivalent of seeing a dumb animal stand up on its hind legs and start using tools. She'd thrown hamburger meat on the pan and in a few minutes I heard the first sizzle of popping grease. The alien turned and walked past me, again brushing past my shoulder like I wasn't there. I fell aside. Fine, I thought. I'd play the game too.

"I'm so glad you cooked, honey," I said. "I'm *starving*."

When the alien came back I was already scraping burgers onto a couple of buns and making an exaggerated, ravenous sound. She watched me with open contempt, and it scared me to think she might attack. Still I couldn't resist goading her and made sure to bump into her as I walked past. With our weight differential, the effect was the same as running into a brick wall, and while I did not jar her at all, I felt elated. I'd made a *stand*. Now in the living room, I found the food barely cooked and inedible. Sounds from the kitchen told me the alien was patiently gearing up again at the stove. I went back to watch.

She stood at the oven cooking like any human. I took my hamburger patties and threw the contents on top of what she had going. "Make sure to flip them every two minutes. I hate char."

I went to the bathroom to see if all the scrubbing I'd done earlier at Scott's house had worked. The alien's blood was gone, but so was something else. Somehow my face seemed more like an outline now. I recognized the shape but the middle was flat and blank, scattered with hints of future design, as in a beginner's unfinished pencil sketch. I turned on the faucet, splashed my face, and peered harder at my reflection than I ever had before.

What did I see in the mirror? Eyes capable of a stare not too different from that of the aliens; a gaze that would rather roam directionless than look straight ahead; a gaze practiced at ignoring unpleasant scenes, in exchanging shadow for sun to string half-assed rainbows across my rainy thoughts. These were eyes that always looked to the right when panhandlers stood to the left while my car idled at a traffic stop. Who was I to ever ignore them? Not everyone could inherit a house.

I sobbed a bit. By the time I recomposed myself, the cooking downstairs was done and the alien had it all on a single plate. I went with perfect nonchalance to take what was mine. I had to tug the plate from her clutches, spilling half of the food on the floor in the process before I claimed victory. I went to the living room, turned on the television, and ate standing up. I wasn't about to sit down and give her a chance to ambush me. As I ate, my hands began to shake, making it hard to balance the plate, fork and remote control. What if she knew all about my star turn with the baseball bat? Was that the reason she no longer seemed to be playing her game with me? Was I a marked man now?

The creaking of floorboards signaled her approach.

The tremor in my hands increased. I was sweating. I dropped the plate of food on the carpet and gripped the remote control with both hands. The last thing I'd clutched like that was the baseball bat, and realizing that made me juggle the remote like a hot potato. But I got hold of it again and began to race through channels, watching a blur of faces as snippets of dialogues played themselves out—

"Won't you marry me?"

"Sons of Scotland—"

"*No sé cuando*—"

"You killed my husband—"

"If you strike me down, I'll become more—"

"And reports of vigilante groups leaving gruesome body counts—"

"You killed my husband."

I looked down as a chill raised the hairs on my neck. The voice did not come from the television. I flipped one more time.

I stared straight ahead and pretended to be interested in a cooking show as my shoulders sagged. I was not as strong as her. Not as strong as any of them. The weakest alien, the oldest and most infirm, had more steel than I'd ever possess. I could not even pretend to watch the show for thirty seconds, while their cat-like talent for watching bare walls never wavered even after several hours.

"You killed my husband."

What did she mean? The indictment was absurd. I'd done nothing wrong at the grocery store. The mob killed him.

I swallowed. She couldn't possibly mean the alien in the basement. That old thing?

"I *know* what you're talking about, but he wasn't your husband. He was much older. He was probably near death anyway."

I turned off the television and stared, shivering, at the blank screen.

"Pretty daring of you to break the rules like this, isn't it? I'm assuming it's a rule?"

If an alien could laugh, I came the closest to hearing it. "Rule? Code? Your language has but one approximation. **Blood**."

I bent to pick up the plate and put it on the coffee table. It bought me more time to not have to look at her. "Is that what you've come for? Is that what you want from me now? Blood?"

Feeling ludicrously triumphant in this remark, I turned my head to meet the alien's gaze. As soon as I did, my lungs just froze up. It was overwhelming, when used to their unfocused glances, to confront such a hard, drilling stare. Such eyes! Seeing them was like watching the film of a shattered mirror play in reverse. All the fragments sprang up into the alien's face, into its triumphant, unifying vision. You realized that you were the broken glass and the alien's gaze was powerful enough to put you together as you were—or as you should be. This was religion, I thought, awash in fervor. There was something holy here—a release, a revealing. Were those beams of light radiating from her eyes? My lungs started to work again, allowing air in short, almost erotic hitches. Hearing myself choking, I brought my hands to my throat. My hands never made it. Halfway there they came together as in prayer and I held them near my chest. Was I about to pray to her? Was she influencing me with telepathy? Her gaze—her gaze… I felt the urge to bend the knee and pray as I might before some magnificent stained glass icon of a saint. A tear came to my eye.

"You're going to kill me, aren't you? That's the nature of the rule. If you talk to one of us, that person must die."

The alien stared.

I closed my eyes and gave in to the desire. I knelt.

"The death sentence falls only on the speaker."

Though blind, I felt the power and weight of her stare leave me. The release was instant.

I opened my eyes. Yes, she had turned away from me. Embarrassed and perplexed, I hurried to stand up.

"You mean you're the one who's risking death by talking to me? That's it? Nothing happens to me if I go out and tell everyone that you spoke?"

"Go out into your streets and tell your people that one of us has been talking to you. Tell them and watch their reaction. Tell them many times and their reaction will be as ours. They will refuse to see or hear you. You will be a shadow to them because what you say defies what they know."

"They'll think I'm crazy, you mean."

"In your language."

"You speak it well."

The alien bowed a little. Since taking her regal gaze off of me, she'd spoken standing in profile. "Languages have always been easy for me. It was in the end the one point of commonality I shared with my husband."

"Can every one of you understand us?"

"No. Most have no knowledge of any communication on this planet. It is gibberish to them. That is preferable. It is easy to ignore gibberish. Gibberish cannot insult or threaten you; gibberish cannot catch you off-guard or distract you. In gibberish is protection."

"Protection from what?"

"From distracting thoughts."

"What you really mean is that if you can't understand how someone expresses their pain, then it isn't painful to hear."

"Did you feel pain when you killed my husband?"

"I didn't kill your husband. I don't know why you think I did."

"He communicated with you. He was killed for it. You are his murderer because you drove him to his decision."

"You mean the answers on my manuscript. I thought maybe you wrote them."

"He wrote them. I begged against it as we argued over your unconscious body. I thought I had convinced him, as I had convinced myself. I left him alone with his decision, as is our way. In the end he was tired of—this—" The alien gestured all around, indicating everything with an encompassing sweep of her arms. For just a moment I thought she meant my house. Then I realized she was talking about life itself.

"Well, I had nothing to do with that. I was drunk. I sure as hell didn't drive him to do anything."

"Your senses were so dislodged that you do not remember your actions. How you begged him. How you cried. Still, this did not bring my husband to do what he did. He had no compassion for you or any of your kind. He was heartless. He preferred war, aggression, and dispassionate violence. He belonged to a different time—the past and perhaps, regrettably, the future. He would have had it over within a month. He despised our sacred ways."

I shivered as I listened and tried to piece together the implications. The true terror was not her words, though, but the tone of her voice. If I could reference the alien's timbre against a human's, I'd say she sounded almost wistful for her husband's preference.

"My husband gave you those answers knowing that I would have no choice but to report it to the Authority."

"Then you killed him!"

"He would rather die than go on with the rest of us. He was discontent and blasphemous."

"So you agree I didn't drive him to do anything."

"Something inside of him responded to something inside of you. Before we came here, his terrible thoughts were always controlled. It was only after entering this house that he grew unstable. I asked him to leave. I said there were thousands of places to go, but he had become obsessed. And now I too find myself falling into the same pit as he. I find myself hating, wanting to be done with you. I dare not share such thoughts with my own people. The Authority is rigid. But I begin to see how all my people show the same strain I confront in my reflection. I fear for us, and therefore I fear for you. Our sacred custom must hold and survive."

"What will you do to us? What do you want from us?"

The alien's smile was again touched with that triumphant air that had so enthralled me moments ago. "What do all invaders want?"

I stepped back. So Scott and the Company were right. And knowing that, why should I feel bad about the alien that was killed last night? It too was an invader. What more absolution did I need? The aliens had to be stopped.

"We'll fight back."

"You do so well. We have lost seventy thousand across your world. Our sacred ways are costly. Some, like my husband, believed they are too costly."

"Seventy thousand," I said in a whisper. I could not conceive of it. Where was this slaughter on the news?

"I am thankful to have landed in your country. There are other places where your armies come for us the moment a rocket lands. They wait until we exit and then they kill us as we march out. Still we come. We have suffered much. We always do."

"We'll kill you all."

The alien made a noise. Perhaps it was a guffaw. It sounded as mirthless as the whooping cough. "You have no idea how many are coming. You have no concept of the waves. Your world lacks sufficient bullets and bombs to defeat us."

"We'll make more."

"You won't be able to enter your factories. They will be filled with us."

"We'll kill the ones in the factories."

"One thousand more wait to take each individual's place, and the place of each individual yet to come. You cannot conceive. You think of the vastness of space by saying the stars are like grains of sand on a beach. But my people are the grains of sand on all the beaches on all the planets that circle those stars."

"This is insane," I said, taking yet another step back.

"Go to your mate. Join his resistance. All of your people will before this is done."

"I—I'll *kill* you."

"I will honor our sacred traditions and sit quietly while you do."

2.

"You do believe me, right?"

Scott continued as if I wasn't there, nonchalantly wiping the gun barrel with a piece of oily felt. Then he pointed it toward the ceiling and lined his gaze up with the aim. His contemplation drifted along the barrel for a few seconds. His eyes blinked, a mental shot, and then he sighed and put the gun in his lap.

"God, I think all the Freudians might have been right. All this time I thought I was gay when what I really wanted was a badass gun." He started to aim at the ceiling again.

"Christ, Scott, don't you have anything to say? I just told you we're being invaded."

"I knew that already."

"That they can hear and see us just fine."

"I knew that, too."

"Some of them can speak our language!"

"How else could it have written your interview for you?"

I put my hands in my lap and bowed my head. The soft friction of the cloth against the barrel resumed, and I closed my eyes and wished he'd give me half the attention he gave his gun.

"They seem to have some kind of dissent going on," I said.

Scott set the gun to his right without relinquishing his hold. "I've been thinking about that. I'd like to go back to your place and meet this alien. Ask her a few questions."

"You mean torture her. Well, it won't work. She won't even be there."

"What the fuck is your problem, Craig? You come here all breathless to tell me what these bastards are planning, you say we have to kill them all, and then you get upset over the idea of some rough tactics? Goddamn, but you're a Laodicean."

I hung my head again, cowed. "You're right. I—"

"Your problem is that you believe every word she said. How can you know if it's true?"

"But the rockets—they keep coming. The *aliens* keep coming. How long can we last? What if they keep this rate up for years?"

"Man up and get some self control. You've bought into this story. For all we know there are fifty million of them. And yeah, that's huge until you put it in context."

"What context?"

"Of humanity. There are *billions* of humans, Craig. So let's say fifty million are on the way. Fifty million arrive tomorrow. From a pure numbers point of view the odds are still staggeringly in our favor and they *know that*. Even if they land a billion, we'd still outmatch them seven to one. I'll take those fucking odds, but we need to fight back immediately. Thin them out right at the start."

"Yeah," I said, starting to believe. That alien bitch had lied to me.

"I think your alien is full of shit. I think there aren't that many at all. I think the aliens are using psychological warfare, coming in wave after wave of small ships rather than a few large ones. Maybe they've parceled out their arrival to make their invasion look larger and—inevitable."

I stood up with a rush of excitement. "I didn't even think about that!"

Scott rubbed his jaw. "I hope some of what she said is true, though. The part about killing them the moment they step foot on earth. Bound to be the Russians or the Chinese doing that. It's ruthless and smart. Our government is still slow on the uptake. At least publicly. I'm hoping they're more competent behind the scenes."

"Doing what?"

"Developing biological agents would be a good start. Something that will kill them while leaving everything else okay."

"You think that would be possible?"

"No. I think in the end it will come down to an awful lot of this." He held up the gun. "But you have to experiment on them first. Mengele-style."

I frowned and Scott just shook his head. He was about to launch into another tirade but I cut him off. "Just because it's necessary doesn't mean I have to like it. Or feel comfortable with the fact that you're making approving remarks about a notorious Nazi."

"You know my heart. It's just that sometimes the only way to have courage is to become an extremist. I ignore everything but the task at hand—especially when the task is unpleasant."

"I could almost think you were talking about our relationship."

"Fuck you." He smiled. "No, you'd like that. 'Fuck *you*.' As long as it's about you in any way at all, it doesn't matter, does it? It doesn't matter if there are seven billion aliens on the planet just as long as there is one of you for everyone to talk about."

"Stop it, Scott."

"You need to hear it."

"You're the one who's trying to twist the conversation! You're the one who can't stand criticism. You've changed. You've become *gleeful* about killing."

He gave me a hard, belittling stare. "You have no idea. Look out there." I turned in obedience to his pointing finger and gazed out the window. An alien had strayed into his yard. Livid, moved by a rage that burned his face past red and into a stormy white, Scott stormed out onto the porch, the screen door wheezing and banging like he'd torn it off its hinge. He raised the gun.

"Scott—"

The alien fell dead on the grass, its head blasted open. Scott bounded off the porch to go stand over the body and put a few more rounds into it for good measure as I watched, frozen, from the door. Some people came, a young mother chasing after two children who'd sprinted over from across the street. For just a moment, the children stood there gaping as the mother caught up to them. The younger child turned to bury his face against his mother's thigh, but she would have none of it. Her posture straightened with resolve. She forced him to look at the body. She was saying something but I couldn't hear her. Perhaps she was whispering or only mouthing some oath. Scott nodded at them with the utmost courtesy and turned back to the porch. When he arrived, he kissed me on the mouth, his hands on my shoulders. He still held the gun, which he placed against my body like it was an equal part of his hand. The barrel was warm through my shirt.

"You and I, we've only just begun," he said, and I didn't know which of the two objects in his hands he was addressing.

Chapter Nine: At the Company Picnic

1.

I spent a week at Scott's place watching the cable news and surfing survivalist websites filled with gruesome pictures and illiterate battlefield dispatches. Scott would vanish for hours on end, just as if he had an office job, and return to see the sites I bookmarked. He read them, dismissing some as fantasy, applauding others as indispensable. Part of my job now was developing the Company's social network and Internet presence. We had to know who were the best people to contact.

The Company had plans to expand.

On Friday, Scott came home early and said we were going camping. His demeanor seemed calmer than I could ever remember, as if he'd decided to quit fighting and just let the world slide. We were in each other's arms right away, like two lovers reuniting after a long war. That was close to true. His hours had gotten ever longer. He referred to his time away as *Company business*, but I knew he'd spent the entire day murdering and torturing. I was glad to have a role in the Company that did not require more direct involvement. It was better for both of us to maintain the illusion of business.

"Where are we going, Scott?"

"Just someplace where the aliens won't be. Someplace where we'll have some privacy."

I'd never been to Lake Dowdy, the place Scott wanted to go, but my limited camping experience in Colorado made me scoff. "Privacy? We'll have a family of five on the right and a camper of sorority girls getting shitfaced five feet from our left." I had a different notion of privacy and suggested we just lock ourselves away in some fancy hotel like the Brown Palace and lose the world beneath satin bed sheets.

Scott shook his head. "We're going to the mountains. You can't get fresh air in a motel room."

"The Brown Palace is hardly what I'd call a *motel.*"

An hour later we were on the road in a Lexus LX, which admittedly felt like a Brown Palace suite on wheels.

"Where the hell did you get this?"

Scott looked askance at me. "I did someone a favor and this is how I got repaid. The Company has excellent employee benefits, don't you think?"

"What was the favor?"

"I think you know," he said, and turned on the GPS.

"What about the stuff in the back?"

"What about it?"

I cast a quick look over my shoulder at the massive red Coleman ice chest that stretched across the entire back seat. I reached and popped the top. It was stocked with more food than most people's refrigerators.

"Exactly how long are we planning to camp?"

"I don't know."

I snapped a look at him. "What do you mean, you don't know? I didn't pack many clothes. That cooler makes me think we're going to build a cabin up there."

Scott laughed and told me to be quiet. He turned on the satellite radio and sometimes hummed along to a tune he liked while I looked at the passing interstate and let my doubts joust with each other for supremacy.

As we neared Fort Collins, I had another question for Scott.

"What do you mean?" he said.

"I mean that all these places book weeks in advance. How did you get a spot?"

"In case you forgot, Craiggers, we're a world under siege here. We're probably the only people thinking about camping right now."

"And how long are we staying again?"

He shrugged.

"Does that mean you don't know or just don't care?"

"It means that we're together on this trip and that's all that matters to me."

This answer and the way he said it almost shut me up for good. He had his priorities right for once and was voicing sentiments that he otherwise only spoke in my dreams.

"It's just the cooler—"

Scott slapped down on the steering wheel. "Jesus Christ! Even by faggot standards the stick up your ass is too big for your own good. Forget about the goddamn cooler!"

"I'm just saying—"

"Well *quit* saying. Stay quiet. Let it ride. You'll enjoy it better, I promise."

The radio stations covered up our silence the rest of the trip, until we turned onto the path that took us to Lake Dowdy. I'd been staring off into space, dimly aware of cars abandoned on both sides of the road.

"Shit," I said. "What did I tell you, Scott?"

The crowds were immediate and thick. People walked about everywhere like the lake was hosting a goddamn convention. Scott slapped at the horn to clear off a few oblivious gawkers strolling in the middle of the road and then sped past them, as if mortified by their presence. I allowed myself a smug chuckle. "Looks like a lot of people here had the same idea."

"But not an alien in sight," he said with a grin.

The road narrowed and turned, taking us past sites overflowing with tents and pop-up campers. Scott, perhaps sensing I was about to talk, accelerated too fast around another curve and everything slid except the cooler, lodged where it was in the back seat, the new stable axis of our world. Scott gave another smart turn and parked. I looked up and saw a pitched tent.

"What's this?"

"Hi, honey, we're home!" Scott said in an exaggerated domestic voice. He took the key from the ignition and opened his door.

I grabbed his arm. "What do you mean, we're home? There's a tent here. This is someone else's site."

"No, it's ours. They pitched the tent for us in advance."

"I never heard of a place that does that."

"Now you have. More Company perks. Come help me with the cooler. It's a heavy bastard."

Scott was already out and around to my side while I fiddled nervously with the seat belt and looked out the window like the air would be poisonous. There were seventy people standing within a few yards of us and I just wanted to return to Denver. Scott opened the back passenger door and ordered me to help him. I got out and for a moment both our hands were on the cooler, tugging. Then I heard a rambunctious laugh to our right. "Phil!" Scott said, leaving my side. I turned and saw him hugging a bear of a man overdressed in full survivalist drag. A curved hunting knife about the size of a Roman gladius was prominent on his belt, useful for taking out any random Sasquatch that might be in the area. As I watched, more people came over to talk to them. I could have laughed. Privacy! Maybe in the middle of Lake Dowdy around two in the morning, but that was about it.

I cleared my throat as Scott finished with his hug. He and Bear Man made a few comments in low, confidential voices and then they parted. Scott turned back to me, all smiles.

"You know him?"

"Small world."

"Where did you meet him? The *Eagle*?"

Another man came up to Scott. The world just kept getting smaller by the minute. Men and women alike went straight up to him and sort of bowed like he was royalty. Meanwhile I could not take my place at his side and introduce myself because my body had become a prop for the part of the gigantic cooler that we'd managed to wrestle out together. My feet kept skidding on the gravel substrate as its weight pressed me.

"Scott," I said. "Are you going to help me with this?"

"Hang on."

He chatted up a few more strangers and then waved off still more supplicants. Then he stood in front of me, surveying the woods and the lake with a serene happiness. "Beautiful up here."

"I can't hold this by myself." I felt red in the face as I lost the war with the cooler's bulk.

"Hmm?" He looked, saw me struggling, and reacted with a smile. Together we got the cooler out and once it was free it sank right to the ground with a jerk on our arms.

"What the *fuck* is in there?"

"You saw it. Bologna, ice, bread, eggs, some milk, plenty of beer—"

"Yeah, but what's beneath all that? What do you have hidden in there?"

Scott pointed across the lake. Several small islands dotted the water, the larger ones wooded and inviting, calling forth the boyish pirate imagination of my youth. "That's where we'll go. We'll take down this tent and pitch everything on that big one right there. I know you want privacy."

"Can we do that? I thought we had to set up on our assigned spot."

"The alien invasion changed everything. The rules are different now. Any place you can defend becomes your space. I'll go find a canoe."

"The cooler will never fit—"

He'd already started off and at once disappeared into a throng of thirty new people who sped toward him, orbited briefly, and then followed along in his gravitational pull. I sat down on the cooler and tried to convince myself how much better it all would be when we did get to the island. Scott was going to take care of me. I should have been proud of our relationship. After all, my partner was clearly the most popular man in the campground. I couldn't help but anticipate a certain pride of place when everyone watched us row over to our own private world.

But after half an hour he still hadn't returned. I figured I'd misunderstood his intent and was supposed to go find him, since he probably couldn't carry the canoe back on his own. I took off in the direction I last saw him and followed a trail around the edge of the lake. Small clusters of people gathered at occasional tents, but as I went I found more and more people joining me as if I had my own disciples. My posture straightened. I walked with purpose, smiling and nodding as if they were all here to see me. Some of the people even smiled back.

I soon had over a hundred people surrounding me as we all went in the same direction. The path led to a far more massive convergence, something like a thousand men and women pumping their fists in the air to agree with the words of an amplified voice that sounded riled and psychotic. I ran up against an impenetrable perimeter of muscular backs. I stood up on my tiptoes and weaved my gaze between necks and heads. At last I saw the rough grandstand that had been constructed right in the middle of the campground. Scott stood on it, microphone in hand. The Evangelist was back, preaching fire and brimstone for the aliens.

Just over my right shoulder, a man said, "Enjoying the Company picnic?"

The voice was familiar in an indistinct way. I turned to find the handsome secret agent standing just behind me. The smart dress clothes from before were gone, replaced by camouflage and an absurd brown bandana that pushed his hair back and up like some forgotten eighties movie character. His face showed a trace of stubble that glinted gold and red in the sunlight. Bandana aside, he looked good and his shirtsleeves, pushed up past the elbow, revealed smooth, muscular arms.

He laughed, noticing my stare.

"Sorry," I said.

He took my arm and led me from the mob. "Nothing to be sorry about," he said. "What red-blooded American guy doesn't want to be admired? I admire you, after all."

"You do?"

"You work fast, Craig. Real fast. I ask you to infiltrate the Company and within a few weeks you get it done. Amazing."

"You're a Company man now too, I guess?"

"Working on it. Yes, that's a good way to describe it. I'm *working* on it. But you're one who is in like Flynn. Did you know the government now considers you a vital resource?"

"Oh?"

"You're in a position to influence what I believe is the most important and dangerous militia to ever form in the United States."

I laughed. "If you want to see influence, I'll introduce you to Scott."

"I think that would look suspicious."

"Why?"

He just smiled at me, as if waiting for my slow mind to catch on. I didn't, so I just played along. "You're probably right," I said.

We started toward my campsite and I told him everything I knew. By the time I finished, my voice trembled in a way that surprised me. I'd become emotional, but it was not the emotion of reliving some of the worst, most violent moments of my life. Instead I felt the stir of confession, the desire to be understood and forgiven. After all the internal blurs of rationalizations, I just wanted to understand myself. I suppose that's all I ever wanted, but when I finished I felt the agent now knew more about me than I did. Perhaps he now knew more than any man, including Scott. We reached the Lexus and I sat down on the cooler, looking at him and waiting for his judgment.

He only said, "You've been through a lot," but it was enough for me. I nodded and let my head drop into my hands. I rubbed my temples.

"What's happening here?" I asked.

"You might say that different units within the Company are getting together to discuss an overall marketing strategy. The Company is spreading. Franchises are popping up in every city. Franchises," he said, repeating the word with a little laugh.

"Did you infiltrate one of the other groups?"

"No, but other agents have. I'm here disguised as one of their friends. I'm a recruit. Not that anyone here would know. Rightwing militia groups are never as suspicious as you might think. They don't run background checks. They don't interrogate you and try to catch you in a lie. Just spout out whatever bigotry they subscribe to and you're automatically in most of the time."

"Are you still going to destroy the Company?"

The agent raised his eyebrows and seemed surprised. "You think we shouldn't? Back there some of them are talking about cleaning out the government once the alien threat is neutralized."

"There are always nutcases."

"When you were telling me your story, you sounded like you felt the Company should be destroyed. The dehumanization you experienced sickened you. How did you put it? Giving up your humanity to prove your humanness wasn't worth it. You'd rather die. Has that changed in the last five minutes?"

"The aliens are here to destroy us. There's no doubt about that."

"No doubt," the agent said.

I raised my hands to implore him. "If the Company is fighting back, we should help them. I don't like their methods, but maybe if sane people can gain control we can change things from within. We'll kill as quickly and efficiently as we can, knowing that it's war. But we won't become Nazis about it. We won't torture."

"Unfortunately a great many have already become Nazis. That's the government's concern. The Company gets rid of the alien threat and then the Company gets rid of the government. The analysis is pretty clear on that point."

"Fuck the analysis. If the aliens aren't stopped there won't be a government to overthrow anyway!"

A jeep came around the corner with a horrible thumping noise, as if its back tires were shredded. The jeep was pulling two aliens on a heavy chain. Their bodies skipped and bounced and flipped on the gravel road. A long smear of blood, fur and flesh chased the jeep's path as it went out of sight.

"The alien invasion has opened up a door of deep psychosis in the mind of the population. The hatred is too powerful. The door will never be closed again. Left in the hands of the Company, we will never know victory. Even if they kill every alien, it will not be enough. Who will be their next target, Craig? Blacks, Jews—gays?"

I made no motion or sound. In my heart, I felt the agent was right.

"It's hot out here," he said. "How about getting us a drink out of that cooler?"

I stood up and opened the lid. I didn't see any beers straight away so I jammed my hand into the ice. About halfway down fingers hand ran into the first strange object. The agent came over and watched as I pulled out the ammunition, the explosives, and the guns. They were stacked in rows, sealed in plastic, and when I finished I realized there was only enough actual food in the cooler to last two days, provided we stuck to snacking. Everything else was munitions.

"This is military issue," the agent said, inspecting a gun. "Looks like we have some people in the army with conflicting allegiances."

"I think a lot of people are having some issues there."

"Not soldiers."

"What about ex-soldiers, then? Sixty percent of the men I've seen so far are dressed like Rambo."

"A lot of them are National Guardsmen. This rifle here came from a Guard stockpile, I'm pretty sure. Your friend Scott, was he in the Guard?"

I shook my head. "But some of the Company men I've seen look like they could be. Then there's Mr. Morrison. He's bankrolling our group. I bet he knows."

"Where is he?"

I realized I hadn't seen him. Surely he was here. Probably up in the front of the crowd, shining by reflecting the light of bolder men like Scott. I offered the agent this hypothesis.

"Get all of that stowed back in the cooler. There's mud around from the melting ice—scrape dirt over it. Don't let anyone know you've seen what's inside. Get it stowed and get back to the rally. We'll see each other again."

"I'd like that," I said, a little too softly. This time the agent seemed less amused.

2.

I finished repacking the stockpile but I did not return to the rally. I walked down to the water's edge and sat on a rock to stare at the island that only two hours ago had housed my hopes for a quiet evening. The sun was setting, its pale orange disc a balloon fragmented and threatened by a million pine needles. I'd welcome nights up here, I thought, if only because one of them would lead to the day when we got the hell out of here.

Scott didn't return for hours. I rummaged through the cooler for actual food, reduced to eating cold bologna to ward off starvation. When evening came, the water rippled from fish even hungrier than I was. Some got too ambitious and jumped into the air, going for the abundance of mosquitoes at the surface. The hitting increased and soon the lake was dimpled with little agitations as steady and constant as rainfall.

As I watched, I wondered how many fish there were just yards in front of me—hundreds? Thousands? So much of life was buried; you never had a true inkling about numbers. You couldn't count the fish in a lake any more than you could count the thoughts in someone's head. You saw hundreds of ants building their castle and thought it the whole of their colony, ignorant of the seventy thousand more working below. Life beneath the water, life beneath the ground, life beneath dull glances. Take it all and multiply it by... I looked up at the sky and the stars that would be there if not blocked by clouds.

Scott came to me and put his arm around me, his palm flat against my chest. "I guess you figured it out."

"I'm not sure."

"We've been studying this invasion for a long time now. We had to get everyone together, to get our spirits up and draw our plans against them. There are groups from forty states here right now. Coordinated retaliation is about to start in earnest. We can't afford to operate like some Klan group that kidnaps and kills in the dark. Now we won't have to. The police will not move to stop us now. Hell, I think we have half the Denver PD up here right now."

"Well, that's good." My voice sounded tired and defeated.

Scott's other hand touched me, rubbing my left triceps, spreading warmth. "There's more, Craig. No one knows what will happen. This place could one day be our last stand. We're stockpiling weapons here. We've been constructing bunkers for them everywhere. There may come a time when we're separated and the whole world seems to be going up in fire. If that happens, if there's no communication, if the invasion throws us back—come here, to Lake Dowdy. I'll try to make it back too. Whatever happens, I will find you."

"That's a movie line, isn't it?"

"Don't ruin the moment by being a smartass, Craig."

I turned and found total seriousness in his expression. His concern moved me and I began to get really happy in his arms. "We'll never get separated," I said.

"But if we *do*, come here. I'll come, too. But even if I don't, there'll be people here to help, to fight at your side. I hope you learn to fight at theirs, even if it means becoming the kind of person that you hate. These are good people, Craig. People with the strength to act."

He kissed me.

Gunshots started going off nearby. I jumped in Scott's hold and he offered a light laugh. "Just some live target practice. A few aliens some enterprising people bundled up for the trip."

A man's voice called Scott's name from behind us. We turned. An old man with a lean face coated in gristly white stubble stood waiting. He had a piece of paper in his hand. The hand shook from what I thought was palsy.

Scott went and took the paper. He seemed to take the man's palsy too, because his own hand trembled as he read.

"What is it, Scott?"

"The most accurate figures we have on the invasion. Some guy at MIT did the calculations."

The old man was already receding into the darkness, his shaking hand planted over his mouth. Scott said one thing to him, an indication that another tent revival was about to go down. I reached for the paper but Scott crumpled it and threw it on the ground.

"We'll mow them down where we find them," Scott said.

I bent, took the wadded ball, and smoothed it against my chest. The mention of MIT made me think I was about to see some amazing computer printout of organized data, maybe printed on stationery with some sort of official seal. What I found instead was a handwritten scrawl of numbers in a few undefined columns. Below the columns were some multiplications scribbled out so poorly the old man might have done it, and all of this written on a piece of torn notebook paper. Glancing between it and Scott's determined look, I almost laughed. Unreality washed over me. I felt like we were playing an elaborate role-playing war game and had gotten too immersed in the pretending.

Scott caught on and flashed his annoyance. "I know it doesn't make sense unless you've seen similar figures before and know what the columns mean. Let me explain." He pulled out a penlight that he used to guide my vision from number to number as his words connected them and guided my thoughts. One rocket falling on average every five minutes, always the same number of aliens per rocket. Two hundred and eighty-eight rockets per day.

Eleven thousand, five hundred and twenty aliens a day.

The date of the first rocket.

Today's date.

I looked at the sky again. The cloud coverage refused to abet my imagination.

"There are minor problems with the data, of course," Scott said. "Not every rocket touches down on solid ground. Maybe two hundred have landed in the ocean and sunk, so those aliens are presumed dead. Hopefully your alien was right about the tactics other countries are using. If the more totalitarian nations have the balls the U.S. lacks and are being aggressive about the situation, then we may be able to subtract a few hundred thousand from the total. Maybe even more. That's a plus for humanity but a negative for the United States. By the time our army gets around to taking care of business, they'll be too overwhelmed. Meanwhile those other countries will have their own interiors controlled by taking early action. Start expecting some land grabs in Europe and the Middle East while we're busy being choked by these fucking weeds!"

"God," I said.

"They're still up against seven billion of us. Remember that."

I did. I also remembered Scott telling me how the aliens were playing psychological games, coming in wave after odd wave to make their numbers seem more formidable. The problem was, the calculations on this paper suggested those numbers *were* more formidable. The highest estimate I'd ever seen for the current alien population was twelve million. The figures on the page were almost double that. A million here and a million there, and pretty soon you're talking about a significant invasion force, even if that force did nothing but stand around.

I studied the paper again. "What's this fourth column? The figures there don't seem so bad. Just a few thousand."

"It's the known number of the wrecking machines that have landed in Asia, Europe and the United States. The *dozers*."

"They've really landed that many?"

I remembered how a single dozer destroyed a skyscraper in Los Angels in less than a minute. It took no effort to imagine it coming to life again, joining a line of thousands rolling across the country to take out our cities and monuments. With so many of them, how long would a block take? A few minutes? If they worked nonstop, how long could a city last against them? A week?

"Scott, I don't want to stay up here. I want to go back now and fight."

"I agree. We have to step up our plans. The longer we're up here doing nothing, the harder it's going to be. We were going to make this last a few days, do some strategy sessions. But there is no real strategy, is there? Ultimately it comes to just pointing and shooting."

I nodded.

Scott ordered me to help him with the cooler. We got it into the back seat again.

"Maybe we should have unloaded some of it," I said.

Scott patted the top. "I was going to put some of this *food* in storage up here. But I think we'll need it all for ourselves now. Don't you agree?"

An hour later, we were racing toward Denver with a few hundred cars following, everyone blasting their horns in triumph to announce the coming Purge.

BOOK TWO
Landlords

Chapter One: Oxbow Incident

1.

Rick killed the first two aliens after I kept missing and the third I shot by accident, since I'd tried to miss on purpose. The alien moved into my misfire as if determined to commit suicide. When it went down, Rick gave me a clap on the back, told me it was nice work and good shooting, and ordered me to grab its legs. Rick was my partner tonight, one of the other ten men in our division. We holstered our guns—I tucked mine into my front pocket—and we bent to take the alien to the blue industrial recycling bin on the street corner. During the second week of our coordinated resistance, the recycling bins began appearing in advance at select street corners, evidence of the city government's assistance with our night's work. Neat and tidy disposal was not the Company's stock in trade. Most of my colleagues would have preferred to let the bodies lie in heaps, as a lesson to the aliens who survived. But disease became too great a concern and so the bins were placed there by some city official for the sake of sanitation. They were emptied by five in the morning and the greater population of Denver, who had learned to ignore the gunshots and who taught their children to pretend they were fireworks, woke to the pleasing sound of water running from the mains as the alien blood was washed into the sewer.

We struggled with the dead weight about forty yards before managing to pitch the corpse into the bin, which was already crammed to overflowing. There were sixty bodies total, some wounded in the extremities, all executed in the head. Blood ran from the four corners of the bin's bloated metal belly like excess rainwater.

"Got another clip?"

I gladly gave the Company man my spare and wiped my hands on my pants. More shots rang out down the street, sparking excitement in my partner's eyes. "Come on," he said, running off. I took the gun from my pocket and followed him. This has to be done, I thought. There's no other way. I wasn't like them, but I wasn't pure either. I couldn't judge anyone for exuberant acts of violence. I felt the same emotions, the same desire to destroy the aliens and protect what I loved. In my heart, I was no less sullied than the Company's most ruthless killer. That its most ruthless killer was Scott gave me no pride, but also made me feel no horror. As I walked, as I acted like I was trying, shooting bullets just to the right or to the left of my target to make sure I missed, I just kept repeating the numbers. And as the bodies fell and others did my killing for me, I repeated the number and subtracted. Twenty million minus one. Minus two. Minus thirty.

Minus two hundred and fifty.

We stood on the 16th Street Mall. I looked toward the D&F Clock Tower, its pale face proclaiming the time was neither wrong nor right. It was two in the morning and our division had had been retaking this section for over two hours. Gunshots echoed through the city as if Denver were Sarajevo under siege. I thought of the people in their homes, in their beds. Were they still terrified by our actions or did they sleep through it now, content to ignore the slaughter, waiting for the sunrise and the sound of water to tell them it was over for now? The official, systematic effort to ignore our actions was almost startling. The papers made no mention of it. No news crews followed us, no amateur filmmaker tried to interview us. The heinous but necessary acts of the Company exceeded the limits of even the most ambitious documentarian. If the human race made it through this invasion, if we had a future, the Company's value to the war might one day be known only through the oral history of the survivors.

Rick stopped for a cigarette. "The cleanup crews are going to be pissed tonight," he said with a chuckle. "Bunch of union fucks."

I nodded, looking back toward the pile of bodies that couldn't be put into the recycling containers. I still didn't know if the Company told the city what zones they were targeting, or if the city placed the bins in the areas they wanted us to cleanse. Some people were going to be outraged at having to get down and fling those corpses into the disposal trucks.

"Let's go," Rick said. That and *Come on* were his favorite expressions.

We went down the Mall. Being here so late at night brought back some old memories. When I was eighteen I had a job with the *Denver Post* that included filling the newspaper dispensers along the Mall. I sometimes did this as early as four in the morning, when the Mall was populated only by the homeless and a few roving teens. The homeless slept or drank while the teens drank or vandalized and looked for easy scores. I had my first sexual experience near the alleyway I stood in front of right now. I got propositioned for ten dollars. My memory of it was as surreal as when it actually happened, a crazy blur of ballet and robotic movements that led me to say yes as if always destined to say yes, and to forsake my newspapers for the dark end of an alley that was as dangerous and arousing as the blowjob itself.

"Snap out of it, Mencken. Come on."

When we reached Scott's position farther down the Mall, we found the Company arguing over the body of an old man. He'd been killed by accident when he stumbled out of an alley. Company men had made similar mistakes in the past. Some wanted him left in the street but the shooter feared prosecution so Scott had them take the body to the closest dumpster. They unloaded several bodies to make room and then flung the dead man inside and piled the aliens on top. No one would see the difference, and if someone did the Company would say the man had been a collaborator, a traitor who deserved the bullet. I stood back, watching Scott manage the crisis, and felt ill. From across the street, I just stared into the dark alley the bum had stumbled from, and I saw the ghost of my youth's face contorted with too much pleasure and carefree disgrace.

We got back to work. Two aliens loitered in front of a window display and Scott's bullets dropped them. One bullet passed through the alien's flesh and shattered the glass.

A Company man fired into the air.

"Police!"

"Ask them for more ammo," Scott said.

Three cruisers came up the Mall, their lights flashing in silence. We did not stop and neither did they. The officers nodded and drove past. Nothing to see here, all as it should be.

"Pigs," Scott said. "Fine if they won't get their hands dirty, but does that mean they have to hoard the soap?"

I shook my head. "What?"

"They won't re-supply us," Rick said. "We're running low on bullets."

Scott was shouting into his cell phone, which he suddenly snapped shut. The gunshots were fading, growing infrequent. Then silence. Scott scowled and called everyone to him. We weren't just low on ammunition, we were out. There was no hope for a resupply for at least another hour.

A woman who'd scouted up ahead came to make her report.

"How many are left?"

"Four, right at the end of the Mall. They're just sitting there, Scott. Goddamn."

"They'll be here tomorrow," I said. "We can just come back."

Scott flashed me a look like I'd just offered our surrender. I looked at my feet as a small argument broke out.

"Who's still got bullets?"

We looked at each other. I still had one.

"Right. Then what about the other three?"

"Knives would be the simplest."

"I'm for the ropes. Makes a statement."

"Knives don't make a statement?"

Scott raised his hands. "Brad, go to the back of the truck and get the ropes. Get four."

"We only need three."

"Four ropes," Scott said, and walked past me.

Soon we were walking to the end of the Mall with four nooses swinging in front of us as we approached the aliens.

"That one first," Scott said. The aliens did not resist. They gave no indication we existed or that they knew they were about to die. Their entire demeanor suggested they had found the street, the city and the world deserted for a thousand years and preserved in dust. We were just the ghosts of a dead civilization. As the nooses were strung about each neck, I had to remind myself that they were quite aware of our intentions. They had watched us kill their own people for the past two hours and made no attempt to escape.

The old disgust and awe returned. Any human would flee in terror from us. Were the aliens so much more courageous? Was superior courage the root of the game they played? As the ropes fell over the necks of light poles; as the men lined up to hoist; as Scott saw me standing there gawking and swore at me; as the aliens went up simultaneously—as these moments passed, I went a little crazy, thinking we were the aliens, thinking we had invaded them, thinking we were slaughtering them for their land. The ropes were tied and the aliens hung limp, limp but not yet dead; they would not acknowledge suffocation any more than they would a slap in the face. The Company men admired their work and receded, off to use knives and bats, off to use their cars to just run the aliens down. I looked up to contemplate what we had done and what we were doing. I stood tiptoe and reached to touch one dangling foot.

"Sickening, isn't it?"

A man stood at the dark edge of the alley behind me. By instinct I looked about for Scott, but he and the rest of the Company had sprinted up the Mall to our caravan. He'll drive down to pick me up, I thought. Once he notices I'm gone.

"How long have you been watching?"

"From the start."

The secret agent stepped into the street.

"I don't believe you."

"It's true," he said, his tone easy considering I'd just called him a liar. He seemed the type to take offense.

"Then you're stupid." I don't know what kept me pulling his trigger. Maybe all the deaths had numbed me to consequences. At some point the hammer was going to fall on a full chamber and set him off.

"What I mean is, you could have got yourself shot. We raided down every one of those alleys to flush out aliens. The Company wasn't being too particular about targets."

"I know. They almost had me. The homeless man—"

He saw my reaction and grinned. "I got lucky. He was lying there half comatose. One swift kick got him up and moving, though. After they gunned him down by mistake I knew this alley would be psychologically off-limits. It was a taboo in their minds and I hid in that taboo, in plain sight. Only you saw me. You were looking right at me."

"No."

"If you say so. But from then on it was just a matter of stealth. Yes, stealth, that's the word I want."

"Christ. How many people do you have with you?"

"No one."

I laughed with outright bitterness. "Fat lot of good you're going to do against the Company! I thought the government was serious about stopping them."

"They are, and so am I. Right now I'm just observing."

"I hope you got a good eyeful."

The agent smiled. "I saw that you're a horrible shot. So horrible it must be on purpose."

"I have mild multiple sclerosis," I said. "Sometimes my hand shakes."

"Does multiple sclerosis make you aim at the sky? Or were you trying to wing the last of man's better angels?"

Lights came at us from the top of the mall. The agent moved to my side, surprising me. I'd expected him to scurry into the alley.

"That's Scott, you better hide."

"No, you're going to introduce me."

"Like hell. I thought you said that'd be risky."

"Not anymore."

The lights splashed us. Seeing me with another man, Scott stopped.

"Here's the story you're going to tell." He fed me the lines and in half a minute I was repeating them to Scott, with a few embellishments to enhance belief. After all, I did not think Scott would buy that the agent was my long-lost brother, come to join our ranks. I would have to write my Congressman requesting better training for our secret agents. This one couldn't lie off the cuff worth a damn.

2.

When I came downstairs after showering, I found the agent and Scott sitting too close on the couch. Scott on the left had stretched his arm across the back to allow his hand easy access to the agent's right shoulder. Between the top step and the bottom I saw him give two bluff, lingering pats. I avoided them with a quick turn into the kitchen.

"Look, Scott, you don't have to be coy with me. Everyone's heard of the Company by now." The agent laughed. "I hope Denver's Solid Waste Management was able to come and clear the mess on the Mall, though. Otherwise some shop keepers are in for a grisly surprise, I think."

"That's all been worked out a long time ago," Scott said.

They shared a laugh. Scott told him things he'd never bothered to tell me. Of course the mess wasn't reported on the news. Most of the reporters were Company employees now, just like everyone else. Atrocity? Mass murder? What atrocity? What mass murder? Our cameras didn't see anything. No, the police don't have any reports about gunfire in the city. The public that didn't know was happier not to know, and the public that did know was even happier being able to ignore it.

"Do the dirty work at night, go on living in sunlight," Scott said. I couldn't see him but I knew he was shaking his head. "At some point everyone's going to have to realize this is non-stop work. The killing has to be done round the clock. The aliens don't stop coming between breakfast and dinner."

I poured some orange juice and had the cup to my lips when the agent said something that brought out Scott's special laugh. His special laugh was a low chuckle of contentment that he gave after being particularly satisfied—by food, by sex and now, it seemed, by the shared reverie of violence. I tipped the glass back and swallowed hard, twice. The orange juice seemed to become a solid block in my throat.

"Yes, I can do the initiation easily. No qualms at all."

"You might feel differently when you find out what it involves. It isn't as easy as pulling a trigger. There's a certain intimacy."

"You mean I get to rape the alien's corpse, too?" The agent's voice carried a faux delight that seemed meant for my ears only, as if he was trying to talk to Scott but communicate with me.

Scott laughed. "That's good. I like your spirit. But I wouldn't let anyone defile their humanity in such a way."

"I just want to show you that I'll do anything it takes to join the Company, Scott. *Anything.*"

I closed my eyes. It's amazing how overheard words can tell you everything about a speaker's body posture, knowing looks, a touch of hands.

"Craig," Scott said.

I raced into the living room and found them sitting even closer than before.

"Craig, check the Company sites for us. One of them should have an update by now. We've already reported our numbers."

I went to Scott's computer upstairs and waited for it to power on. Down below, Scott was telling the inquisitive agent all about the Company networks and information sharing, the secret websites that gave the slaughter figures in each precinct across the nation, wherever the Company operated.

"We only moved four hundred and five units in Denver last night. That's under our—"

"Moved?"

I was bringing up Firefox now.

"A joke. Craig sort of came up with it, really—he's a bit of a writer. It seemed fitting to use corporate euphemisms. Each alien is a unit. Each moved unit is an alien corpse. We call shooting *shipping bullets.*"

I hated Scott for revealing that. For all his talk of sacred initiation rites, I had a much greater belief in earned intimacy. Through Scott, the agent was getting a shortcut to all of the Company's traditions and in-jokes. It was like when two people have a friendship that transcends all other relationships. They have their own terminology, their own private references. Then one takes a lover who on first introductions pretends to be in on all those secrets just because they were shared with him. How could I not feel cheated and betrayed? Even if the agent was not an imposter, he did not deserve to walk into the initiation room already knowing the Company's secret handshake.

I typed in a long, memorized URL.

"I shipped sixty-five bullets and moved sixty-one aliens last night," Scott said. "Lousy shooting night for me. I'm disappointed in our supply chain, though. *Supply chain* isn't a euphemism. We need to get better logistics if we're going to maximize our nights. You can't fight a war if you're running out of ammo, and bluster aside it's simply too hard to work without bullets. You can only stab and beat so many before your arms are exhausted. And running them over isn't practical most of the time."

The website finally began to load. I entered a password.

"I've heard some groups are resorting to poison."

"Gas?" Scott said. "That seems—"

"No, no. They simply put a cyanide capsule into the alien's mouth and force it to bite down. Or they inject the alien with a syringe. Yes, a syringe. That's right."

"Very interesting."

I stared at the number columns on the screen.

"Of course, several of our poisons were found to have no effect on them at all. But cyanide—"

"Scott!" I rushed downstairs and found him standing, the agent still on the couch.

"What is it? What's happened?"

"The figures are in! Twenty more dozers fell in the United States last night."

"Hell," Scott said, "you sounded like you had *good* news."

"I do! The alien rocket count tracked exactly the same. That means just over eleven thousand aliens—"

"So?"

"Let me finish. The Company kill reports aren't all in yet, but they already total over *fifteen thousand*! The alien population actually dropped last night!"

The agent was forgotten and Scott was mine again. We stood locked in each other's embrace as if the two of us had just overthrown the invasion by ourselves. Looking into his eyes, seeing hope and excitement there, I felt like we had won. His embrace turned last night's gore and slaughter and moral horror into sanitized subtraction and glorious victory. Light had replaced the tunnel. I thought I could kill tonight. To keep the look in Scott's eyes, I could shoot and not miss. Killing was necessary. We were in a war and we *could win*.

Behind Scott, the agent rose and contemplated us with a pale, somber face. I tightened my embrace on Scott and watched the agent, certain I could kill him too if he attacked.

"Why the long face?"

Scott pulled away, confused. "What?"

"You don't seem happy," I said to the agent.

The agent blinked, obviously thrown. Did he think I was about to betray him? *Wasn't* I going to betray him? Did he think I was ever on his side? I wasn't, was I?

"I feel great. I can't wait to join up with you guys."

"Tonight you will," Scott said. "And feel proud. You'll be among the last of a select few to join through the ritual. That makes you sort of special. There's too many joining now to spend our time with ceremony. We'd only be killing about five aliens a night if we did. The new recruits—their hearts are in the right place, but they'll never be pure the way ours will be."

The agent looked at me, his eyes aglitter. "Tonight," he nodded—and I wondered if the Company was about to see a hostile takeover.

3.

Scott lay deep in sleep beside me, his body sometimes twitching as he dreamed of retaking the world. He succeeded and now the last alien towered over me, a splintered baseball bat in her hands. She swung to kill me in vengeance. That's when Scott fired, tearing her skull apart. Then he and I were on our island at Lake Dowdy, watching the campfires dot the shoreline as fireworks finger-painted the entire sky. Scott held me and said he was not unhappy the Company was disbanding. It was only right, with the planet secure again. We were no longer warriors, but citizens and voters. We were survivors. Such a nice, gentle word, *survivor,* a breeze-floating word, and on our island there was a perfect sigh among the trees. He shifted and cradled my head in his lap with spotless hands, and we sang a song to each other as the knights of old might have—a ballad composed and tested by war.

I lay awake for five minutes staring at Scott's face before realizing that it was not his dream but mine. I just liked the dream better when I could place it inside his head.

I went downstairs. In honor of his initiation, Scott had invited the agent to stay. I found him asleep on the couch. He had stripped down to just a pair of boxer briefs. I could have just stood over him and stared, memorizing all that beauty. Instead I sat on the bottom step and held my head in my hands.

Whose side *was* I on? Did I really not know the answer? My immediate response had always been "Scott's side." But that could no longer suffice. He had once been my private universe, but private universes no longer existed. Humanity's side, then. The nation's side, the planet's side. My thoughts still reached out, looking for something even greater. *God's side?* But if God existed, He'd made the aliens too. That was the terror of trying to be on the side of ever larger things. You ultimately came to something so large it included everything and there were no sides at all.

Right and wrong, I thought. I am on the side of right. The aliens are wrong and we're...*wrong too.* But aren't we *less wrong*, having done nothing to provoke or cause the invasion? If the aliens had asked, we would have shared. The aliens did not ask. The aliens did not acknowledge our existence. The aliens placed us so far beneath them that we were just the crazy bums on the street, the kind polite society ignores. They would convince us we didn't own all the buildings. The aliens must be driven back. The aliens must be *destroyed!*

I kicked my heel into the stair step loud enough to wake the agent. He sat up with a start and looked around. In a few moments he calmed, remembering the room. He blinked at me.

"Getting an eyeful?" He stretched himself elaborately, every muscle taut and toned.

"I know how much you red-blooded American guys like being admired."

"Not as much as I admire *you*, Craig."

I shook my head. "Haven't we had this conversation before?"

"It takes a lot of thought to betray your people and the ones you love for something you believe is greater than yourself. We're kindred spirits."

"*Be quiet*," I said. I took a deep breath, trying to be calm. "I haven't betrayed anything."

The agent smiled.

"At least I'm not collecting a paycheck for it. Anything I'm doing is the result of soul searching."

The smile continued. "I'll make sure the government reimburses you for your expenses."

"Oh, fuck off."

There were keys on the coffee table. I swiped them and stormed out the front door with the agent calling after me. This would wake Scott. *Fine.* I hurried, fumbling for the largest key. I turned off the agent's car alarm and got in. I didn't back out into traffic with the same grace the agent had shown the first time we met. I rammed the back bumper into the Sutters' fence, straightened, and clipped the mailbox accelerating. I drove with no destination in mind.

Chapter Two: The Citizenship Test

1.

I ditched the car when it ran out of gas and spent the rest of the day starving and stumbling around Denver like a drunk, keeping the nameless, silent, uncountable and unaccountable company of the aliens. These streets had been cleared last night; now it seemed like all those corpses had resurrected to reoccupy all their old haunts. We're losing, I thought. Everything we erased at night was scribbled back in at sunrise.

I kept looking at my watch and wondering if Scott was okay. It never occurred to me that when I left, Scott would be alone. Had the agent seen an opportunity to kill him straightaway? Only the promise of the initiation ceremony gave me hope. The agent wouldn't risk anything that kept him from penetrating the Company further, even killing it's leader. But a reckoning was coming. Maybe it would happen tonight, at the ceremony itself. In my imagination I saw the government's SWAT teams moving in, capturing Scott and the Company's leadership in one swoop. I felt in my pocket for my cell phone and discovered I'd run out without it. I had to do something to warn them.

I found a pay phone and dialed Scott's cell. He never picked up, but I kept talking. I'd call, talk until the voice mail timed me out, then hang up and call again. I kept talking, making a fragmented recording of my confession, deepening the hole I'd dug for myself. If Scott was fine, I knew I was basically talking myself into an execution. Even if Scott forbade the Company from killing me, he'd never want to see me again. At that moment, such a fate felt about the same as death.

In the end I had to lay my neck on the line. When night came, it found me at the warehouse. I stood alone in the initiation room, alone in the place where I stabbed the alien with the shard of a baseball bat.

No one else was there. My God, I thought, the agent did it. He killed Scott. The Company, the resistance movement, was finished.

I went back to my house. No one was there, either. No note, nothing. If Scott wasn't dead, he was either captured or hiding.

We were finished too.

Over the next five days my landline rang constantly, followed by an immediate click as soon as I answered. The calls were not traceable. I kept telling myself it must be Scott calling, testing or tormenting me, but in my heart I was sure he was dead or imprisoned. It was the agent calling instead. He and his men were coming for me now. I checked the secret web sites and found most inaccessible. The Company's network had been smashed. I cried and barricaded myself inside my house and went numb to the phone's shrill ring.

The alien said nothing, though I had to believe she knew everything. She knew exactly when to come and go. With Scott gone, she had asserted her presence in my life again like a secret mistress.

She and I watched the cable news shows together. Sometimes I would speak but she never responded. It was as if her revelations to me had never happened. Sometimes I wondered if this was even the same alien.

"You don't have to act like you don't know me," I said. "You've already torn down the fourth wall. Why try to build it up again?"

Her liquid black eyes were cold.

On the news, her last words to me were proven to be truthful. The actions of other countries had come to light. The video footage looked like a documentary film of concentration camps from World War II. Soldiers stood grinning in front of a mound of bodies piled twelve feet high. Soldiers stood grinning in front of a trench lined with alien corpses. Soldiers batted at limp aliens swinging off ropes. Russian soldiers, Chinese soldiers, Egyptian and French and British and American soldiers. *American* soldiers, I thought with some relief. The government was getting things done now. The Company had to be destroyed in the process. I turned off the television and let my head hang. At least the fight is on now. What the Company did will be trivial next to the type of killing a government can do.

To my left, the alien continued staring at the dead screen.

"I'll turn it on again if you want to watch. Flap your ears twice if you want the television on."

The alien got up and walked toward my bedroom. I followed.

"Did it bother you that I used to watch you and your husband have sex? Well, too bad if it did! It's *my* bedroom and *my* bed. And you ruined it with your...your...your *secretions!*" I pounded the wall once, twice. The impact was hollow. I couldn't stand that sound. It was like striking a shell, a lie. I swung a third time with everything I had. This time I struck the alien in the back of the head, right where its cranium met the neck. The alien did not give me the courtesy of acting affected, even as I shook the pain out of my hand. The knuckle of my index finger had split open.

"I know you're a liar," I said. "It's all a hoax—the numbers you spouted off. It's all a trick to make you look like you've got more people than you do."

The alien inserted two fingers between the Venetian blinds and scissored open a four-inch incision to the outside world.

"Please talk to me. I can't stand the idea of knowing you can understand me but won't answer. Before, I at least had the illusion that maybe you didn't know I existed or somehow couldn't see me. But now... It's rude. It's fucking rude. We're being invaded by a race of passive-aggressive pricks!

The alien kept staring down out through the blinds.

"Goddamnit! Say something!"

"We are surrounded."

I went to the window. I don't know what I expected. Police cars or army tanks or the aliens themselves. Instead I saw a fleet of cars and trucks parked up and down the street and in my neighbors' yards. There were empty cars in the middle of the busy road, left to snarl the traffic. Horns exploded up and down the street, and I saw innocent drivers fleeing through their passenger sides as militiamen poured out around them. Three cars swarmed into my driveway and yard. One was Scott's. I strained to see him but the shadows fell in all the wrong angles on the windshield. I couldn't tell if he was inside or not. I could hardly see anything specific in the action happening everywhere Car doors and house doors were opening and slamming. People were getting out of truck beds and belting weapons across their chest. I saw little Ryan Sutter at the edge of his lawn, looking on in awe at first, and then jumping up and down in a war dance when his father marched out of the front door with enough armament to stop the Terminator.

The telephone rang.

"*Hello?*"

"You ready to take the new citizenship test, Craig?"

"Scott!"

"It's simple. Bring out the alien and you get to keep your citizenship with the Company, the country, and the planet. You'll get to keep your house, too."

"Scott, the agent—"

"Never mind the agent."

"The alien isn't here."

"Strike one, Craiggers. We see it in the window."

I turned to find the alien brazenly pulling up the blinds to display the crazy world outside.

"What do you want her for? What do you intend to do?"

"Strike two. You're really making us wonder about your loyalties, Craig. Now, if we have to come in there and get the bitch, I'm not sure I'll be able to protect you. Your house will definitely be torched, but they might spare your life. Then again—"

Through the phone and the window I heard police sirens. I had a moment of unfounded hope, thinking a neighbor had called them after seeing this paramilitary assault on my house. I started to breathe a sigh of relief as five cruisers pulled up to discharge cops dressed in SWAT gear. Then they went to reinforce the militia.

"Okay! I'll bring her out…give me a second."

"I'll do even better and give you a minute. Because I *love* you."

I threw the phone on the bed and spoke at the back of the alien's head. "What now?"

The alien didn't turn.

"They're going to kill you." My nerves made my voice disintegrate. Every syllable shook. My body felt loose and decayed, unraveling and frayed. "They'll torture you until you scream. You *will* scream. You think you won't, but you will. They'll take their time and the more you resist, the meaner they'll get. I've seen it."

She stared.

"Well, aren't you going to *do* something? Can't you summon help?"

She sat down on the bed.

"Please do something. Save yourself. God, I don't even know why I care. I mean nothing to you."

"That is not entirely true," she said.

Now I couldn't talk at all. What could I mean to her? Was this more bullshit, more manipulation? When the minute elapsed I was drenched in sweat. My mouth made a queer bleating sound like a small, injured animal might make. I listened to the sound of myself shrinking up, shriveling away. The Company was coming. I heard their sharp rapping on the door. It wasn't a polite gesture. They were using batons.

I rushed about in a circle. Wild thoughts seized my mind. If I was just an inch tall I could hide anywhere and they'd never find me. Why was I so large? If I was an inch tall I could hide in the dirty clothes in the closet, crawl into a shirt pocket, and climb out when they were gone. Why was I so *visible*?

I hid in the closet and curled up on the floor. A small explosion seemed to happen downstairs. Had they dynamited my front door? I kicked at the floor and pulled the closet shut. Footsteps trampled up the stairs. I whimpered and grabbed at shirttails and pants legs and coats, bringing a rain of clothes and hangers down on top of me. Shoes, shoes! I got all the shoes and added them to the pile, then burrowed down and held my breath.

I listened to the rampage happening outside the closet. This is how a king felt when his castle was breached, when the barbarians stormed the gates. My mound of fabric did nothing to mute the sound of their fury. They conquered every room. They had occupied the living room and kitchen. They had taken the bathroom and guest bedroom. All that remained was—

The bedroom door smashed open. An unexpected silence happened. The Company men must have been staring at the alien sitting there on the mattress. Maybe they deliberated her fate. The deliberations did not last long.

The strike sounded brutal, unrestrained. A baseball bat. On the back of her head. I closed my eyes, bringing my buried body into a fetal position. The sharp impact of her dead weight on the floor sent a rattle through the closet.

"That's one problem solved. Now where's the traitor?"

The men conversed right next to the closet door. Though terrified and eager to grasp at any hope, I wasn't fooled. They had found me and this act was just sport for them. Their amateurish terrorism numbed me as I found myself stirring. A bullet in the brain and it wouldn't matter. The clothes fell away like a molt of old skin as I stood up to end it all. I opened the closet door and found six guns pointed at my face.

2.

Though blind, I knew where they led me. We were going down into the initiation room in the warehouse. The sound and feel of the steps had a quality I couldn't explain. I remembered them with a vividness that was almost instinctual and strange, a sort of genetic memory. On the final step my legs crumpled and my handlers had to drag me along the floor. When we stopped, they put me on my knees with the rough sack still cinched over my head.

"I came here after I called you, Scott. I waited! I didn't want anything to happen to you, but you weren't here!"

"Should we execute him now?"

I cringed, becoming bony edges, elbows and shoulder blades and kneecaps, sensitive parts with little protection. My body was a collection of prized pain targets. The sack muffled voices and made them indeterminate, but I thought I knew my eager killer's name. It was Ralph Morrison.

"He was sheltering the enemy."

"Then most of the people in the country are guilty too!" My words ran around the inside of the bag, trying to find sensible ears. "I wasn't sheltering, I was being occupied! Scott, the agent—"

"I always thought this guy sounded like a Company man when it's convenient. When it'll save his life."

A sharp jab, probably a steel-toed boot, struck into my thigh. I rocked myself on the floor without a cry. I hadn't been kicked hard, but the hurt went beyond speech. The pain went down to the bone and rang out across my body in a violent, feverish shiver. Mr. Morrison wore boots with steel toes.

Mr. Morrison had kicked me.

As I recovered, I heard another sound close to me and felt heavy footfalls. It seemed like I was no longer the center of attention, and then—

"Tell us everything."

"I—I did—"

"Not you, asshole." Another kick got me in the side, between the hip and ribcage. I rolled over and moaned. Nausea like a huge solid square forced its way through my intestines. I didn't even get a chance to steel myself. There was no warning retch. I vomited fully in one motion, right into the bag that threw it back, stinging hot and acrid, into my face and eyes. I coughed and struggled to breathe past the fumes. My eyeballs seemed to dissolve under their lids.

For a few minutes I must have gone mad. I heard the alien's interrogation as a series of disconnected phrases spoken in many different voices. But it was questions only, questions followed by violent incentives to answer. There were no answers. I listened for them as my world shrank back smaller even than the bag around my head, and as my consciousness drifted away for what I felt would be the last time, I quit struggling and let the poisoned, stinking air seep into my mouth.

"Shoot the bitch now. We've wasted enough time."

"Shut up, Morrison. Quit acting big."

"Scott left me in charge!"

A power struggle. The men jostled. I tried to roll away. Maybe I rolled right into them, because a foot struck my head, right in the temple. I shrieked and tore at the bag. My hands were bound, my fingers inflexible. The shouting got louder. There was a little opening, a tear in the bag that had moved from the back of my head to the front because of my exertions. Through it I now saw Mr. Morrison raising his gun. He was nervous with it, moving it from side to side in unsteady jerks, as if he felt the need to cover every angle. The men around us had all fallen silent. The world inside the bag began to blacken and calm again. I coughed once more and willed myself into the darkness that seemed about to take me.

"Are you going to help him?"

Her voice, low and steady, but penetrating the bag more clearly than any man's shout. Like a bit of smelling salts, it put strength in my bones and roused me. I craned my head, trying to see more through the rip. Then the bag was torn off my head, revealing my face splattered with vomit. But *their* faces were more hideous and sickening.

"She talked! The fucking bitch talked!"

The Company men became thin and dark retreating wraiths. I blinked. The alien stood unvanquished among them. They were cowering and ashen-faced before her, as horny men might be before a queen they both feared and desired. The alien was like She Who Must Not Be Named. I knew she had turned her gaze upon them, locking them inside that glorious, almost blinding concentration. I wondered if men, straight men, felt a difference when she looked on them like that. Did they see in her, despite her appearance, a perfect wife, a perfect lover? All but Mr. Morrison seemed affected. Perhaps he saw only Liz's face, and that made him raise the gun.

"Look out, he's going to shoot!"

But she ignored me. She offered no comforting hand, gave no smile or assuring nod. As she went on just looking at them, more Company men began to recover. Two more guns were trained on her. At first they did not feel threatening. The hands that held them shook and made the guns seem more like lucky charms or religious totems held up by superstitious primitives. The alien did not seem bothered by them at all. For one disheartening moment, I thought that she had slipped back into the game and awaited death, content to have her brains add to the nasty fresco of blood and flesh on the masonry walls.

I took the sack that had been my hood and used it to swipe more vomit off my face. Then I stood up as straight as I could, though my body flooded with pain. I limped over to her as if we were allies. Until we got away, I supposed we were.

"Let's go."

She turned and headed in the wrong direction, away from the stairs and toward the place where the initiations happened. I yelled for her to stop but a crippling cramp in my abdomen left me gasping. The alien went farther back to the one place that was an absolute trap.

"Don't," I said, my voice not even a whisper.

She stopped and stared at the scene before her. The Company had grown increasingly uninterested in cleaning up after its ceremonies. The corner now looked like a charnel house. She kept staring even as I stumbled in front of her to put myself between her eyes and the gore. Her vision lanced through me to the violated remains of her people. There was blood like different coats of paint and there was worse besides the stink of severed parts, bone bits and strewn internal organs. Her stare became so focused that my own flesh seemed to melt as if exposed to a laser. I fell back with a whimper and turned for the stairs.

Mr. Morrison and his men had blocked the exit.

"Kill me or let me go, Ralph. Either way I just want out."

They didn't react.

"What's it going to be, Ralph? You going to tell them to shoot me?"

He shook his head like he was falling apart inside. "I didn't believe they could talk. She *talked!*"

"Of course they talk. Didn't you read my interview?"

"That interview was made up."

"Not all of it. Yeah, they speak to me. They've been speaking to me for months, telling me their plans."

"Scott said they talked if you put the screws to them. But I never heard it, not once. I thought he was just making it up… Goddamn, she spoke perfect English!"

Two thugs moved toward me but Mr. Morrison stopped them. He wanted me for himself and grabbed me by both shoulders, driving my back into the wall. I seemed to be the only one who even noticed the alien. Her ears had turned a deep auburn color and twitched in a way that reminded me of a cat's tail, when the cat is pissed off. She wasn't playing the game now. She wanted blood.

Mr. Morrison wanted blood too. He was shouting at me with a rage that had nothing to do with the situation. "Liz said you were a untalented piece of shit, but I gave you a break. You fucking owe everything to me!"

"Where's Scott?"

Mr. Morrison put his hands to my throat and squeezed. "He isn't here."

"I don't—don't—believe that." Scott and I might be finished with each other but I didn't think he'd walk away from my execution. If anything he'd be the one to do it. He'd say it was the only way he could live with the past.

The alien's nostrils flared like a bull that was revving up.

Mr. Morrison released me and turned to the alien as I slumped to the ground. "Goddamn, I'm so sick of this. Let's waste the cunt."

"Ralph—Ralph, don't."

He had no idea what he was getting himself into. He thought the alien would take whatever violence he intended to afflict.

"Ralph!"

"Put a bullet in her goddamn leg. That'll make her talk!"

"*Ralph—!*"

Now the Company men, likewise emboldened, encircled her with cocky and smug expressions. One of them grabbed his crotch. "Let me put this in her. That'll make her talk. She'll say all kinds of shit."

A thug knocked Mr. Morrison aside and stood in front of the alien. "You ever had a human's dick up your ass, bitch?"

The alien's black eyes gleamed.

I clawed the wall trying to stand. Mr. Morrison, deposed and shaken, as if he had no idea how he'd got here, grabbed me by the shoulders again. All the anger, so explosive a minute ago, was gone, replaced by limp fear. "I didn't want this to happen. This isn't my fault."

Another thug hawked phlegm up his throat and spat it across the alien's face. She ignored it. Her gaze stayed trained on the grisly floor and I thought she must be evaluating the entire course of her life. She was doing it in a methodical, scientific and dispassionate way—weighing the reasons for the game against this cruelty; weighing ancient doctrines; weighing her husband's death. How many invasions had she seen? Were we the most violent race, the most venal she had ever encountered? Had all other civilizations accepted the invasion as logical and just acquiesced, surrendering with the same pacific silence that had conquered them? Were anger and resistance only human traits, unknown throughout the rest of the galaxy?

Something like a new fiery sun was birthing in the black universe of her eyes.

"We have to get out of here quick."

"I know, I know—"

"Because if I'm right, she's about to kill us all."

Chapter Three: Stargazing

1.

"Kill us all?"

I nodded.

"She's heading for a breakdown. We have to get her out of this place before she goes psychotic."

He was naturally dumbfounded. "She's going to kill us all, but you want her to come *with us*?"

"It's important, Ralph. I owe her."

"You don't owe her anything except a lot of misery."

"She saved my life. And invader or not, I won't sit here and watch someone get raped!"

That was the line for Mr. Morrison too. Shooting the alien was one thing. Sexually violating it quite another. "But I can't stop them."

"You're still the authority here"

"No, I'm not." Bitterness hardened his tone. "They don't need my money anymore. I can't do anything."

"Goddamnit, Ralph. They think she's going to passively take it. What do you think is going to happen the moment one of them tries to penetrate her? That'll be it. We all die. It won't matter where we go. She'll kill us. They'll all kill us."

"They—they won't really do it. They're just threatening her. To get her to talk."

"She won't talk."

"She just did."

"Trust me, Ralph. I know her. She's the toughest of the bunch. But it's not even about interrogating her anymore. It's just a sport now."

A Company man got tired of seeing the two of us conspiring by the steps. "You, front and center!" Before we even had a chance to move, two more goons came and grabbed us. Merciless fingers dug into my shoulder and had their way with me. Ralph was taken to the left and I was placed next to the alien.

"So supposedly the alien cares about this little faggot, huh? We're supposed to make her talk. Well, she talked but we didn't like what she had to say. What will it take, sweetheart? What will make you say what we want to hear? Will hurting the faggot do the trick?"

"It won't work!" Mr. Morrison pleaded.

The goon ignored him, bending down to peer into my eyes. "Why does she care about you? Are you fucking each other? Is that it? You got so tired of man ass that you went in for some alien shit?"

"Jesus Christ."

"Fuck off, Morrison. There's a real man to run things now."

The goon tore my pants down to my ankles. Then with his implacable grip he maneuvered me into a sickening position and laughed as I struggled. To the guys at his back, he said, "Bend the alien over. Break her legs if you have to, but get her bent the fuck over."

"No," I screamed, "I won't do this—"

"We're going to watch you two go at it."

"Like hell—"

He smacked the back of my head and I saw stars. It shut me up.

"We can't get her to budge, John."

"Well, like I said, guys. Break her legs."

One of the men produced a two-by-four from around the side and drew it back. I shouted for him to stop but the whistle and thwack of the board on her magnificent leg dissolved me to sobs. She wavered once, tilting slightly, but did not go down. The board wound up for another release.

"Ah, come one. Give her a little kiss to make it better."

He smeared my mouth up against the alien's back, mashing my nose flat against her spine.

Thwack!

I closed my eyes. Her body shifted more, dipping as her leg trembled on the verge of collapse. I felt like a tree hugger clutching at a trunk about to be logged. Only my tree suddenly righted itself. I opened my eyes.

"That's right," John said, joined by a chorus of hoots from everyone but Mr. Morrison. I could vaguely see Ralph, or an idea of Ralph, standing frozen as he had been off to the right, restrained but not struggling.

"Yeah," my goon said. I gasped when he gave my dick a strong, loveless squeeze. "Go and get it up. Show me how to fuck her. Show us the way."

His grip forced my crotch against her. God help me, but I responded. I responded like a stupid puppet. "Stop this," I said, crying. "Stop this, stop this." I don't know what strength my voice had. The bastards were crowing so loud that any sound I made must have seemed a wordless whimper. I kept repeating myself, realizing I wasn't talking to the humans any more. The alien was the only one who could end this. How her control had lasted so long was beyond me. It eclipsed human explanation and reason. Certainly it eclipsed human emotion. When was she going to kill us? When would her fuse ever light? I could not comprehend the burn of rage I'd detected in her eyes against the old stoic obliviousness she now endured. If they forced me to rape her, would she simply let me do it? Would even *that* mean nothing to her? "Stop this," I said. I kissed her flesh, licked it, breathing heavy. "Stop this." I bit into her with words, with teeth. My arms attempted an embrace. This too made the Company bastards cheer. "Stop them from doing this. Please. *Please.*"

The alien reared back like a bronco and all sound ceased. She whirled, her big hands outstretched like oars lashed to helicopter blades. The Company men took the sudden blows to their torsos and face. Each hit devastated the body. Bones shattered. Lungs collapsed. Hearts stopped. I lay on the floor, bunched up, arms over my head. The alien was nonstop movement. She was everywhere. I saw Mr. Morrison flee upstairs. Another Company man had a gun and aimed it, but her ruthless hands fixed him. She disarmed him and threw him into the wall with a force that cracked the concrete. She moved even faster, like a spinning top twirling so fast that she might be levitating. Then I was in her arms. She stopped to pick me up. She shifted me onto her back and I clung to her neck. This happened so fast it did not even seem like a break in her berserker rage. Her hands found two more men and dashed their foreheads with a forced that left both skulls shattered.

Her assailants fled or dead, the alien climbed the staircase in three graceful strides with me still gripping her like a baby koala. We burst into the warehouse floor and bounded past an astonished Mr. Morrison, who lingered in paralysis. The alien increased her speed. We were outside. The wind in my face froze my lungs in anticipation, like cresting the first hill of a roller coaster. Bullets went past her. The world turned upside down. I started laughing despite myself, marveling at her superiority. She ran down the street, jumping over and on top of cars. She cleared a city bus like it was just a hurdle on a high school track. I don't know how it happened, but suddenly we were standing on an isolated rooftop. Her pace had outrun my senses. She had carried me so far, jumped so high, and run so hard, but I was the one winded. She reached and pried me off her back.

"Th-thank you."

She lay down and stared at the cloudless sky.

Panting, I clutched her shoulder. "Please don't play the game—not this time. Please talk to me. I—I owe you my life."

"You owe your life to your people."

"I owe my life to the guys who were about to kill me?"

"If your death improves their chance to survive, then you must surrender yourself. The individual owes that to the many."

I laughed in bitterness. "Is that what your people believe? You didn't seem to buy into it back there. Not that I'm complaining. I'm glad that you aren't so representative of your people."

Her gaze seemed to flicker a moment, as if considering. I looked up at the open blue world above us, wondering what she saw there.

"I am only too representative of my kind."

I sat beside her and listened to the city's sounds. Sirens and gunshots rang out. A fleet of cars was gunning down the streets. Maybe the Company was after us. Maybe it was something else. Beneath it all, from far off, I heard a persistent low rumble, like the stuck recording of a thunderstorm. I'd never heard anything like it.

There were more shots, a burst of machine-gun fire followed by so many heavy thuds that I could estimate the body count without looking.

"Listen. That's your people dying. What's the point of it all? I'm not saying I want you all to fight back, but...*why* don't you fight back?"

"We hold to our ancient values."

I sighed from an inner stirring of sadness for myself and for her, for the world and even for the universe. It was the same sadness I felt after a breakup. I looked over at my alien's lounging body. Did she give me these feelings? I was closer to being her hostage than her lover, held here out of fear that I could no longer survive on my own if both Scott and the Company wanted me dead. But even Stockholm Syndrome is a type of love. I felt like she and I had perched on this rooftop like cultists expecting the end of the world. These days only the cultists were sane.

"Ancient values. What's so valuable about letting yourself be slaughtered? I guess your freakout back there was a violation, then? Is it the same kind of violation that your husband committed by answering my interview questions? You ratted him out. Who'll rat you out?"

"I will surrender myself, should the time come. But it will not come. It was necessary to violate our customs to discharge the greater responsibility that is my burden alone."

The low rumble became just a bit more pronounced. If it was like thunder, the storm was getting nearer.

"What responsibility is that?"

"Your survival."

I gaped at her. I asked her to repeat what she said, but she refused. The idea of my survival being anyone's responsibility was too exotic to comprehend. What did she mean by it? I tried to formulate some logic for it, some explanation, and found myself ambushed by exhaustion. I lay down on the roof and stared at the broad sky. Rockets streaked across my vision, silent points of light darting toward another state, another country. The view was clearer and deeper than I could ever remember. The alien stared straight up and her vision seemed to be farther off than the sky, farther off than moon. Her ears were fixed in the same direction as her eyes.

"What do you see?"

I wanted her answer more than anything, but it did not come. I yearned for the sound of her voice. My gaze strayed along her form, as if to read her body and translate it into a speech she might make, a speech she carried inside her. So much of her looked too animal to be anything else, and then you came upon the parts that were too human. I put my hand on her thigh and we stargazed together.

"That reddish spot there is Mars, I think. I was obsessed with Mars when I was a kid. All the best science fiction is about Mars. Have you been to Mars?"

She stared, her eyes glassy and dark. Darkening. In her eyes I saw the sky reflected perfectly. I saw a shooting star and turned my head to seek the actual thing.

I leaned away, settling onto my back. Another shooting star made me smile and I crossed my arms over my chest. Together we really might have been hesitant lovers trying to find something above us that would sweep away a final doubt. A star to call our own. That was the wonderful thing about stars; each could be named and renamed a thousand, a million times; they could be claimed by generations of lovers. Those small points of light were big enough for that. Another shooting star came arcing to our right. Again I traced its streak in boyish excitement. Her gaze did not deviate. She seemed even more distant, no longer just ignoring me. I bent closer to her face, wondering if she might have gone into some kind of stasis. A notion came, a thought that closed up my throat and choked me.

She was dead. She'd been dying all that time right beside me and I didn't know it.

I put my head against her chest and listened for a heartbeat that wasn't there.

"I pray to God sometimes. I only do it at night. That's how I prayed as a boy, at night listening to the sound of my parents sleeping. My father snored. Sometimes he would stop snoring and I'd get so scared. I'd think he had died in his sleep and I would pray to God that he didn't die. Sometimes I would offer my life to God in exchange. Every once in a while my father's snoring would start up again just when I made the offer, and I always felt like a bit of me had been taken. God didn't need the whole thing right away. Sometimes the snoring wouldn't start and I had to get up, quietly as I could, and tiptoe close to their room. Sometimes then I could hear the snoring and it had just gotten too low to be heard through the wall. But sometimes even then I couldn't hear anything and I had to open the door—the hinge always whined. I had to crack the door and peak in. He was always alive in that house. He died outside of it, like my mom.

"It's not having the faith of a child—it's having a child's fear. God looms over you like the night that's in your bedroom, amplifying every noise, making every sound unfamiliar. You become a teen, you start losing that fear. You listen for the noise of your father's snoring because it means he isn't awake to hear all the new sounds you're making. You're glad for the dark because it makes you blind and being blind lets you see your fantasies so much better. You laugh at the idea of praying to God and want to prove God's absence. You look at the lamp on your nightstand and think, 'Tonight I will pray to *it*.' After a while you've prayed to every piece of furniture in the room; you've prayed for rain or sunlight, prayed to pass tests, prayed that the friend you like somehow likes you back. And the results are always the same. Your mattress answers prayers with the same efficiency as your television set. You get better test scores reading your textbook instead of your Bible.

"And then *something* happens—a disaster—and you're an adult in the little kid's darkness, and the snoring is something else—something roaring at you. Something that wants to get you. It is the old God. And you beg God to take everyone else before you. Take my father, my mother. Take my grandmother, she's past her time. Take my neighbor, take my best friend Nathan. Exchange their lives for mine. Take them instead of me. Everyone, you see, but Scott. When we were together, I'd lie awake in that old darkness and hear his light snoring. Sometimes it stopped and I'd swallow hard and wait for it to start again. I'd count to twenty. I'd roll over—I can still hear the bedsprings creak—and I'd snuggle my ear against his chest. His heart was always beating. Then I'd smile and thank the God I claimed not to believe in.

"Even right now, I can't hate Scott. He's always had a hurt inside him that he doesn't know what to do with. The Company has perverted him. All he wanted was solutions and the Company offered him Final Solutions. It doesn't have to go down that route for either of us. Do you understand that? Not for aliens or humans. If calm heads get together, they can reason out a peace. We'll share resources if that's what you need. Maybe—maybe there can even be an alliance between us." I rose off of her and thrust my finger at the reddish spot and stared, soaring. "We'll go out together and terraform the planets. Think of Mars!

"Eventually one of us will fall in love with one of you. Isn't that possible? Isn't that happening someplace even now? Perhaps right here? There'll be a way for them to conceive children. Once that baby is born, both races will set their sights on greater things. Like Mars," I whispered.

Her ears swiveled and twitched. I scrambled away from her.

"That is not the fourth planet."

"What? What do you mean? That's Mars. Right there." I kept pointing.

"That is a carrier ship, still many weeks away."

"A carrier? Like your rockets? Carrier? Carrying how many?"

"Five million."

I jumped up. "Five million? Weeks away?" I swallowed, started to move left, then right, finally going nowhere. "At least it is just one ship. We can surely absorb five million. Africa alone—"

Now her finger rose and I followed its direction, squinting. Her finger moved in a jagged line across the whole sky, tracing a new, terrifying constellation across the ecliptic. I saw them at last—Mars. Fifteen to twenty Marses scattered across the sky.

"God," I whispered.

"You realize now that those are not shooting stars you see. They are our rockets, landing. Always landing." I heard in her tone the softness of contemplation.

Tears came to my eyes. "There are so many planets. Why do you have to take ours? What about Mars?"

"We are already there."

I sniffed and dry-heaved.

"The end of your surviving is at hand." She sat up. "Tonight begins the full-scale destruction of your cities."

I backed away, nearly falling off the side of the building. "What right do you have to do this to us? Who are you people?"

Now the alien brought herself to standing, a beautiful motion like that of some lubricated unfolding mechanism. "Many times in our history, we have invaded planets that had at least one culture sufficiently advanced in science and mathematics to know and give name to the transcendental geometric constant. In each instance, we assumed that given name for ourselves, for that is how those cultures experienced us. It is how you will experience us. In your language, then, we are the *Pi*. We are the endless numbers that follow the decimal point marking your people's last generation. Our population cannot be totaled. We will fill this planet and move on to the next. We are survivors."

Trembling, I looked over the side and down to the street. The fate she sketched was so terrifying and certain that I intended to jump and kill myself, but the silence arrested me. Here the alien was talking about the destruction of Earth's cities and everything around me seemed serene. Was she lying?

I began to realize what might be causing the persistent rumble. Back in I-25, the dozer had come to life.

"How will you destroy the cities with so few dozers? Even if we just sat back and let you do it—which we won't!—it would *take years*—"

"We have years. We are the *Pi*. Our boundless numbers fall like drops of water on stone. Our constant pressure reshapes all to our will."

"And humanity is just supposed to sing 'Raindrops Keep Fallin' On My Head' while you crowd us out?"

"No. You will kill many of us, as you have already. We will not stop you."

I stepped away from the ledge, powered by a surge of vengeance. "That's right! You've made a huge mistake coming here. *We're* the survivors. Nobody's going to take Earth away from us. You got millions? Well, we've *got billions*—"

"We are trillions upon trillions upon trillions," she said.

I blinked, my rage blunted a moment. "Fine. I guess we'll just have to start breeding a lot. Hell, even I will hold my nose and pitch in."

"Reproduction must stop. Those who survive your cities' destruction will be separated according to gender."

I laughed. "What are you going to do, deport all the men to the North Pole and drop the women off at Antarctica?"

The look she gave me had an air of grim finality. "Those living will survive as best they can. Then your race will end."

Chapter Four: The Pi

1.

The alien quit speaking. I needed to hear no more anyway and I left her on the rooftop, gazing up at the night sky with its new constellations of coming invaders. Getting home proved a challenge. I passed through isolated riots and skirted acts of mob violence. Men and women moved about in gangs with clubs in their hands. They beat aliens to the ground and pulverized them. Sometimes I stopped, unable to look away, wondering why I still felt any compassion for the creatures getting pummeled. Perhaps I admired them in a way. I admired their ability to suffer so much torment in silence. Many men and women, entire generations of minorities, had done so as well. But the defining human characteristic was the courage to shout. The *Pi* would always suffer in silence.

They would conquer by it too.

I reached home at last and found Scott alone and drunk in my ransacked house.

"I'm sorry," he blurted.

"Get out."

"I can't. I don't have anywhere else to go."

"Mr. Morrison has a big place. Try him."

"Ralph's dead."

I stared at him. "Bullshit."

"I swear."

It had been only ten hours since I last saw Morrison in the warehouse. I broke into a sweat. "Did the Company do it?"

"No. He did it to himself—in the basement. Everyone thought he had come along, chasing after you like the rest. But he didn't leave. And when they came back…"

"He did it in the initiation corner, didn't he?"

Scott squeezed his eyes tight and dropped his head, nodding. The sensation of horror welled up and then collapsed all at once, leaving nothing.

"Well. One down, the rest of the Earth's population to go."

Something dimly luminescent, like light reflecting off dark glass, hurtled toward me. I ducked and the bottle exploded along the wall.

"Fuck you, Craig." He bent over in his chair and mashed his face about in his hands.

"We're certainly fucked," I said with a coolness that was almost glib. "Have you taken a peek at the night sky? The Company better start investing in atom bombs if you plan on mounting an insurgency."

"There's no Company. Not one that I recognize, anyway. When we started, our methods were violent and coercive but we had solid values and reasons behind them. For a while I was a leader but it started to seem like I had to follow everyone else in order to stay at the top. What happened to you—I didn't want that. But it was going to happen anyway and I needed to stay on top of it. I got burned."

"That's what you get for trying to plug a volcano with your ass."

Scott nodded, tried to stand and fell back in the chair. I glanced back at the shattered glass to try and see what he'd been drinking. It looked like scotch.

"Stumble home and sleep it off, Scott."

"Like I said, I've got nowhere to go."

"Then go to hell. It doesn't matter. No one will pull you over and if you kill someone it'll just be sparing them the future. I'm half tempted to get in the back seat and let you drive me off a cliff. But I'm a coward so instead I'm going to bed. You can come up with me if you want. We can die in our sleep tonight when the roof comes crashing down."

"My house is gone."

"The Company take it from you?"

"No. No—you haven't heard? You don't know anything about what's happening, do you?"

"I know more than you do," I said, annoyed. "I know what's coming."

Scott's loud laughter edged toward hysteria. "What's coming? I'm talking about what's here! Their machines—the dozers. They're moving. They started up all across the world simultaneously. The one that's been blocking I-25 for months just suddenly came to life, took the Colfax exit and has been bulldozing half of downtown."

"I know." I kept my voice quiet, as if their machines might hear us and come.

"You know," he mocked.

"Just a few hours ago she told me it would begin."

"Oh, you're a great one for information. You cozy up with the aliens directly and indirectly. You know all their plans."

"I haven't betrayed us."

"What about your friend? The so-called FBI agent."

"I don't know what agency he worked for. And I did everything I could to warn you—"

"He wasn't with *any* agency, Craig. He was a sellout. We took him to another place for his initiation but instead he was tortured. If you can call it torture—he broke so easily. He claimed you were the point man, the Benedict Arnold. You talked to the aliens, you arranged a deal with them to spare you. He wanted in on that."

"He's mad."

"Schizophrenic is more like it. The Company wanted you dead and for a while they wanted me dead too. I had to go along with it!"

I again looked at the broken bottle. "Too bad you wasted it. I could use a drink."

He stared off in disgust.

"Look at this place. The dozers might as well not bother with it."

"Christ, quit giving a shit about your goddamn house."

"I'm just trying to focus on any question besides the one I want to ask."

"What's that?"

"Why weren't you with them in the basement?"

"I couldn't," he said.

"You knew they were going to kill me and you couldn't stand to be there?"

Scott pulled at his hair. "I can't believe you'd ask that."

"Guess that's a yes."

"No, it isn't."

Suddenly neither of us had anything to say. The argument left me too wired to think about the sleeping suicide I had planned.

I hurried and turned on the television. Two of the local stations were dead. The other three showed an avalanche of destruction across the nation—across the world. There was footage of a dozer destroying a house while a group of people threw rocks at it like a bunch of Neanderthals. In other places the human response was more muscular but just as ineffective. Scott and I watched scenes of tanks moving, helicopters swooping, Predator drones firing.

"Report now of dozer activity in Fort Collins—"

"Capital building destroyed. The governor—"

"The damn thing took a Tomahawk missile right in the side and as you can see there doesn't even appear to be a scratch—"

I switched to the cable news. Fox now had footage of a different type of counterattack. I recognized the scene at once. There was no military. The fight wasn't against the dozers. Mobs were assaulting individual aliens, beating them, stabbing them, shooting them. The aliens did not hide; they did not fight back even when someone doused them with gasoline and lit a match. Fox's reporter struggled to talk over the chaos. He claimed the people of Baltimore had decided to purge their city of the aliens once and for all. Thousands of their bodies were being loaded into trailers and dumped into the Chesapeake. Behind the reporter, the only mechanical thing moving was a dozer, just rumbling into the edge of the picture.

"Too many months too late!" Scott growled.

I allowed myself to nod despite my disgust. There was no doubt the aliens deserved it and yet I did doubt it, to the core of my being. I looked away thinking of my alien and wishing she were here. Hopefully she was still on the rooftop where I'd left her. She wouldn't be discovered there.

"My God," Scott said.

My attention came back to the television. The footage had changed to Washington, D.C. A single dozer moved on the White House. The footage scrambled between shots—helicopters and roving news teams all angling to record the end of history. The dozer just rolled steadily down Pennsylvania Avenue through a torrent of firepower. Machine-gun fire, tank shells, guided bombs, and rockets tried to pierce the alien alloy. The screen filled with smoke and we had only the descriptions from the embedded correspondents. One jumped the gun and, determined to give himself strength, announced he could see the dozer was burning. Others joined in, a hopeful chorus that refused to sing the grim tune of reality. The dozer was blasted to bits; the dozer was smoking and severely damaged; the dozer was blackened and at least seemed to be slowing down; the dozer had a minor dent in it. The smoke dissipated and we saw the dozer was fine and glistening, emerging from the haze like a Cadillac exiting a car wash. My hands found Scott's. We watched a tank position itself in front of the dozer. I had seen the dozer on I-25 many times but I never felt overwhelmed by its size the way I did now. The tank looked like a toy, a St. Bernard against a charging elephant. The tank fired once and rolled back but the dozer preyed upon it. The tank broke apart like an eggshell.

The dozer turned and crashed the White House gates. A reporter said the troops had been told to hold fire now for risk of damaging the bulding. The reporter repeated that, talking to himself now with a crazed laugh. On screen, a platoon rushed in front of the dozer and put their hands and shoulders against it, as if to push it back. It ran them over, oblivious to their existence. An attack helicopter swung into view and fired its entire arsenal in a glorious display that lasted several minutes. The ordnance did nothing and the dozer offered no counterstrike. It seemed to have no offensive armament at all in the expected sense. I remembered the movie theatre and the woman in the row ahead crying as, on screen, the Martian machines floated down the street blasting every building. The reality was so much more banal. No missiles, no lasers, no flak rose up to drive off the sorties our military threw against it. Like some stoic mammoth it pressed on, content to let the swarming insects get in their little bites. Another helicopter fired without effect. The pilot must have gone mad. He pressed himself full throttle at the most fragile-looking part of the dozer, the tower that directed its devastating wrecking ball. The helicopter burst apart on it and the dozer moved through the horrific fireball unscathed. The crane swung around and the ball, held aloft in its strange magnetic field, shot forward at hundreds of miles per hour. The columns of the North Portico disintegrated as the structure exploded into rubble and splinters. The entire building lasted less than ten minutes, about the same length of time I spent mowing my lawn.

I started to turn off the TV.

"Keep it on!"

I handed the remote to Scott. "You watch it if you want to. I can't."

"Where are you going?"

"To find my alien."

Scott showed some life. "And kill her?"

"I left her on top of a building. She showed no sign of moving but she told me to run if I wanted to live. There was a dozer coming. As I ran home, I wondered if the dozer would spare that building if it knew she was on top of it. I thought it would. Now I don't think so. She stayed up there to commit suicide."

"Let her," he said.

"For whatever it's worth, I owe her. Because of you, I owe her."

"But you can't just leave me here."

"You wanted to stay, so stay."

Outside my door, about seventy *Pi* dozed in yards or walked casually here and there, budding masters of all they pretended not to survey.

2.

I managed several miles in my car, weaving around endless debris and abandoned vehicles and piled *Pi* corpses. I was reduced to driving on the sidewalk before I came to where the I-25 dozer was operating in the city. The destruction towered up on every side, so thorough that it seemed to have erased even my memory of what used to be there, the familiar storefronts, the vintage clothing store, the comic book outlet. Most of the street signs were gone. I knew I was on Colfax. The capitol building should have been just up ahead but I couldn't see even an outline in the dark. Maybe the morning would reveal the heaps of its once proud dome. My headlights ran up against a blockade of large chunks of concrete and tortured pieces of iron and steel.

The rest of this journey was taking place on foot.

I continued on, clumsily scaling my way along the path of the dozer as disgust and anger swelled inside me. The sound of the single dozer, still a mile in the distance, gave the ground and air a reverberation felt bodily. I closed my eyes and thought of what the alien had said. *Trillions and trillions.* Once their full numbers arrived, the Earth would always have this shaking even after the dozers quit. The aliens' feet would be its source.

I passed dead *Pi* and live ones. The dead had all been executed at point-blank range. Somewhere a resistance still existed, unorganized, shooting wherever there was a target. Humanity's last gasp, gang violence. The living *Pi* ignored the dead and continued their bland disinterest. Amid the ruin of one city block an alien stood staring at a slab of ruptured cement like it was a piece of modernist art. Had I been armed, I would have shot him through the neck. Instead, I whispered my name into its ear. Then I whispered Scott's and Mr. Morrison's and every other person I could remember. I wanted it to know the names of its victims.

They're going to do it, I thought. Their machines are going to destroy us and they're going to play the game until the end. Even as this agenda became clear, I continued to doubt the truth. So effective was the mask of their aloof, vacuous behavior that I still could not believe they had looked across the vastness of space and drawn such a plan against us. This was soulless barbarism suggesting some deep core of evil. This was violence! How could they not recognize it in themselves? Why didn't they just conquer us immediately instead of this absurd delay and so many unnecessary deaths on their side? I thought of all the invasions I'd ever read about. Even some within the Nazi army had broken under the strain of the suffering they inflicted upon others. The *Pi* showed no signs of breaking. Perhaps they knew the secret to success after all. They balanced the craven disregard for the terror they inflicted upon others with a callous disregard for their own safety.

A military helicopter swooshed overhead, went into a static hover and unloaded a hell storm of ordnance at the dozer that was still beyond my vision. The whole world seemed to roar and shake as if some angry god was emerging from the ground. Staggered and knocked flat on my back, I got up to see blistering bursts of light, different colors mounting each other into the night like rungs on a gigantic ladder. The helicopter swiveled and danced back a hundred yards before making a half turn back toward its target, like a boxer stopping on the way to his corner to check his opponent's swagger. The helicopter buzzed away as if the round—and the match—was already over.

Scott limped up behind me. He told me he'd stolen a truck to follow me. "Did you see that? Christ. I thought the dozers were fast. The helicopter destroyed the entire block in record time."

"Maybe that's part of the plan. They move their machines into the cities, get the military to fire upon them. The artillery doesn't hurt them but it speeds up the city's destruction considerably."

He walked with me and we helped each other navigate over the larger debris. The flames farther ahead heated the air in stark contrast to what the dozers left behind.

"It's amazing how cool to the touch everything is. I thought the destruction would be super hot."

"Not from them. Their destruction isn't like our destruction. We drop bombs, blow things up. We use fire."

"They don't exactly use ice," I said.

We moved on about half a mile with the temperature rising as the wind drove ash and superheated air at us. There was silence up ahead, raising Scott's hopes that maybe the helicopter had won. He went on about how the army wasn't stupid and how we'd had all this time to work on developing something that would penetrate their machines. That was the great failure of the aliens' plan; it gave us time to prepare. We weren't primitives waiting for household gods to rescue us; we had split the atom after all. I nodded and nodded, a hollow person eager to fill myself with his hope. The silence became more powerful and I grew convinced. We had won this battle and if we won this one then we'd win the next one too. Score one for the White House. Score another for the state capitol building. Who knows, maybe in Paris they were scoring several for the Louvre right at this moment.

"I'm telling you. Did you see those explosions? It had to be something experimental. It had to be a new kind of missile," Scott said.

We came to a block corner occupied by a ten-story office building with WELLS FARGO displayed prominently across the front. We must be around Lincoln Avenue, I thought, smiling as a sense of familiarity returned. The building stood preserved and untouched, ready for banking hours. As long as it remained unbroken, symbolic, we knew we had our economy, our livelihood—our lives. That was it then. I made a grand gesture to Scott as we turned the corner. It was time to see what victory looked like.

"No!"

The backside of the Wells Fargo building looked like a gigantic scalpel had descended. We saw the girders, the halved office spaces with furniture still inside. Aided by the moonlight and fires, I felt myself peering in upon secrets. It was like a doll's house opened to reveal all the compartments. Here's where Barbie works. Here's where Barbie takes a smoke break. The dozer was nestled up against the façade, quiet and dark. For a mad moment it seemed like the dozer was in the process of constructing the bank instead of destroying it.

"At least we got the bastards, just as I thought," Scott said.

"I don't see how. The fires are way down there. This whole area would be destroyed if it was the target."

We exchanged glances and then we crept toward the dozer, stupidly staying close to the building wall that was more likely to collapse upon us than give cover. It *is* dead, I thought. I didn't care how or why. The dozer's surface wasn't smudged or scratched. It wasn't the missiles but maybe something else—perhaps a chemical component all the ordnance had disguised. Scott reached forward to touch it and I started to warn him off. The weapon could have been anything, a virus or bacteria.

"All ours," Scott said, patting its side. "Once the aliens are gone we'll have these and their rockets to reverse-engineer." His hands rubbed together.

Scott saw the shadow before I did and grabbed my arm. An alien came around the side of the machine and with apparent weariness leaned up against it with arms and legs lightly crossed. It wore something on its head. I squinted to focus better. Yes, it was a construction worker's yellow hardhat cocked to the right on the *Pi*'s oversized head.

"Son of a bitch."

"Let's get out of here," I said.

"It's a game to them. All of this is a game."

"Before it sees us," I said.

"It's like if an adult put on a cowboy hat to ride a hobbyhorse. It's—it's…condescending. They're mocking our destruction."

The *Pi*'s ears snapped up from its eyes and for just a second it stared right at us, all pretense abandoned. Its lips curled in what I interpreted as a silent chuckle. Then its gaze swept past us and became the familiar gray, unfocused seeing that either never landed on anything or else intensely focused for hours on the mundane and barren. For half a minute the alien lounged there. With the absurd hardhat balanced on its head, it looked like a union man taking one of a hundred daily work breaks. Then it turned and without hurrying went around the side to re-enter the machine. Rooted as we were, we did not see how it got in, but within seconds the enormous dozer powered up as quiet as a new Lexus. The air hummed again but whatever engine powered the machine made no discernible noise at all. Then there was a horrific screeching and grinding as the dozer tore back and the building began to sway. Scott grabbed me around the waist and flung us away on the heels of a total collapse.

Scott held to me through a storm of dust and noise. As the scene cleared, we saw the dozer heading up the ruined street to smash the next building. "I think that's where she's at," I pointed.

"We're nowhere near the old warehouse."

"How do you know? Look around. Do you know what street this is?"

"No. She won't be there anyway, Craig. She's one of them. She's been lying to you the entire time. She's been faking empathy. They're master actors."

"She wasn't faking," I said. "She doesn't need to. She doesn't have any. A touch of sadness, maybe, but not empathy."

"Then why are you trying to find her?"

"She saved me from your own goons. But it's more than that. She opened up about what her people were doing. She gave me a glimpse—"

"At our own destruction," Scott said with a harsh laugh.

"Yes. But that's something, at least. I just—I have to *understand*, Scott. That's all I've ever wanted, to understand. You, me, her, *them*. The universe. Even if it's just for a few minutes before I die, I want to know what it's all about."

"The universe," Scott repeated, pressing his lips tight. It didn't hide his reaction. The hysterical, mad laughter came out of his eyes.

As we argued, the dozer reduced its next target to a cold heap. All I could do was stare. I'd come all this way, taken all this action, just to end up paralyzed at the critical moment. If she was still on that rooftop—if it was even the *right* rooftop—then she had probably just died. Knowing I could have done nothing helpful in the first place gave no solace. I could not have reasoned with her; I could not have forcibly removed her. At that moment I began to understand why so many people facing a crisis act like nothing is even happening. We're taught, or we instinctively know, that we can do nothing to change the situation. It is therefore better to just ignore it.

"I should have killed it," I said.

"What?"

"The dozer's driver. That was the best chance we had. We can't hurt the machines from the outside. We probably can't ever get inside them or someone would have figured out how. But the driver was right there. I thought they were remote controlled, but they're not. I could have killed the operator and hijacked the dozer. Then we'd have something to fight them with."

"You don't know there's only one of them inside. Besides, do you have a gun? You'd have needed a gun."

"Not if I was like you, Scott. If I was like you I could have acted and I wouldn't have needed a gun."

He was quiet a long moment. He looked at all the destruction. "In the end, I'm glad you aren't like me."

I broke into a long, deep sob. Scott held me gently at the right shoulder and held something up in his left hand. It was his gun. "It was loaded and I didn't fire. I thought about it. So blame me, not yourself."

Given world enough and time, I probably would have.

3.

Hours later we discovered the anomaly. As we made our way back to the car, we got lost in the maze of destruction and found ourselves among a growing mob of stragglers that literally ripped apart every *Pi* it crossed. Scott stayed quiet and somber, no longer interested in butchering. He walked with his head down. I kept my head up enough to notice the occasional stray building still standing amidst the carnage. Their survival made no sense until I made the connection when I saw two buildings left untouched on opposite ends of the block and compared them. They were both churches. The others had been churches as well. And not just Christian churches. All the holy places seemed to have been spared. The churches, the synagogues, the mosques—even a storefront Christian Science Reading Room—remained standing amidst mountains of rubble. The dozers were surgically precise in excising them from the ruin. I told Scott and he only shrugged. A few others noticed the pattern too and began to speculate. It could not be random chance. What did it mean? Why offer such respect to these buildings, and by extension our religions?

People began attributing it to God. The idea rippled through the mob and drove them forward in righteous certainty that our small band could overcome the invasion with the power of faith.

"It's a sign! God has not abandoned us! God is with us even now!" These words came booming from the doors of the Cathedral of the Immaculate Conception, where a few hundred people were piled around, forming a sort of pyramid up the steps to the pinnacle of the entrance. The words rang out simultaneously from within and without through enormous speakers lashed to the front of the building. The voice was powerful but solemn and, despite the moment, somehow uninspired. My church experiences had always been of the Southern Baptist or Pentecostal sort. I'd only been to church four times in my adulthood, always seeking out the most radical and conservative, sweating out sermons that condemned me for loving another man. My friends called me crazy when I told them afterwards, saying I must be a masochist. My friends all went to churches in Boulder where the apostle Paul had the last name McCartney. Their churches had no sense of judgment or outcast and everyone lived in one big happy neighborhood.

But I knew better. It takes a barn-burning preacher to show you the nature of the universe, not female pastors who sometimes played the guitar and interrupted their sermon to break into a verse of "Eleanor Rigby" if the spirit moved them. But Father McKenzie was inside the cathedral right now calmly telling the mob that it was now obvious God had made His presence felt. A Pentecostal would have seized the moment and forged us into His army, His arm. We would become His smiting fist. The priest inside the cathedral was too reasonable and certain, appealing to the logic of faith rather than the emotion. "God has surely stayed their hand against the churches. God gives refuge from the aberration that has come upon us." No, his voice was too calm to be effective, though people wept with rejoicing all around me. They nodded and gave themselves to God and hatched grand schemes about building nothing but churches. Shopping malls, apartment buildings, banks—all would be housed in churches, vast sprawling churches that God would protect. The aliens outside, we inside, and life would soon become normal.

"Look at that."

We all turned our heads toward the sound of a precise, uniform marching. The *Pi* were coming at us in a vast line, their arms linked to make a chain that must have extended a quarter of a mile. This chain, this net, came at us with slow assurance, not rushing, not discernibly urgent. It had the fluidity of an ocean wave, every alien in lockstep unison even though several had to scale heaps of rubble while others had a clear path. Our crowd shared a murmur of alarm, all of us too fascinated with the image the aliens presented. It was like being assaulted by a chain of paper doll figures. When the *Pi* got within three hundred yards, we went silent, all except the priest, whose calm promises now seemed sinister in the face of even calmer devils. His assuring voice now seemed closer to that of a concentration camp official telling us to disrobe and step into the shower room.

Scott pointed. "There's another line behind them. And a third— I'm sure of it. Like a phalanx."

"Do you think this is it? Are they going to kill us?"

"I guess I would, if I was them. There's not much good in holding back now."

A couple of people who overheard Scott broke into a run. A few others, seeing them flee, decided to join. Under any other circumstance the domino effect would be complete. We'd all be running. If it were a tornado coming down the street there'd be no question. But we stayed. Almost all of us stayed and I guess we meant to fight. The *Pi* still weren't armed and as they got to within seventy-five yards our side started picking up anything sharp. Many had guns, of course, and the firing commenced. The priest's voice snapped quiet and we were American Revolutionaries again at Bunker Hill with arrogant lines of Redcoats marching straight at us, impressively oblivious to the artillery we rained down upon them. When one *Pi* fell the line closed up immediately. Rocks struck their heads, crude spears put out their eyes. The *Pi* continued and then they were too close for guns, too close for rocks. It became a fist fight as we punched their bodies. The *Pi* suffered our attacks, never letting go of each other's hands. Their line surged and began to drive us. We turned and ran. The ends of the lines sped up and swung forward and in. Scott and I tripped and the *Pi* stepped over us in their silent pursuit of the crowd. We watched in astonishment as their line now closed into a circle with at least a hundred men and women trapped within. Frenzied hands waved through the narrow spaces between the alien bodies, which stood so close together not even a child could escape through the crevices in this living sheepfold. The alien circle moved in the same lockstep uniformity, taking their human captives with them. The second and third lines came to gather the bewildered stragglers. Now the *Pi* broke into smaller groups and made smaller nets to capture individuals and couples. They worked their bodies in unison and forced the people to move. If people refused to move, the circle just stopped, content to wait. Likewise if a human within the circle tripped and fell, the alien prison waited for that person to stand. I heard people shouting, calling for help as they beat against the impassive bodies of their captors. Inevitably the mobile prisons kept moving, sometimes fast, sometimes inches at a time.

Scott and I watched them pass us by. A final line came and we stood there, prepared to be captured. But when they got to us the *Pi* casually lifted their arms and let us slip through the net. We were fish they did not want to catch.

"What happened?" Scott asked as we watched the last circle leave. "Why were we spared?"

A few ashen faces peered at us from the cathedral door. Like their dozers, the *Pi* had ignored everyone actually inside the church. I saw their suspicious expressions and shrugged. What had we done? Ignoring us couldn't be an accident. Had we done something to deserve being spared? *We're collaborators.* That's what the people in the church must think, that we were alien sympathizers who sold out our people to survive. I started up the stairs but the door slammed shut and locked us out.

"It's not what you think!" I shouted and collapsed on the steps. Scott sat down beside me.

"I don't understand," he said. "I've killed more of them than anyone. Don't they want revenge?"

We just sat there looking at the ruins of Denver.

"What do we do now?" Scott said.

"Go back to my house." Then I laughed because I'd answered so automatically, a portion of my brain still in the fantasyland destroyed several hours ago.

"It's probably still there," Scott said. "Unless more dozers have arrived, it may take weeks for the one to flatten all the suburbs."

"Do you know how to get back?"

"You've lived in Denver your whole life. Do you really need street signs and landmarks?"

"Sorry I'm not a goddamn homing pigeon!"

He frowned and began picking at stray rubble on the steps. I lifted my head and watched him. It seemed criminal and irresponsible—hideous, even—to desire him now. Sex was a thing of the past, a faded pleasure. What could it say about my humanity, to want sex as our history went down building by building? Still I could not help watching him and thinking about everything that ever attracted me to him. He was lean but not incredibly fit. He possessed a natural masculinity that expressed itself in a carefree aura, a confidence to try anything and shrug off failure with a smile. Before the invasion, these same attributes had also led me almost into despair that he would never take anything seriously. I did not want our love to be something he could walk away from and think *Better luck next time.* Unfocused in our relationship, unfocused on a career, his attitude always suggested he was just loafing and waiting for everything to work itself out. The invasion had changed that part of his personality but now he seemed to be reverting. We might have been sitting by a lake skipping rocks, not quite hungry enough yet for a picnic on our island.

"Our island!"

"What?"

"Remember Lake Dowdy? Do you think they've gone up there? Up to all the camps and up into the mountains? Do you know if the Company had other places where it stashed weapons?"

Excitement stirred in his expression. "Hundreds of places. We always said if there was a disaster we were to get to a stronghold."

"There are humans there," I said, and the words made me shiver. The people in the church were already dead to me. It was as if only Scott and I existed on the planet.

"Some. But how many could have made it?"

"Thousands!"

He grimaced. Skepticism.

"Why not?"

He just shrugged. "You think we should go for it?"

"There's nothing else for us to do."

But first we had to get home.

Chapter Five: Days

1.

First Night, as it came to be known, ended across the world as each respective time zone hit nine in the morning. The machines powered down everywhere, sometimes in the middle of streets and highways, more often in the middle of someone's house. Scott and I, ragged and staggering, found our way back to my house by following a few remaining landmarks and extrapolating from memory. What should have been no more than a two-hour hike took four as we scrambled over rubble and made countless corrections. Some neighborhoods were flattened while others stood serenely still like comfortable islands dotting a raging sea. I detected no pattern and that frightened me because I could not guess at what I would find. But then I started to know where I was going and the confidence gave me an energy Scott lacked. I started to run. I couldn't help myself and there it was, my house, standing untouched amid the surrounding ruin. Every house flattened but my own. I stopped and gave Scott time to catch up.

"Why?"

"It's just like the nets," Scott said, an edge of distrust in his tone.

We had seen one other occurrence of the net phenomenon on our journey. The few humans on the streets found themselves being rounded up like the crowd outside the cathedral. Scott had been the one who needed to experiment again. Only now, at the end, was he curious enough about their ways to forgo any sense of danger and give up all other plans, even joining the resistance in the mountains.

Seizing me by the wrist, he led us into an oncoming alien line and waited. The *Pi* again lifted their linked, implacable arms and let us slip through. No one else escaped.

"There has to be a reason."

"What are you implying, Scott?"

He looked down at his feet. "I don't want to say it."

"Then don't. I've done nothing to make them want to spare me. I've killed aliens. I hated the Company but never enough to turn against my own kind."

"Still, there has to be a reason," Scott said.

"I don't see why. There's no reason to anything else they do."

So First Night ended with my house still standing and Second and Third Night did, too. Most of Denver and the suburbs were gone by the end of the Third Night. For the first time in my life I could step outside and see the mountains as clearly as if I lived in Boulder.

I was outside staring into the distance as Third Night ended when Scott returned, weaving between increasingly thick crowds of Pi strolling to and fro. He was looking more and more exhausted, ashen and thin. He wasn't sleeping well and our food supply consisted of uncooked scraps. There was no electricity. The phones did not work. The previous day Scott's cell phone burst into song and we scrambled over ourselves to answer it, but no one was there and we sighed into each other's desperate faces.

"I almost forgot my way," he said. "Everything's gone except the churches."

"No cars?"

"Nothing. We'll never get to Lake Dowdy without a car."

"What about people?"

The *Pi* went past in both directions, never straying into the confines of my yard.

"A few people here and there, still clinging to the churches."

I sat down on the porch and stared out at the aliens. There were more today than I'd ever seen before and I guessed one of their carrier ships had touched down at last. I had worried about Scott going out alone but he insisted. The *Pi* did not make their nets but they knew how to use their numbers to press against you, to squeeze you with their weight and suffocate you as they pretended not to notice.

"We could walk. How long do you think it would take?"

"We can't walk," Scott said.

"But how long do you think it would take?"

"More than a week. More than we could survive with no food or water."

Scott went inside. I hoped he would lie down and rest but I could hear his stomach rumbling as he passed. I hoped he would find my rations on the table and eat them.

2.

We found Mr. Sutter the next day. I hadn't thought about the Sutters and little Ryan but I had assumed they escaped. I had no reason to think so but my mind just couldn't accept their deaths. Mr. Sutter swung a pistol back and forth and staggered, shrieking that the invasion was our faults. The story he told us—who knows of it was believable. But I dry heaved after he finished his rambling confession of killing his wife and then little Ryan, shooting them both in the head and then turning the gun on himself but being unable to fire. The same instincts that led him to kill his family also fueled a powerful self-preservation and here he was offering us the gun, telling one of us to execute him.

"No," I said.

"Yes," Scott said, and over my shouts he and Mr. Sutter went around the side of my house and the gun rang out. There was nothing for a while, no sound, and when Scott did not come back a fear seized me. I ran around the side and Scott was standing over Mr. Sutter's body, just staring like all the answers were at his feet and seeping into the greedy soil. Both his hands were empty and I could finally breathe again. He had thrown the gun away.

I went inside after Scott and I found him obsessing with the radio. We wouldn't have it much longer either once the batteries faded.

"What are you doing?"

"At one of the churches they talked about new resistance movements. I don't know. Sounded crazy."

"You're trying to pick up a broadcast?"

"A guy—he was wearing this tattered army uniform—said the government had been moved to a secret place to continue to fight. The military has given up on attacking the dozers directly. They can't penetrate them. And some countries have tried using nukes—on their own cities. Can you imagine?"

"I can't imagine there are any cities left at all," I said, though I knew there must be. The dozers were efficient but even if there were twenty thousand of them it would take months—even years—to systematically plow the whole country down. I stared at the ruin of Denver and could not accept that other American cities still stood, probably abandoned but largely untouched, perhaps even with power. Was the Internet still viable? Did television stations still broadcast someplace? If so, perhaps the cities were not abandoned after all. I imagined the people there entering a mass psychosis, a hysterical amnesia. They would go about their lives in those cities as if nothing had happened, as if the sky were empty, and wait for the dozers to come claim them in their homes.

Scott kept fiddling with the radio knobs. Sometimes a tantalizing burst of static different from regular snow arrested his dialing and he would wait for minutes listening in earnest before cursing and chasing hope up and down the bandwidth.

"The army's plan now was the Company's plan all along. Mow the individuals down wherever we find them. But it's too late, isn't it? I don't know. I don't know anything. I never did."

"Scott, calm down."

"Nukes," he repeated. "Sounds like aggressive chemotherapy on terminal cancer. Pointless. The body's already dying so let's make sure to kill the spirit, too. We were the spirit, Craig. The Company and all those good men in it."

Scott went on telling me what he'd heard. Three carriers had set down two days ago and the lines of aliens still went unabated day and night. Smaller rockets fell at a rate of five hundred a minute across the globe. I could not believe that even though I had proof in what I saw constantly overhead. At night the sky never went dark now from the rockets. Half a million stars seemed to have been added to our heaven in just a day.

Scott switched from static to static and finally hammered the radio off with his fist. He dropped his head into his hands and sat comatose.

Here's where I cry, I thought, staring at his back. I might have shed tears for all the destruction and all the deaths—I had probably wept, shrieked, and laughed in madness countless times over the past week. But now I would cry because Scott's will had been broken and because he could see no bright future for himself, and therefore none for me. How many times had I relied on seeing through his eyes? They saw darkness now when I craved light. So I'll cry for us and the aliens and the world they've conquered, I thought. Let my tears mean that we at long last have no anger towards them, only pity that they are so vicious, so callous as to destroy us without even acknowledging us.

The front door opened.

"You!"

The alien entered with two full brown bags, as if she'd just taken a stroll to the corner grocery store. She walked past and walked into the kitchen as Scott roused himself.

I followed her.

"You're alive! On First Night I went out to try and find you. I thought you were in trouble because of how you saved me. I wanted to repay the favor."

She sat the bags on the table. I looked in them and got another shock. Each was full of food—human food. Eggs, milk, hamburger meat, all cold. Where had it come from? I asked but of course she did not answer. She did not acknowledge me at all.

"What is this?"

She walked out of the kitchen as Scott stumbled in. I helped him, putting an arm around his back. He felt so thin. I showed him the food. "Isn't it wonderful? We can eat. You can get all your strength back."

"I don't want it," he said, turning away like I'd offered him rotting garbage.

"We need this food. You have to eat."

"I'd rather pick through piles for scraps than be fed by them." He twisted away from me and stormed into the living room where the alien sat on the couch acting comatose.

"What do you want from us?" Scott demanded. "Why are we being kept alive?"

The *Pi* leaned her head back as her ears folded over her eyes and stayed there.

"Goddamn you!" He struck her across the face, knocking it to the left. Scott rubbed his knuckles.

"Scott, please calm down—let me cook something. Then we—we can do something. We can think better after we eat."

"We're not staying here."

"I know we're not, we're going to the mountains."

"No! We keep *saying* we're going to the mountains. But in your mind you've already settled in here. I see it in your eyes. You're an amazing man. I've never seen a man who could rationalize and adjust like you. It's the best survival skill. It's always the best of all possible worlds wherever you park your ass."

"That's not fair—"

"Don't tell me about fair."

"Okay," I said soothingly. "We leave right now. We take off walking and if we find a car, that's great. We'll bring the food with us."

"No."

"It's completely impractical to think we can walk that far without food. You're the one who keeps telling me that."

We argued a few more minutes and then we found ourselves staring at each other, each anticipating one final joust.

"Good bye, Craig."

Tears filled my eyes. "I'm coming with you."

I latched onto him and pressed my forehead against his chest. He stood still but I felt the muscles twitch. His right hand reached for something, tugged and then the arm lifted. I pulled back in time to see Mr. Sutter's gun.

"No!"

He fired but I broke his aim in time to send the bullet to the *Pi*'s right. It struck an inch off her head to the right. The gun clanged on the coffee table and made a soft thud on the carpet.

"You're dead to me," Scott said before running out the door.

Chapter Six: Nights

1.

The *Pi*'s right ear flickered up, revealing her liquid black eye. Its intense, belittling stare paralyzed me. "Your partner will return."

"No, he won't."

"His food is here."

"Didn't you hear him? He'd rather starve to death than eat what you brought."

"That is not the food I mean."

I looked around, puzzled, until her stare made me look at myself. "Me?" I laughed. "What do you mean? I'm not his food—"

Her ear closed over her eye, releasing me. I sank down and lay on the carpet, succumbing at once to all the exhaustion I'd been pushing off. Nothing worked, my muscles inanimate, my bones a burdensome steel with rust at the joints. I closed my eyes, but despite the heaviness of my slumber I slept fitfully, coming back to awareness again and again but unable to do anything useful with it. Had she done something to me? Was the food tainted? But I had not eaten the food. Her eye, her eye—she hypnotized me. She did something to me. She—

When I woke again, the *Pi* still sat serene on the couch, both her eyes uncovered and glittering from the little bit of light in the room. I sat up and looked out the window. At another time I would have guessed it to be a little after twilight, but it felt much later and I knew the sky was deceiving now, lit by a universe of descending metal.

"Scott," I whispered.

I stood up—too fast. The rush of blood sent me tottering and I managed to grab the wall and steady myself. A minute passed with me just breathing long and deep as my insides settled. Then I stepped onto my little porch and peered out. Aliens walked to and fro in great silent lines that stretched as far as I could see. Their rows went on and on and it seemed I was looking upon a mutant field of sunflowers on a windless day. Even their footsteps were quiet, as if they knew I'd been sleeping and tiptoed accordingly.

"Scott," I said, calling into their masses. I had a wild image of his head, his pretty human head, suddenly leaping up out of that mob and shouting back as we made our way to each other.

I crept around to the side of the house and behind it, hoping Scott might be hiding out.

I went inside and rushed upstairs, praying he'd come back while I was asleep. But the bed was empty. I came down to see the *Pi* still sitting on the living room sofa. I stood in front of her.

"So what happens now?"

She looked through me.

"Please say something. There's no reason to play the game now, is there? We have too much between us. Hell, you're my *guardian*."

She stood and went into the kitchen. I followed her and watched as she emptied the bags. One package was hamburger meat that would go rotten soon since there was no refrigeration. She took the meat in two large gobs and dropped them both into my largest skillet. She set the skillet atop the cold burner and then turned to me.

"Eat."

"In case you haven't noticed, there's no electricity. Am I supposed to eat it raw?"

I stalked her into the living room. "Why are you so eager to have me eat? Is the food poisoned or something?"

"Leave my house."

"But this is my house and it will always be that way until I'm dead." I held my breath on hearing these bold words. In that moment I knew I had said too much, had crossed some line. *Given her permission.* I was certain of it, but the *Pi* did not stir.

"Leave."

I sat down on the sofa and glared at her. "I'll make a deal. If you tell me where Scott is, I'll go. Forget about whatever obligation you have to me. I just want to finish this with him. You promised he'd come back, but he hasn't. You must know where he is. How many other humans are around?"

"Your partner has joined the others."

"The resistance? He made it to the mountains? That's impossible. Unless he found a car. I cant believe he wouldn't come back for me."

"Leave now."

"If he can find a car then I can find one too. And we'll be back. Then you die."

She said nothing. She would not force me out. She *couldn't*. I could go upstairs and sleep if I wished. Instead I went to the door. Maybe she was the landlord now, but I was evicting myself.

2.

I slept in the yard and made raids into the house whenever she hosted a party, which she did often. Her guests always walked right past me, gazes fixed straight ahead. The door was never locked and when I entered I found myself in a gathering of mannequins, their manners always silent and cold and stiff with indifference. Something about it reminded me of the few parties my parents used to throw, loud enough to wake me, and when I came downstairs in my pajamas the gathering hushed in astonishment, as if Mom and Dad had told them they had no son. I lingered among the aliens, glad to disrupt their gathering and force them into the game. But their patience was perfect and I always broke first and returned to the yard.

Five times in the past month I slept on the floor and finally, seeing her leave and thinking her absence could let me hold a fantasy together, I slept once in my old bed with the comforter pulled up and had my last cry in that old familiar, stolen dark. No one and everything had died on that mattress and I could not help but think that I had slept through history.

When I woke up there was the same brown bag of dry goods left at my feet, prisoner rations that showed up regardless of where I slept.

I cannot properly record how American society ended. There was no more television or radio, no supermarkets and supermarket tabloids, no Internet. I found Scott's cell phone in the front yard. In his rush he either dropped it or it slipped from his pocket. I tried it but there was no signal. The towers must have been leveled too. I looked up into the sky and wondered if the last remains of humanity's existence would be our satellites trafficking in their freeway orbits. Or had the *Pi* disposed of those as well?

I got my news through rumor. With increasing rarity, I sometimes encountered a man or woman the *Pi* had also ignored. But these people always seemed nuts, spewing the most unbelievable story. One evening I strayed away farther from my house than usual and found a man wandering among the *Pi*, who carried on in silent, self-imposed obliviousness. I described Scott and asked him if he'd seen him. Staggering, he seized my shoulders and spat his stinking breath into my face. I could only stare in terror at what by all rights should have been my face in a mirror. Unshaved, unwashed, gray and gaunt—a better face than mine because it showed the scars of survival. This was a man who had slept on rock and dirt, uncovered, since Third Night at least and maybe even long before the First. I wondered about his abilities. Perhaps he had always been homeless and used to being ignored. Those years of torment had strengthened him now for humanity's last days. I could not fathom his ways and it sparked a deep, crimson shame. I had slept in a bed, I had eaten my rations, and I had shaved. I had only three days of stubble since my electric razor still had enough charge to shear away the weeds of encroaching barbarity. At least my breath stank. It had been fully two days since I last brushed my teeth, using a portion of the bottled water the aliens included in my food bag.

"The government's relocated to the Northwest Territory," he said.

"I guess it's pretty desolate up there. No aliens?"

"The aliens are *everywhere*," he replied with a conspiratorial whisper, as if we were not surrounded. We were having this conversation amid hundreds of *Pi*, who were pretending not to hear us.

"There's hope for us if there's still a government," I said.

"I don't like it. Our government in another country? That's not American. But there's much to be proud of. We've killed millions of them."

A *Pi* walked close by and he hawked a loogie on it. The *Pi* passed without brushing off the slime.

The man smiled. "Cowards. Even if we don't have guns we still have our weapons, eh? Our disgust. Our indignation. Our dignity! *Fuck you!*" He turned, screaming at them. He kept screaming until the veins bulged in his neck and I thought he would collapse. I put my hand on his shoulder.

"Did you say millions?"

"Yes! I heard about a battle where over a hundred thousand were killed by just one hundred soldiers."

"What happened to the soldiers?"

"They ran out of ammunition."

"They ran away, then?"

"No, they stood and fought. Bayonets, knives, whatever they could fashion. The aliens kept falling but new ones would replace them and they locked their arms together and formed a circle. They—they—the soldiers were *herded* to someplace. They fought while they were being herded and the herding continued despite everything. No one knows where they were taken. Those poor brave bastards."

"I've seen the aliens herd people, too," I said. "Have they tried to herd you?"

"No. I'm too smart for them."

I remembered what my alien had said about keeping humanity from breeding. "I wonder where they take everyone. You think a concentration camp or something like that?"

"They eat us," the man said. "I've seen them do it."

"I don't think they're eating us."

The man ignored this and told of other victories that seemed plausible enough. But why the aliens continued to show such passive indifference on an individual basis astonished me. The man talked on and I felt like how warriors of old must have felt, listening as the words of the shaman-poet charged their blood with tales of battlefield glory. But finally his madness and his desire for extravagant hopes got the best of him and the stories became fairy tales. The government was now in Reno, Nevada, not the Northwest Territories. Next he moved Congress to the Florida Keys and minutes later to Hawaii. Attack helicopters were mowing the aliens down from the sky. He'd seen fields of their corpses rotting away. The purge of Denver would come soon. The big cities had to get it first. New York and Los Angeles and Chicago. Chicago was so bad they just dropped the Bomb and wrote it off. He pumped his fist in the air. "But L.A., ah, L.A.! We drove the bastards into the sea there! Did you know the Hollywood sign is being rebuilt? We'll have new movies again by the summer."

His grandiose fantasies oppressed me even more than reality. I now realized that our government no longer existed, and whatever victories remnants of the army achieved were small in comparison. The stockpiles had been exhausted and with the standard means of production ended, there were to be no replacements—no new humans, no new human equipment.

"Tomorrow," the man said, "is the end of everything. Nuclear war. The end of us. The end of *them*."

I looked up to the sky by reflex. It was bright blue and cloudless except for the endless streaks from rockets entering the atmosphere, crisscrossing above us everywhere like super-powered flocks of birds. As I stared, the man explained how the United States government in Comoros had reached consensus with the other nuclear powers to initiate a full-scale exchange. It would kill most of the aliens on the planet and make the Earth uninhabitable to human and alien alike. Humanity's final *fuck you* to its conquerors.

I started to walk away. Maybe he was right, but probably he had made it up weeks ago or heard it from another madman. Did I even care if the world was blown up tomorrow? I asked myself this over and over and hated concluding that I did care. I did not want to die in atomic fire any more than I wanted to be shot or stabbed or starved. The bottom-line human instinct is to stay alive, just like any animal. Implicit in that instinct is a desire to write the future. The future is written by history's survivors.

"*Scorched earth!*" the man shrieked. "If we can't have the Earth, no one will." He stumbled off, muttering that I was a damn fool and promising the bombs would cure my stupidity. I waited for the lesson to fall on my head.

Chapter Seven: They Paved Paradise

1.

I woke up hearing the rumble from far off, towards where downtown Denver used to be. I got up off the grass and placed my hands over my forehead to shield my eyes from the sharp early sunlight. For a moment I could visualize all of downtown as it used to be, the jutting skyscrapers that always made the city seem deceptively larger than it was. I dropped my arms, realizing I wasn't hallucinating. The skyscrapers were there again—there and taller than before. In fact they were being constructed right in front of me.

Did I die? Is this heaven? The *Pi* had treated me as a ghost for so long it was easy to think I might be dead.

I did the most dangerous thing. I broke into a run straight toward those towers. My safety perimeter ended at my yard. Beyond that the *Pi* massed, their numbers growing by the hour. The throng of their bodies was so dense that navigating among them was like trying to ride a bicycle through an impenetrable forest. To run among them was close to suicide, for they never acknowledged me nor gave way if I blocked their movements. Their bulk easily brushed me aside or knocked me down. I had fallen once and only just managed to avoid being trampled to death by unconcerned feet. Moving among the *Pi* was like being thrown in the path of charging buffalo and expecting them to part for you. You had to navigate using patient strategy, moving with their flow, seizing small openings here and there while always jostling for a bit of space to the left and right.

But that morning, I just ran.

I charged forward like a linebacker, easy evidence of incipient insanity. Even the smallest alien outweighed me by a substantial margin, and I'd lost an unhealthy fifteen pounds since I last saw Scott. I ran toward the towers thinking of him, certain he had made it to the mountains to formulate a last stand with the rest of humanity's survivors. I thought that somehow he could see me running and know my spirit was not broken. The new skyscrapers in the distance, even if they were alien, seemed a beacon that I associated with Scott. He stood taller than those buildings in my mind, and if I could cross the distance to reach them, then someday I could cross even greater distances to reach *him*. The towers waited for me. Scott waited for me. *Push on.* Step by step I did, twisting and sliding through the silent, loitering alien masses.

I was bruised and battered by the time I reached the construction. The skyscrapers were going up very fast, almost with the ease of a child stacking blocks. New machines, similar in size to the dozers but clearly designed to erect rather than demolish, were creating a new city right in front of me. The tons of rubble from the previous civilization were gone—hauled away or converted into new material—and replaced with strange prefabricated housing constructs that seemed to stack and snap into place. *Legoland*, I thought.

I am living in Legoland.

The buildings up close had a cheapness about them, a phoniness that belied an otherwise incredible feat of engineering. The machines worked in threes, one placing a floor as another placed walls. There were no girders, no support structure of any kind that I could see. Each wall locked into place with the faintest of clicks. There were no discernible seams and the walls stood in place straight and sturdy. Once all four walls were in place, the first two machines moved away and the third came forward. The third machine had a crane arm that, like the dozers with their wrecking balls, employed some kind of powerful magnetic field. With astonishing speed, the crane arm levitated smaller pieces and placed them within the four walls, partitions that created interior rooms. Three partitions were added, all of them clicking into place. At that point, the third machine moved away and the first returned to place a flat roof over the structure. The roof served as the floor for the next level of identical cubicles.

Story after story rose in this fashion. The labor, like the product, continued in uniform succession and each unit took less than ten minutes to complete. Upon completion, twenty *Pi* would enter through the one doorless opening and not come out from what was evidently their assigned home.

Watching the *Pi* build was like observing an ant colony or beehive through glass. The uniformity of the design depressed me. They laid thirty box units in a square, each unit approximately fifteen feet tall and containing about six hundred square feet. When the thirtieth unit was done, the machines returned to their original corner and added the walls, interior, and ceiling for the next course. There were no ladders, no walkways, and no elevators that I could detect, but somehow more *Pi* reached and inhabited the next story of cubicles. I saw one standing in the opening, staring at the sky like a self-satisfied man in a country cabin. How did the alien get up there? How would it get down? I figured the center of the thirty-unit block must be hollow, creating a courtyard that let them move around behind the scenes. I crossed my arms at the chest and watched the towers rise and rise. The magnetic fields in play allowed the machines to move materials with perfect precision even half a mile into the air. I wondered how high these towers would eventually reach. I thought of the Tower of Babel. The *Pi* seemed intent on building hundreds of them, and God—as if I needed more proof—did not care.

I walked on, finding new fascination with the exactness of *Pi* construction abilities. I found more machines working everywhere. I could make out the basics of a grid and the spaces that must have been designated for streets. Everywhere else the perfect towers rose with the same uniformity, the same inevitability, and the endless walls rose higher and higher until the sun was eclipsed and I got dizzy if I craned my head back to follow their reach into the heavens.

They still left the churches and synagogues and mosques and Christian Science Reading Rooms, and all the other places they had not destroyed before. These old buildings were now wedged into the crevices of the *Pi*'s skyscrapers, fitting so well that I could not slide a piece of paper between our architecture and theirs. I entered into the cool dark of a chapel and stared at the empty pews and the cross high above the altar. The cross was life-sized, and a model of the crucified Christ stared skyward in agony, as if to show him asking God why he has been forsaken. I'd never seen the Crucifixion so rendered. Most showed Christ's head hanging low in exhaustion, his glorious task accomplished. What church ever focused on the uncomfortable moment of Christ's doubt? I fell into a pew and my gaze lingered on that face. Christ too had the stare of an alien, the ability to look at and through surfaces. He might have been staring at the ceiling, but his eyes watched the falling rockets carrying creatures who had not heard of him, and for whose sins he had not died.

Or had he?

"Don't forgive them," I whispered, and bowed my head.

2.

I stayed in the church for two days, resigned to die there. Hunger pangs struck sharp for several hours and then magically subsided, and I knew my body had begun to consume itself. When I woke up on the third day, I found a brown bag containing a water bottle and bread and peanut butter on the end of my pew. I hunched over it, ripping the bag open and taking pieces of bread to dip into the jar. The chunks were smeared so thick with peanut butter that I could barely swallow them. Each bite revitalized me, but with that satisfaction came a throat-closing guilt. I looked at Christ again and felt I was taking the devil's communion. Almost vomiting, I ran outside, knowing I was not being chased but feeling something on my heels. Smears of peanut butter remained on my hands like a stain.

I thought it was twilight at first until I noticed the sky. I had to look almost straight up to see the ribbon of blue the *Pi*'s towers threatened. I realized that from now on the only sunlight I might ever see would be at noon, when the sun was directly overhead. Resigned, I stepped away from the church and risked joining the alien throng again. The *Pi* moved here and there with no seeming direction in mind, their footsteps as muted as the *clicks* of their erected buildings. They did not look at me and I began the old dance of dodging and weaving to avoid being trampled. I knew they wanted me gone. Trying their patience was my only reason to live. I imagined millions celebrating as soon as I was dead and this game of theirs could end. But until then they waited—and fed me.

I fought my way through miles of their hordes. It was much harder than before, the towers forcing me to keep to the streets of this new city. I battled suffocation and claustrophobia on every step and countered it with memories of the mountains. I thought of Pike's Peak. Was it still there, or had the dozers triumphed there as well?

My legs cramped. I stumbled against the side of a tower and panted from pain. At once about forty *Pi* pressed closer to me, ruthless in working their weight to grind my spine against the wall. I pressed myself flat, squirming, crying out as their nonchalant brutality threatened my rib cage. I wriggled, punching at them as best I could. I was moving. All at once the wall ended and I fell through the unit's one opening, landing on my back inside the unit itself.

The interior had the same uniform color as the outside, a dull orange that made it hard to tell where walls ended and began. I picked myself up and squinted, trying to forge some sense of boundaries and difference. Instead I became dizzy, swooned, and hit up against another wall I hadn't known existed. I edged along the wall until I found myself falling into another room. Several *Pi* were there and I wedged myself into a corner with the same burst of fear I'd have felt stumbling into a lion's den. But the aliens showed no reaction even now. Three of them paced to and fro as if in the middle of some great and silent philosophical dilemma. Four more were lounged on the floor. One had its ears folded over its eyes while the others stared blankly at the ceiling or the wall. Not even their breathing made a sound.

I became more curious than fearful and began to explore. There were four identical partitions, devoid of any function except being filled. There was no bathroom, no kitchen. I realized by all rights the rooms should have been pitch black because there were no light bulbs and no windows, no openings at all except the entrance. But the ceiling glowed with an orange light that rendered the aliens clearly visible amid the hazy colored sameness of the room and its illumination.

Two of the *Pi* began to fuck on the floor next to the others, who paid no attention.

If I could cry, I would have shed tears in pity for them. They had traveled so far in their cramped, identical rockets. They must have suffered greatly on their mission to invade this beautiful, spacious world. And now that they were its masters they limited themselves to life in these little identical, featureless boxes. They were like birds mesmerized by their nest, content to peer at the sky but never try it. If they were still playing the game only on my account, why did they not kill me? They had no ethical qualms about destroying our cities; why should the outright murder of a single person give them pause? But I stood among them, these new owners of Earth, and did not feel in the least threatened. They had made me a shadow on the wall.

Chapter Eight: Return of the Secret Agent Man

1.

I made my way back to the church and explored it further out of boredom. In the business office I found a spiral notebook. The first few pages were filled with attempts at a suicide note. All the lines were crossed out and I wondered if the pastor himself had written it. If so, it would seem that faith won out and the idea was abandoned. I pondered the notebook for a moment and ripped out the used pages. Then I began to write about everything that had happened.

I returned to the chapel and saw a brown bag on the first pew. The *Pi* knew my every move. I went for it.

"That's mine!"

The bag spilled open on the pew as I jumped back. "Who's there?"

The man came out of the dark, moving along on his haunches like a SWAT officer. He lunged at the food and began to devour it. As he ate, his head turned and he seemed to address his shoulder. "Yes, good. That's just the right term. It tastes good and it is good for me."

I still hadn't seen his face but there was no mistaking the agent's voice. "I thought you were dead."

He looked up and recognized me. "You—the writer. The gay guy."

"I thought the Company killed you."

The agent laughed as he tried to swallow and began to choke. I slapped him twice on the back. His body felt as solid and nice as I remembered it.

"I know you were never with the government. What did you want?"

He stood up. I thought he was going to answer but instead he said, "Are you hungry?"

"Yeah. But you ate my food."

"The *Pi* gave me two. The other one's over there." He pointed to the right, three rows down, but I didn't look. I was shocked that he knew the aliens' name. He went and got the bag for me. Inside was more peanut butter, bread and bottled water.

"When he gave me two bags, I knew there must be another human. Another collaborator."

I threw the bag down. "You've fucked with me since the day you showed up on my porch. Scott said you were really working for the aliens."

"We both were."

I swung at him. His reflexes let him grab my wrist and spin me into the ground on my knees. He could have broken my arm but he didn't apply much pressure.

"Why?"

"I wanted to be a spy," he said. "The government wouldn't even let me try. Doctors always said I had a mental problem. Everyone judged me. When the aliens came, they didn't judge. You could be with them all the time and everyone was equal in silence. I preferred them to us. At first, anyway."

"What happened?"

"I started staring at one. It was staring at me so I stared back. I kept staring until its lips sort of made this movement—almost like a horse's lips smacking. I thought it was a smile so I smiled. And then it just started talking to me."

"I don't believe that."

He jerked on my arm then and kept jerking until I said I believed him. Then he let me go. I cradled my elbow.

"I was alone with the alien all the time. It spoke perfect Spanish. Gave me assurances. Told me I could help. Help them and they'd help me. Yes, help. That's right. Help. *Para ayudar.* See, I happened to know Spanish."

"Well, good job, man. They own us. So that explains why they're keeping you alive. What about me?"

"Didn't you *ayudar* too?"

"Fuck no I didn't *ayu*—no, I didn't help them. I *fought* them."

"Then I guess you're just lucky," he said, pointing at the bag.

I thought of the bread and peanut butter. There was no question I'd eat it. I bowed my head.

2.

The next two days we didn't leave the church and he kept talking, telling me about his life and how he hoped for better with the aliens. Then the dozers came and destroyed everything and the aliens got themselves together and made these living nets and patiently cast themselves among the humans to catch and drag them away.

He looked up at Christ. "He made them fishers of men." He started laughing in a way that would have been scary if he didn't look so damned enticing. He'd taken off his shirt now and had the best body in the room. Even Jesus's sculpted abs finished in second place.

He told me how he spent an entire day following a small group of *Pi*, about ten who had joined hands to imprison five men. He thought the group would have to stop and rest but the *Pi* kept going, mile after mile, driving the men toward an uncertain destination. He kept yelling at them to slow down, saying he knew everything; but the aliens ignored him. Worn out and depressed, he'd made his way back to Denver and took refuge in a synagogue. A brown bag of food and water was there for him in the morning and he knew he had not been forgotten.

"What about your alien contact? Wouldn't he say where they're taking the people?"

He bent over and spat in the aisle. "He won't talk anymore. He just feeds me. But two weeks ago he left me this."

He went and lifted up a pew cushion and pulled out a beautiful dagger. I got up the moment I saw it and put some space between us. "He spoke his last to me when he gave me this. He said it was a *contract*—that's what the writing on the blade means. He didn't explain it all but I got the gist. The contract is between him and me, because he did something he wasn't supposed to do. Talked to me, I guess. Under their laws, he has to give me food and water. Nothing else. Just enough to survive on my own. My biology has to hold up. If I get sick, there's not going to be any medicine. But they won't herd me off. I have my freedom."

"*Freedom?*"

He shrugged.

"What do you do with the knife?"

"He didn't say. But the way I see it, there's only one way this contract ends. It ends up buried in his heart or mine. One of us dies and the terms of the contract end. The terms…yes. The terms. That's the right word. The crazy thing is, I don't think he cared how I ended it. I think he'd be just as satisfied if I killed him instead of myself. And he'd stand there and let me do it. He wouldn't raise a hand to stop me."

"You should do it."

"How would I eat with him gone?"

I held up my bag. "I'm willing to share."

God help me, I was imagining a life with him. I couldn't help myself. His magnetism remained even if he was crazy. Maybe his craziness made him even more attractive. I'd spent my life passive, preferring men who took charge. Seeing him and spending more time with him made me want to take charge of him and give comfort. I loved Scott. If Scott came through the church door I'd cling to him and never let go. But Scott wasn't coming back and there was only the silent church and a silent life and Christ hovering above us, the second handsomest man in the room.

"We could live here together. There are board games in the rec room—Checkers and Scategories and Life."

I thought that if only I'd met him years before the invasion, when he was just a schizoid loner feeling rejected by the world, I could have saved him. I could have kept him from making the mistakes he made with the aliens. Made him sane somehow.

He stared at me. I could see he was scared.

"I know," I said. "I understand if you're not gay. But these are special circumstances. I promise I could make it good. You could close your eyes and pretend. We can show those bastards that *we* can adapt."

He began to cry in silence. I tried one final push.

"We'll live our lives in freedom to honor all of humanity. And we'll love, man. We'll love so much it'll shame the *Pi* into leaving."

3.

I went to bed with him as a lover after we ransacked the place for cushions and pillows. The seats in the pulpit where the elders and deacons and pastors sat had velvet padding that he liberated using the *contract*. We sliced the pads free and brought them down the central aisle to make our bed. Then we made love and my penetration was a *contract* of its own. I was not used to being the dominant partner. His hands were clenched throughout and he became tighter and tighter as I tried to turn pain into pleasure. He was extraordinary and I loved him in full. His back was amazing, smooth and muscled, capable of handling any weight and burning with fever. I climaxed biologically and intellectually. I came into a new understanding of myself and my potential. That's all anyone wants from any experience, some new understanding of himself. Only afterwards did I consider how rude it was to climax in him without permission. I asked him if he was okay and he said yes. I asked him if he regretted it and he said no. His voice seemed very shy. I turned him over and pleasured him with my mouth. It was very quick, which gave me hope for our future together. We fell asleep in a mutual embrace after promising ourselves to each other.

I slept long and dark, dreamless and naïve. In some romances everything depends upon who wakes up first. If I had woken first he would not be dead, but because I slept he had time to wake and look at me and think about what had happened. I don't know what he thought exactly, whether he was horrified or just lonelier after experiencing me than he ever was before. But he took the *contract* and he ended its terms a few feet away, far enough that I wouldn't have to worry about his blood running across my fingertips. I can't say how long I stared at him before moving again, knowing I could never take his body from the church nor stay here with it. I was about to leave when I found my bag at the end of my pew and his bag at the end of his. I'd like to think he saw his bag before he ended the *contract* and that leaving it was his message to me. Before leaving, I took both bags and sat down beside him. I imagined us staying in for the day and in silence I enjoyed our couple's meal for both of us.

Then I took up the bloody dagger.

4.

I walked out of the church and the *Pi* were there, strolling back and forth or just standing stagnant and mute. Not a sound from the thousands of them. I took the dagger and went to the alien nearest me. I drove the dagger into the base of its neck, right up to the hilt. It staggered, quiet. "You *will* scream," I said, twisting the knife as hard as I could. It was lodged in bone and sinew that cracked to my satisfaction. I jerked it out before the alien could fall back on me and I stood over it until I was sure it was dead. *Pi* went back and forth and still others were standing and looking without looking. I gutted one from the groin to the heart. The dagger solved the problem of their flesh quite well. I stared straight into the alien's liquid black eyes as I killed it and this time I was not satisfied.

They must know torture first.

I went straight into the first unit of the nearest tower. Two *Pi* fucked right on the floor while others stood around pretending not to notice. The female was on top and I slit her throat and she died still astride her. I watched the male to see if he'd continue having sex with her corpse. He did and I screamed and killed him too. Then I killed the other aliens, my hands beginning to tire from stabbing them. Six were dying on the floor and I was about to leave when I heard the faintest noise in another room. Alien or no, I recognized the sound of a baby.

I went around the partition with a tight grip on the knife. I had seen young *Pi* before, carried in their mothers' arms on the streets.

The aliens multiplied with a speed that made rabbits seem infertile. But even those babies had been silent in my presence, as if they were born into the world aware of the game and waiting for me to die before crying out for mother's milk.

In the other room, I found a female *Pi* on the floor. She had just given birth. A male *Pi* held the newborn in its hands. The aliens seemed in the process of making a silent decision with their eyes as I came into the room.

I took the baby from his hands and put the knife against its head. The *Pi* gave no reaction.

I swallowed and let the dagger's tip touch the infant's skin.   "All of the children. Every last one, for what you've done!"

Both *Pi* glanced just a moment at the child, allowing me to see a trace of awareness and pain. Then their eyes showed all the sentimentality of someone looking at a rag doll, and their gazes turned to the wall as they waited for me to murder the child.

I dropped the dagger and put the infant atop its mother's chest. "You win."

Chapter Nine: The Long Death

1.

I stepped outside with no hope and no plan. I stared at the *Pi*, watching their silent movements. Then I saw one alien who stood still in the masses. The alien looked right at me and I felt the familiar thrill of superiority in the gaze. It was her. *My* alien.

I went toward her and she took off. I trailed her through the crowds knowing she wanted me to follow. She could have lost me any time—I was thrown back three steps for every inch I gained and constantly had to shift and slide and tackle my way through bodies. The aliens were everywhere. There were millions here now and none of them made a sound. I lost track of her every few seconds. The one reason I never lost her was because whenever I stopped moving, she waited for me.

It went on like this for hours as she led me painstakingly to a final series of towers where my old neighborhood once stood. I knew it because my home was there, just like the churches, sitting snug between the skyscrapers. My house and my yard were the only spaces no alien occupied. I pointed at the absurd scene and laughed. This is insane, I thought. I'm insane. There was grass in the yard, brown and sparse from lack of light but grass all the same. I painted it green with memory. I knelt and watered it with tears.

This dying patch is *not* the last grass on Earth, I promised myself. Somewhere there still existed amber waves of grain and Scott was there, lying on his back to see a spacious sky. I'd find him. *Somehow* I'd find him.

The alien walked past me, stepped onto the porch, and went inside.

2.

Over the next week, I dreamed of escaping the maze they were building and of finding Scott. I dreamed of this every night and every morning before I woke in my front yard with my face smeared with dirt. Clumps of dead, brown grass were in my hands. I'd pulled them out in my sleep and they drifted to the ground like hair lost from chemotherapy. Soon the yard would be nothing but cracked, bald earth. When had it last rained? Had the *Pi* done something to the atmosphere to prevent rain?

I'd look up into the narrow strip of sky overhead and ponder. Sometimes I'd hallucinate that an Air Force jet was streaking past, and then I'd jump up and holler. Maybe it wasn't a hallucination, but I came to accept that a hallucination was preferable. I wanted there to still be pockets of humanity left, a resistance, some semblance of the past. But it was hell to think that I alone suffered as I did. I could not stand the implication that somewhere life continued as I'd always known it.

While I dreamed of escaping, in reality I did nothing. Daily I woke and either sat on the yard or moved to the porch to eat the food now left each morning by my head. The contents were a cruel joke to me now. Half of the food was inedible because I had no way of cooking it. Raw steaks, raw hamburger meat and chicken. Was my provider obtuse to the fact I could not eat meat uncooked, or did she just know how best to taunt me? My other provisions now consisted of bread and bottled water, which I'd taken to sharing with the dead grass, hoping to revive it. I only made mud. I often debated going inside. What was the point of living outside my house, exposed and aching, when I could sleep in my own bed? But I just couldn't bring myself to do it. The house wasn't mine anymore. Stealing inside would just reinforce the idea that I was a trespasser.

But finally a crisis drove me inside.

I had made a few more excursions into the *Pi*'s skyscrapers, venturing into those towers that sandwiched my house. These petty invasions were my way of avenging their far greater one. One day I caught three aliens eating a food I'd never seen before. It was a red-colored substance with the appearance and consistency of seaweed. It was crunchy despite the slimy appearance and curled the tongue with its foul taste. Yes, I ate it. I snatched it from one alien's hand and I ate it right in front of him. I don't know how it affected the *Pi*, but I found my hunger stimulated to the point of a craving, and I stuffed myself with the red weed until I could only stumble away, doubled-over with stomach cramps.

I reached my yard and tried to vomit. I could feel the red weed inside my belly as if it were a living thing, a thing with tendrils that probed and anchored itself inside me. I was nauseated but I could not puke. I jammed one, two and then three fingers deep into my mouth. I retched again and again as pain brought me to my knees. I gagged myself with even greater force as hot tears came from squeezing eyelids. The food stayed in me, burning.

The burn spread. "Oh God..." I started to crawl to the porch. My right hand found and turned the knob in a blind grope. The old familiar smells of my life with Scott rushed over me as if the house had been preserved in an airtight vault. For just a second I forgot the pain and sighed with relief. But my stomach jerked on its internal reins and cracked its interior whip, and I was up again. I raced up stairs and ripped my clothes away as the terrible happened. I retched and vomit came out in thick strands of reddish-purple hair algae. I was suffocating. The viscous weed was lodged in my throat. I plunged fingers into my mouth and began to pull. The weed dislodged in little pieces, like cotton candy. I panicked, colors bursting in my vision, my heart pounding. Then my fingers caught the weed in the right spot and instead of tufts, the whole mass dislodged.

My throat cleared. My whole stomach suddenly seemed in my hands and I flung it to the floor. I collapsed over the sink, chest heaving. I was greedy for both the air and the familiar scents of a passed life. My eyes shut, I seemed to leave my body and drift ghostlike through both rooms and time, through loves and arguments. I saw my first dinner with Scott in the kitchen. He cooked it. I watched us watching movies, when we were just friends; I watched the night my right hand dared out of its pants pocket to stroke his leg. Back further. Back before Scott was in my life. I saw my parents living here without me, wondering where I was or perhaps not wondering. Back further. Myself as a gloomy, lonely adolescent. Myself as a boy, crying. Had I never laughed? Myself as a newborn. As a fetus. I saw my parents young and happy in a world where I did not yet exist.

I opened my eyes in the bathroom and saw the red mess on the floor was shriveling up and drying fast, becoming a sort of wispy husk like the grass in my yard. Hunching over the sink, I turned the faucet knob by old instinct. Of course the days of running water and plumbing were long over. Except water *did* shoot out, cold and crisp. I ran trembling fingertips through the stream. How was this possible? It had to be an illusion. I tried it and laughed at the cold sensation of water dousing my face. A few last red flecks of weed came from my mouth like bits of ash.

Renewed, I explored the house, finding nothing and everything changed. My alien had touched no furniture. The bed looked exactly as I had left it, unmade with the topsheet twisted at the foot and the comforter mostly on the floor. Dust lay thick on the furniture. But there were changes. Attached to the hallway light switch I found an odd flat device that looked like a refrigerator magnet. Round and about the size of a half dollar, it was white except for three small blue luminescent partitions. When I touched it the blue light faded and the device came free in my palm. It had little heft and no discernible components. I positioned it back on the light switch and tapped it. The device reattached to the surface and the blue lights returned. Entertaining a wild hope, I flipped the switch. The hallway light came on.

A generator, I thought. With growing excitement I roamed the house looking for similar devices. I found them on every lightswitch and outlet. I found them on the kitchen and refrigerator. I opened the refrigerator door—the light came on and I found the shelves packed with identical brown bags. *That bitch*, I thought. She could have told me I could cook the raw food inside instead of leaving me to figure it out or die. I tried the stove. All four burners worked. The dishwasher worked.

I entered the living room.

There was a generator attached to the television.

I stood in front of the dead screen, genuinely fearful. What would I find if I turned it on? Were there still transmissions? It seemed impossible. But why else would the alien bother to power the television? I took the remote control and my finger hovering on the power button. What if I turned it on and found every channel exactly as it had always been, except replaced by *Pi*? Aliens in suits doing the news; aliens in sitcoms; aliens in cowboy drag having six-gun shoot-outs at the OK Corral?

Moment of truth. I winced, half-expecting a trap. The television was rigged to explode when activated. I squeezed my eyes tight and waited. Silence. Had I not hit it after all?

I opened my right eye a fraction. The television was on but showed only muted white snow. I raced through the channels in disbelief. Had she really expected me to be entertained by dead air after all? No channel had a picture: final proof that my civilization had died.

Sighing, I started to walk away when I noticed generators attached to both the DVD player and the VCR. An old tape was waiting to be played. I bent down and paused. Whatever was on it might be among the last vestiges of human history. Proof that humans had existed. I pushed the tape forward and the player accepted it. I pressed *play* and the television flickered and showed a picture.

That's when I screamed.

3.

My alien came home and found me sprawled on the couch. I must have looked dead and oblivious like her, drained bloodless and with empty eyes. The frozen picture, which I stared at until I no longer saw, showed Scott's birthday party from two years ago. I remembered taping it. I'd started with the video camera before passing it around for everyone to use. The picture caught Scott and me standing together and kissing in front of his cake. His eyes were closed but mine were wide open, leaving a still-frame ghost of myself peering back at me these past few hours.

The *Pi* looked between me and the TV for a moment. Then she removed the power device and the screen died.

My gaze darted to her as she sat on my ankles and stared at the wall. A minute passed as the pain of her weight grew in my pinned legs. I remembered her and her mate eating my food, fucking in my bed, pretending I didn't exist. Outrage and pain combined in a fury against her and the *Pi*'s cold, cowardly invasion. I shrieked out, a cry for the whole world: "Goddamnit! Quit living on me! *Quit living all over me!*"

I bent toward her, my arms helicoptering. Before I knew it my fists were pounding against her solid flesh and it was like the globe of our Earth smashing itself to pieces against an impossible galactic wall. I tried to kick but her weight held me fast. She did not turn to regard me until I fell back exhausted and defeated, my knuckles pulverized. In that moment I realized how weak I'd become. She offered one look of acknowledgment.

She did not give me another until I asked her, in the quietest whisper, to kill me.

I could barely see her eyes. My head was too heavy to move so I trained my sight straight down my nose and just caught a piece of her face. Her voice came at me in matter-of-fact probes.

"Do you desire self-destruction?"

"Yes."

"Do you consider it a release?"

"Yes."

"Then you will give it to yourself."

She held a dagger out toward me. I don't know where she'd been keeping it but I supposed she knew that I understood its meaning. The *contract*. I laughed with little strength and tried to reach for it. She was still sitting on my feet and my stomach muscles wrenched as they tried to lift me. I fell back, panting and laughing even more, despite the pain. Then my bowels exploded in my pants. An instant stink flooded the room and I sputtered in shock. My alien kept the *contract* outstretched toward me.

"I can't," I panted. "I want you to do it."

The dagger trembled. The disruption ran like a wave down the shaft, into the handle and up her arm. She jumped up like a shot and stumbled, for once graceless in retreat, her gaze still trained on me like I was a thing immensely dangerous to her. I registered this hazily through the pain and shame and surrender that seized me.

"Are you afraid to kill me?"

She didn't answer

I lay staring at the ceiling and noticing details I'd never bothered with before—stains and divots and dust webs. At first, I thought noticing these things meant something had changed within me, that in my acceptance of death I could see through assumptions and beliefs and take things as they were, with all the imperfections I had always willfully ignored. Then I realized it was just that I rarely rested on my back in life, trained by the television since childhood to lounge on my left side in dutiful submission. I rolled to face the dead screen now, edging my soiled, damaged body in small shifts, until I finally rested on my shoulder and stared at my alien.

She was scared—terrified, and willing to show it. Her dread ran deep and filled the room. I felt it on me as I would feel damp walking through a fog bank. Whatever I had done to her intrigued me and put a bit of energy in my muscles. I moved my body again, inching my body off the edge of the couch. Fresh pain shot through my belly. I was going to die. I'd somehow managed to escape illness and injury until now. Her obligation to me didn't include medicine. There'd never been a drug in all of those brown food bags. There'd never even been a beer to numb the pain. I didn't know exactly what the pain in my guts was, but I didn't think it was gas. I'd ruptured something.

I got to my knees and moved toward her on all fours. As I got closer, her gaze readjusted and focused on me like I was some overpowering, slithering predator instead of her crippled charge.

I hit the first stair step, pawed at it, and hoisted myself. My body was too beat down to straighten and turn to face her, but I mustered enough dignity to say, "I'm going upstairs to my shower. *My* shower. *I'm* going to use *my* shower. Do you understand that?" I stopped, coughing and winded. She didn't react. But it was a different type of non-reaction. She seemed too afraid to respond. Even as I fought for courage, I knew there were a million ways that she could instantly reduce me back to total serfdom. She could say, "Fine, try your shower; I will take away your water." I had no response to such a castrating answer. But she stayed silent as I inched upward, made it to the top and crawled toward the tub. There was a generator attached to the showerhead and so I gave a small turn of the knob and hot water spat forth. I ran my hands under the water expecting a final trick, expecting to be electrocuted at last. But instead I was soothed and massaged.

    I fell into the tub with my clothes still on. As the water saturated everything, I found little threads of energy that I saved and worked into a ball. The ball was in my hands, working the buttons, tugging at fabric; it was in my legs, telling them to pump and kick the clothes away. I closed my eyes, preparing for the eternal rest. I entered the world naked and wet, I'd exit that way too. The water came down taking away pain and filth. Then I was naked and I resolved to lie there and let my life flow from my body and swirl down the drain with the water. It fell and fell, never cooling, the same pleasant heat. I thought if I closed the shower curtain I could trap the heat better. I reached blindly toward it and my hand found flesh. I opened my eyes to see the *Pi* standing over me with the *contract* in her hand.

4.

"I'm ready," I said.

    I draped my right arm over the side and leaned into an exaggerated pose, like that painting of Marat. I waited, quite serene, momentarily past pain and regret. The tub, the house, the world—I was drowning in illusions. The best I could hope to do now was to die in the façade and let it collapse over my head, a coffin lid.

    "Do it," I said. I gave up my throat, open and undefended for her blade.

    Again the knife wobbled. Once again, her entire arm convulsed like she was at war with herself. I waited out the minutes with closed eyes and a rocketing pulse.

    "Please take the contract and cease your suffering. I offer this gift to you."

"No. You took everything else away from me. Now take my life, too."

She waited so long in silence that I finally gave up my pose and bent forward to reheat the water.

"Answer a few questions for me before I die."

She just stared.

"I'll take the dagger and kill myself with it, but only if you answer my questions first."

"Yes." Her tone was eager for the barter. "But take the contract first."

I saw no harm in that. I held out my hand and she rushed to give me the knife. She closed my fingers around the grip and pushed my arm back toward me. I meditated on the glittering symbols that decorated the blade.

"First question—is this writing? What does it say?"

"One side describes how and why the contract was made. The other side, the terms of its breaking."

"The knife itself is some sort of legal document?"

"There is no exact word in your language. **Contract** suffices."

I turned the blade in front of me, as if I had some sense of the different markings. "You're bound to ensure my basic survival needs. The contract ends if I stop wanting to survive. If I kill myself."

"Yes. The bond—the burden. I despise it so. My husband—"

"The one you sold out."

"You have participated, without realizing, in two of our highest laws. That we shall not acknowledge those whom we replace; that we must revoke the charter of anyone among us who acknowledges those whom we replace. As a condition of that sacred vow, which I upheld against my husband, the life of the one who was acknowledged became my charge."

"Me."

"Now plunge the contract into yourself and release us from its terms."

"I have more questions. Is there a mark on me somehow, a warning to others to keep away?"

"That definition will suffice."

"I want it off. Take it off."

She motioned at the dagger.

"Not that way."

"It is the only way." She moved toward me and I held the dagger between us. I rose out of the tub with the point aimed at her.

"I have more questions and if I understand our situation correctly, you must answer them."

"Ask."

"Why the churches? Why are they still standing?"

"All religion is sacred to us."

"And your religion?"

"Inviolable."

"Tell me about it."

"Our religion is survival."

"Is it in your religion to take over other planets, to kill off the people? What kind of God do you worship?"

"Survival. There is no choice, there is only survival and reproduction and seeding. Once there was violence that put our survival at risk. I have seen the records. All of us see the records, a warning to ourselves about what survival can make us to do. That was our past; we shall not taint the future with what came before. Only a few, like my husband, would embrace the old ways. It is not holy."

"Holy?" I spat out in an incredulous laugh. "Is that what you call your methods? Passive resistance is one thing, passive conquering is quite another. It's like Gandhi leading the Mongols."

"Survival is precious to us." Her fingers gestured at me. "Even your survival, in its own way. Our cherished beliefs keep us from denying someone else's survival until it is absolutely necessary. We have sworn to a way without violence. We each lay our bodies to its sacrificial altar though it conflicts with every instinct, every urge. How many times did your people beat and kill mine, destroying them with a slow pleasure? We felt every blow. We cried out but kept it inside us, to remain faithful to our vows. And we did not fight back even as your savagery split open our skulls. That is **our** dedication and we have lost billions of ourselves in exchange for giving natives one more year, one more month, one more week or one more day of survival."

"But when the end comes, you throw all pretense aside. You raze cities, you get your revenge."

"It is not revenge; it is survival. As surely as plants give way to other plants."

"Weeds," I shot back. "You're nothing but strangling weeds."

"But we are also kind gardeners. We have plucked the weeds and put them in other gardens to survive until they wither and fade, according to nature."

I stirred, catching her meaning. "Where are they? All the humans you've rounded up—there are billions of us. Where could you put them all?"

"In places where we honor their will to survive."

"Like concentration camps? Are they given shelter—food and water, like I am? What about babies? You didn't really separate all the men and woman on the entire *planet*—"

"Reproduction is ended."

"But reproduction is survival. It's the root of survival!"

"We have debated the issue among us many times, on many worlds."

I flashed the dagger in front of her. "How do you stop them? Do you castrate the men? Inject the women with drugs?"

"They are not allowed to commingle."

I listened to this and the simplicity of her tone and I started to laugh.

"You would have been happier there with your mate."

I jolted. "What?"

"You and your mate do not reproduce. We do not hinder non-reproductive enjoyment on the way to extermination."

"I doubt we'd find your prison camp very erotic. It doesn't matter anyway. I'm here and Scott's in the mountains someplace with the resistance. Or he's dead."

"Your mate is not dead. He is confined."

I flashed the dagger again. "*Where is he?*"

"He is with the others. Surviving."

"You took him?"

"When he renounced you, the protection that had been extended to him through you was ended."

"I want to see him."

"That cannot be allowed."

"Why?"

"The bond—"

"Fuck the bond," I yelled. "I can be protected in some camp just as easily as in this house. Is he okay?"

"He is surviving, and will survive until his mind ceases."

I listened to her simple, emotionless words and verged on tears. "Please—I've got to see him. I want to spend the rest of my life with him. Even if the rest of my life is one day, I don't care. It's over. You've won." I tossed the dagger to the ground. "The *contract* is over. I'm annulling it. Now take me—"

"No."

"Goddamn you, I'm begging!"

Her large black nostrils flared and her ears flicked rapidly over her eyes. "This place was my reward for informing on my husband. So significant was his crime—and my faithful response—that even choosing this as my living space was granted. Otherwise it would be unthinkable. It is not without price. No one else would consider it a reward. I am shunned in some quarters but not openly ridiculed. My deed is considered too heroic and orthodox to allow vocal dissent. As for the food—" She allowed herself a smile. I could not believe how it transformed her vaguely humanoid face into something almost recognizable, an impish delight. "I have come to like the foods of this world. But that is not allowable, no matter the deed. You are the excuse I use. I must make sure my burden has access to its accustomed food."

"But you want me to kill myself—"

"I can conceal your death." She bent in a flash for the dagger. Somehow I got there first.

She was not a practiced killer. As our gazes locked I saw into her eyes and for once it was I penetrating her, looking into the core of her beliefs. She had not lied to me. Until the moment she rescued me from the Company's warehouse, she had never directly taken a life. She had seen her closest friends die, fallen in wars of attrition in which her people never fired a shot. I knew in an instant she could not put the knife into me. Maybe the entire idea of a contract was something she fabricated on the cuff to take psychological advantage of my despair. Her people were cowards and they had forged their cowardice into a deep religion that kept them from dealing with any conflict, even on a galactic scale. I told her this. I told her and she had no reaction. That's when the knife was fully in my hand.

"Define us as you wish. You slaughter us unopposed by anything except your own resources. Again, we show we are not hypocrites. The faith of our survival is a sacred wall. You kill five thousand of us and twenty thousand arrive to stand for the fallen. **Billions** are still on the way."

The number—the idea of the number—fell between us and punched a hole through the floor of our argument. A hole, a whirlpool of eternal silence into which we both must go. I gazed at the dagger. Would she? I could not help but wonder, for all her talk and for all my assumptions, if she would play the game one final time and let me stab her. She could disarm me without effort. Even at my best I hadn't the strength to fight her if she truly opposed me. *Billions.* To her it was the number of the present. To me it was the past, the tally of the dead and dying, the number of the forgotten. Of Scott. I could still be with him, in a sense, if I added myself to the figure. But I would honor him first. Killing her would also kill me, and Scott would want me to kill her.

I raised the blade between us and stared at her face. Who was she? What was her name? How old was she? Did she have children? How many invasions had she lived through, how many worlds had she seen overthrown? Or had she never set foot on a world until now? Had she traveling on one of the *Pi*'s sardine-tin rockets all her life? Had she been born on it, nourished on it, programmed and taught within it the mechanics of the vacant stare, the automatic disinterest in the world she would ruin when the rocket's door finally opened?

I looked down at my hand as it moved. The knife was inside her. It was not as difficult as I expected. It was like jabbing into tender pulled pork. The *contract* was very sharp. Her hand closed around mine. Her hand did not descend to stop me; it did not intend to pull me away. Her hand—not mine—had guided the knife. I looked up from our clasped hands. She had tears in her eyes. It was horrible to behold. It was like seeing one of the faces on Mount Rushmore crying.

As I stared into her wet eyes, I felt the pressure of her grip grinding my bones into the dagger's handle. I winced as she forced me to turn the knife counterclockwise to disembowel her. I fell to my knees but she kept me holding the handle. Her blood spurted into my hair.

She held me like that for many minutes, and when she released me I tried to escape. Her body got in my way. She slumped against the door, slamming it shut and blocking the exit. She slid to the floor, taking up much of the narrow space. I realized right away I was too weak to move her. I'd never get the door open again.

Her gaze stayed trained on me for a minute, but her focus shifted. I only just detected it. Once more, instead of seeing me, she seemed to look through me. *Past me.* I could swear she gazed at time itself, the endless building blocks of survival that looked like slow erosion and finally decay, as if survival itself was just an illusion of permanence. Perhaps it was. But I saw also in her fading gaze a larger picture of absolute need. When she said *survival*, she did not think in small terms, individual terms. I saw now, as she died, everything she had tried to explain to me. The individual was erosion and decay that rose up again, reborn in the continuation of community and species. I took the knife from her and as I did her hand came up one final time. Wasn't there something else to say, some little lesson, some tiny regret that, after all, nothing survived the death of the individual—*for the individual*? She held the handle as her gaze returned to the present, and we stared at each other, both wishing we could ignore the reality before us one final time, and wondering how we'd ever managed to count ourselves among the living.

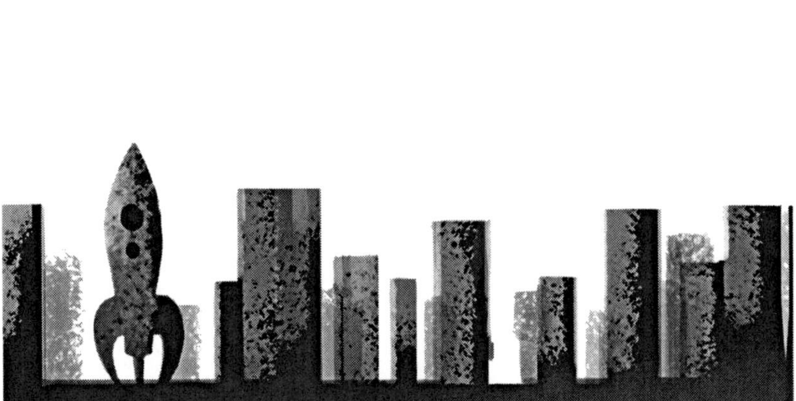

Acknowledgments

There are several people I would like to thank. First and foremost, Steve Berman for taking a chance on *The Survivors* and for his encouragement and hard work in bringing the manuscript to press. I also thank Alex Jeffers for the interior design for the book and Niki Smith for the fantastic cover. There are many more people I wish to show gratitude to for always giving me an honest opinion on whatever piece of writing I shove in front of them. They include Paula Peterson, Cassandra Greenwald, Darren Buford, Linda and Dirk Anderson, Carter Wilson, and John Shefflin. And a special thanks to Ed Bryant, a great teacher.

About the Author

Originally from Kentucky, where he received a Bachelors and Masters degree in literature from the University of Kentucky, SEAN EADS is now a reference librarian in Denver, Colorado. Besides writing, his interests include golf, two cats, and tasting new beers. You can follow his blogging attempts at seaneads.blogspot.com.

```
FICTION EADS
Eads, Sean
The survivors


R0119935378              PONCE
```

PONCE DE LEON

Atlanta-Fulton Public Library

JUL 1 6 2013